June 1987

To Jerry.

with all good wishes,

E.F.bett

Tales from a Greek Island

Alexandros Papadiamantis

TALES FROM A GREEK ISLAND

TRANSLATED, WITH AN INTRODUCTION AND NOTES,
BY ELIZABETH CONSTANTINIDES

THE JOHNS HOPKINS UNIVERSITY PRESS
BALTIMORE AND LONDON

This book has been brought to publication with the generous
assistance of the Andrew W. Mellon Foundation.

The Johns Hopkins University Press
701 West 40th Street
Baltimore, Maryland 21211
The Johns Hopkins Press Ltd., London

The paper used in this publication meets the minimum require-
ments of American National Standard for Information Sciences—
Permanence of Paper for Printed Library Materials,
ANSI Z39.48-1984.

∞

Library of Congress Cataloging-in-Publication Data

Papadiamantēs, Alexandros, 1851–1911.
Tales from a Greek island.

Translated from the Greek.
1. Papadiamantēs, Alexandros, 1851–1911—
Translations, English. I. Constantinides, Elizabeth.
II. Title.
PA5610.P345A23   1987   889'.32   86-20957
ISBN 0-8018-3333-7

To Jim

οὐ μὲν γὰρ τοῦ γε κρεῖσσον καὶ ἄρειον,
ἢ ὅθ᾽ ὁμοφρονέοντε νοήμασιν οἶκον ἔχητον
ἀνὴρ ἠδὲ γυνή

Contents

Acknowledgments

I would like to express my gratitude to a number of scholars who have helped me in the preparation of these translations. I have drawn on the notes and glossaries in the editions of George Valetas and N. D. Triantafyllopoulos. Especially valuable has been the four-volume study of the customs, manners, and idiom of the island of Skiathos, *Skiathou laikos politismos* (Salonika, 1958–70), by George Regas.

I owe much to friends and colleagues who read parts of my manuscript: to Professors Anne Farmakides, John Rexine, and Gregory Rabassa for their helpful comments, and particularly to Professor Peter Bien for his constant encouragement. I am indebted to Professor Susan Spectorsky for translations from the Arabic.

I am grateful to the Research Foundation of the City University of New York for a faculty grant toward this translation and to

Queens College, CUNY, for releasing me from some of my teaching obligations during one semester.

Finally, I would like to acknowledge the greatest debt of all, to my husband, Professor James Tetreault, who from the beginning, as reader and adviser, helped me see this work to completion.

Introduction

Alexandros, elder son of the priest Adamantios and his wife, Angeliki, was born in 1851 on the small Aegean island of Skiathos, then on the geographic fringe of the newly founded Greek nation. Under his patronymic, Alexandros Papadiamantis, he was to become famous in Greece as one of its most eminent prose writers—some say the most eminent—and the finest Greek representative of nineteenth-century realism. Papadiamantis's major work, excluding three early historical novels of small literary value, comprises one short historical novel, *Christos Milionis,* and about one hundred seventy stories and sketches, varying in length from two to one hundred pages. The great majority of these stories deal with the lives of the inhabitants of his native Skiathos. As the author of works that depict in a realistic vein the outlook, manners, and speech of a given locale, Papadiamantis did for his island what Thomas Hardy, Alphonse Daudet, Theodor Storm, and Giovanni

Verga did for their homelands. The large number of his stories places him in the company of other prolific short story writers such as Chekhov, Maupassant, Pirandello, and Henry James, who by the abundance and variety of their characters, plots, and settings create a unique, recognizable world of their own.

The stories of Papadiamantis are noted for their acute character portrayal, their careful observation of the daily activities of life, and their loving descriptions of folk traditions and the natural environment. Steeped like many another Greek author in the literary heritage of the Hellenic past, Papadiamantis frequently presents the world of his narrow island society with strong mythical and symbolic overtones. He surpasses other representatives of Greek realism not only in the breadth of his vision but also in his felicitous combination of humor and ironic detachment with compassionate understanding.

Taken as a whole, Papadiamantis's stories represent human life in microcosm, a world imperfect and sinful but at the same time full of beauty and in the end redeemable. His outlook was informed by Christian ethics and doctrine, particularly as they manifested themselves in Greek Orthodoxy and the Byzantine tradition. With profound charity he describes the prodigious difficulties faced by the poor and humble, and especially the lot of village women, toiling all their lives at home and in the fields, burdened with society's high expectations of them, married in youth according to the stringent demands of the dowry system, and bereft of sustenance in their widowhood when their male children have emigrated or gone to sea.

Though the world Papadiamantis portrays is a traditional island community, where class distinctions are not as marked as in a more urbanized society, the characters that appear in his stories are of every disposition, age, and circumstance: innocent babe, mischievous child, neglected child, coy adolescent girl, rowdy adolescent boy, marriageable maiden, lovelorn youth, loving father and husband, devoted mother, heartless mother, good stepmother, bad stepmother, charming widow, wronged woman, prosperous landowner, simple laborer, gruff shepherd, stalwart fisherman, honest tradesman, captain, seaman, usurer, the sick, the maimed, the derelict, the eccentric, the simpleminded, and many, many others. Papadiamantis's preference, as is often remarked, is for the neglected and the lowly, for those who find themselves without the comfort and

security afforded by a happy family and adequate means. This is
true both of his island stories and, especially, of the thirty or so
stories set in Athens. Yet even the grimmest of these tales is relieved
by his omnipresent humor, sometimes gentle, sometimes broad,
sometimes sardonic, sometimes parodistic (as in the poem in "Love
the Harvester"), sometimes even macabre (as in the grave episode of
"Fortune from America"). Irony is pervasive in the stories, often
appearing in the contrast between the characters' professed and real
motives and in Papadiamantis's dry authorial comments and digressions.

Greek writers, living in constant awareness of their classical
predecessors, have often invoked their ancient myths to illuminate
contemporary Greek life. Long before T. S. Eliot celebrated James
Joyce in 1923 as the discoverer of the "mythical method," Papadiamantis had used myth as an organizing principle and had made, to
quote Eliot on Joyce, a "continuous parallel between contemporane-
ity and antiquity." The most obvious example of the mythical
method in Papadiamantis is "The American," a modern-day re-
creation of Odysseus's return to his faithful Penelope. "The American" parallels in miniature the second half of the *Odyssey* in its plot,
its characters, and some of its details. The hero of the story returns
unrecognized to his native island after twenty years' absence and
finds his parents dead and his house in ruins. But he is reunited with
his betrothed, who has remained faithful to him these many years.
The Homeric Eumaeus, Eurykleia, and the suitors all have their
counterparts in Papadiamantis's story, as do such details as Odysseus's treasure, the scope of his travels, and Penelope's weaving.

Papadiamantis, with his conviction that the great writers of
pagan antiquity were a fundamental source of human wisdom that
complemented, rather than clashed with, the highest Christian
ideals, makes frequent use of these mythical parallels. Part of "Love
the Harvester" is a reworking of the myth of the nymph Galatea and
the herdsman-giant Polyphemus as it appears in the pastoral poet
Theocritus's *Idyll* 11. The poet-lover, the sorceress, and the goatherd
are all characters known to ancient pastoral. The domain of the
pagan fertility gods, Dionysus, Pan, and the Satyrs, is evoked in a
number of ways: the springtime lushness of nature, the abundance
of flowers, the frolicking of the goatlike children, the primitive impulses of "Wildman," the crowning of the old woman, and in many
other details. In "The Haunted Bridge" the persecuted child is

explicitly compared to the sacrificial victim described in a well-known Greek folk legend, and she is implicitly linked with the classical myth of Iphigeneia and Agamemnon. Often Papadiamantis's symbols derive their force from their mythical associations: in "The Homesick Wife" the heroine Lialio, white-clad, alluring, and subtly dominating, is by implication associated with the moon and its mysterious power and with the sea and its divinity Leucothea, the White Goddess of Homer's Odyssey (Book 5).

Papadiamantis's long story "The Murderess," one of his masterpieces, is a penetrating psychological study of a grandmother whom poverty and family conditions have driven to madness and infanticide. Many of the shorter stories also take an uncompromisingly harsh view of the traditional Greek obligation to provide marriageable daughters with a dowry. In "Fortune from America" brother, sister, brother-in-law, and even mother take unscrupulous advantage of a young man's willingness to dower his sister. The resentment felt by the islanders toward female children because they are a financial burden also appears in the tale of the hated stepdaughter in "The Haunted Bridge." Both in "Fortune from America" and "The Voice of the Dragon" the crass demands of the bridegroom for a sizeable dowry are accepted, albeit resentfully, by the bride's family as an inevitable part of the marriage arrangement. How different the fate of the well-dowered girl is from that of the dowerless can be seen by comparing Lialio of "The Homesick Wife" with Mati of "Love the Harvester." Both are beautiful, virtuous, and intelligent, and yet Lialio is unhappily married to an elderly man because eligible youths "do not marry poor girls," whereas Mati, the daughter of a prosperous landowner, is able to make a suitable marriage that is also a love-match with her ardent suitor. Among Papadiamantis's many tales of humble women caught in the rigid bonds of island morality and customs, the story of the charming widow in "The Matchmaker" provides a refreshing contrast. By her work at the loom Kratira has been able to earn her own living and win for herself a measure of independence. She is thus in a position to reject the marriage offer of an undesirable egotist and, by her winsome yet prudent ways, to elicit a proposal from a more attractive suitor.

Another theme that recurs frequently is the frustrated yearning of the romantic, isolated youth, such as Mathios in "The Homesick Wife" or the young herdsman in "A Dream among the Waters." In

"Love the Harvester" there are two such young men, the sentimental, citified student and the dim-witted, beastlike goatherd. Each adores the girl with a long-nurtured passion, but though the one is a romantic hero and the other a would-be rapist, the author cannot altogether withhold his sympathy even from the latter in this May Day celebration of life.

"Love the Harvester" is also an example of Papadiamantis's occasional inclination to parody the conventions of romantic fiction, with its helpless maidens, love-struck swains, villainous seducers, and heroes to the rescue. The poem that Kostis sends his beloved is a tumultuous jumble of phrases plucked from island love songs; the scene at the sorceress's home is not unearthly but rather a humorous depiction of the distraught lover's gullibility; and the description of the attempted rape, with its overwrought writing and frequent breaks in the narrative can hardly be taken as a description of a criminal act. Papadiamantis's rejection of melodrama is forcefully illustrated in a passage from "The Homesick Wife" where he deliberately interrupts his narrative, breaking the artistic illusion, and asks the reader to imagine several possible melodramatic turns he could introduce into the plot "if only the literary conscience of this author would allow it."

Papadiamantis's attitudes on religious, political, and social questions can be described as conservative, or rather, more precisely, as reactionary, in the vein of other nineteenth-century reactionaries such as Balzac and Dostoyevsky. Although his priests are pious, dutiful men, he found much to disapprove of in what he considered the departure of the contemporary Church from traditional Byzantine practice, and he sometimes inserted digressions excoriating the hierarchy for their innovations. He considered democratic voting procedure as an exercise in disorder; one of his funniest stories is a satirical account of a local election campaign. He saw only venality and incompetence in the recently reorganized Greek civil service, he vehemently decried the emancipation of women, and he repeatedly sang the praises of the good old ways. His country's noble traditions were being corrupted, in his eyes, by "European" ideas and habits, from political institutions to matters of dress and comportment. On one occasion he goes so far as to deplore (or at least he seems to deplore) the abandonment of the veil by Greek women. It should be noted that Papadiamantis holds this view of the liberal European West as decadent and corrupt in common with several other writers whose thought was deeply tinctured by Eastern Orthodoxy, most notably Dostoyevsky and Tolstoy.

Though Papadiamantis defends the traditions and beliefs of his Greek island, with its strict moral code, scrupulous observance of religious rites, rigidly hierarchical society, patriarchal family, and suspicion of foreign manners, his stories nevertheless illustrate the dark side of that life as he perceived it. Females are the victims of their male kinfolk and husbands; males, in turn, are blighted by poverty, lack of opportunity, and their own fecklessness. For women there is no escape, only adaptation to circumstances; for men the principal escape is seafaring or emigration. There is no inherent contradiction in Papadiamantis's view of his world. As a Christian he considered all men after Adam to be born in sin and doomed to suffering. Salvation lay in faith in Christ, moral integrity, self-sacrifice, and *engarterisis*—a combination of patience, endurance, and forbearance—the principle virtue of many of his heroes, and especially his heroines. Nothing could be further from Papadiamantis's outlook than the materialist, positivist, optimistic thinking of many of his contemporaries. Human society, as he saw it, was not perfectible, and such "European" notions as progress through science, universal education, the emancipation of women, and democratic elections would do more harm than good to the ordinary Greek, who was not ready to assimilate them. Since many parts of Greece were still not free, the time, he thought, had not yet come for Greece to consider itself a modern nation, though he felt that the Greeks were well rid of their Turkish overlords, as is clear, for instance, from "The Bewitching of the Aga."

It is thus not surprising that the fundamental moral question for Papadiamantis was the meaning of evil. "The Voice of the Dragon," the story of a young wife accused of bearing an illegitimate son and of the son's persecution as a bastard, examines the problem of evil and original sin. It is an indictment of human intolerance, replete with moral ambiguities, contradictions, and uncertainties: the narrator's voice never rules on the mother's innocence, the lawyer who defends her does more harm than good, the boy lives on the margin of his society, both figuratively and literally—he climbs to high places and goes into a cave to avoid his persecutors—and even the monk who counsels him has dubious moral authority. The one voice of good sense is the boy's aunt, yet even she has no answer to life's injustice except her faith in God's goodness. The narrative

itself is distorted by the frequent wrenching of chronological se-
quence, and these dislocations stress how impossible it is for man
to understand the meaning of evil and the ways of God to man.

Though Papadiamantis, like most European authors after Flau-
bert, usually narrates his tales from the point of view of one of the
characters, he does occasionally interrupt his story to comment in
his person. But since these comments are for the most part in
general terms and are seldom judgments on characters and their
actions, he cannot be said to employ the older method of the
omniscient narrator. Instead his authorial interventions concern
politics, social customs, and ethical and religious matters. Such, for
instance, are the remarks on the introduction of card playing
("Civilization in the Village"), the arrival of the new liberal morality
("The Murderess"), and the inevitabiliy of a child's corruption as
he grows to manhood ("The Matchmaker").

Whatever subtle distinctions one may wish to make between the
"implied author" and the flesh-and-blood writer (as Wayne Booth
does so usefully), there can be little doubt that these comments
represent the genuine judgments on public matters of Alexandros
Papadiamantis. In addition to these general views, details from the
writer's own experiences are woven into the fabric of many of the
stories. Like Mathios in "The Homesick Wife," for example, and
Kostis in "Love the Harvester," Papadiamantis was a student who
did not make good. The problem of dowering sisters, the loneliness
of a shy bachelor's existence, frequent attendance at religious rites,
longing for the unattainable woman, all common themes in his
stories, were also the central facts of his own existence. It is very
naive, nonetheless, to conflate, as some Greek critics still do, Papadiamantis the historical personage with the male characters of his
fiction or with his narrators, and to view his stories reductively as
sources for Papadiamantis's biography.

The details of Papadiamantis's life are well documented. A large
number of his letters, particularly those to his father, have survived.
His principal biographer, George Valetas, included in his monu-
mental study of the author (first edition, 1940) the comments and
impressions of many of his friends, acquaintances, and family members. Even during his lifetime Papadiamantis's character and habits
were a subject of interest among the Athenian literati, and many of
them left accounts illustrating his reported faults and virtues: his
pride, his piety, his moroseness and avoidance of social contacts, his

fondness for drink and the company of humble people. There is no doubt that his life was full of hardship, material and spiritual. His father was poor—Greek priests at that time did not receive a salary, and if they had no family means were obliged to depend on contributions from parishioners. As the elder son, Alexandros was intended by his father to be the chief support of his large brood, four daughters and another son. His father hoped to make him a high-school teacher, but though the boy had studious inclinations, his schooling from grammar school on through university studies in Athens was continually interrupted because of his ill health, his rebelliousness, or his family's lack of funds. Poverty was the constant excuse of the young Papadiamantis when as a student he wrote to his father about his slow progress. He attended the university for only two years and left without taking a degree. Though eligible, he did not even take the examination that would have qualified him as a grammar-school teacher. It is clear that he had already decided to become a writer and that he refused to shoulder the responsibilities of a routine professional existence and of providing for his father's family. It is equally clear that throughout his life he felt a deep guilt for his inability to live up to his family's expectations, and particularly for his failure to provide dowries for his sisters. Of the four girls, three never married. Papadiamantis lived most of his adult life in Athens, usually alone in run-down boarding houses, fitfully employed as a translator, frequenting tavern and church, composing his stories, and longing for the unspoiled beauty of his native Skiathos, to which he retreated for long stays when bad health or homesickness oppressed him. Finally, weakened in body and spirit, he returned to Skiathos, where he spent the last two and a half years of his life, surrounded by the affectionate solicitude of his sisters. He died in January 1911 of complications, perhaps of pneumonia, following an attack of influenza.

During his lifetime Papadiamantis was, by all accounts, extremely popular with the reading public—that is, with educated Greeks, both those who lived in Greece proper and those who were settled in large Greek communities abroad, particularly in Alexandria and Constantinople. The turn of the century was a time in Greek history when patriotic feeling, irredentism, and a desire to define the nature of modern Hellenism ran especially high. The pioneer Greek folklorist Nikolaos Politis not only aroused general interest in folk traditions and the life of the peasantry but also sought to prove that modern Greek customs and folkways were in many instances descended from those of classical antiquity. Papadiamantis therefore provided his contemporaries with just the sort of regionalism that was altogether welcome. The editors who published his stories in the newspapers and periodicals likewise gave him generous praise. After his death critical notice of Papadiamantis's work was still more laudatory.

It is significant that among his admirers have been the most eminent Greek poets of the past hundred years, including Constantine Cavafy, Kostis Palamas, and the Nobel Prize winner Odysseus Elytis. In his essay on the stature of Papadiamantis as a writer, Elytis points to the combination of realism and symbolism, sensuality and mysticism, topicality and universality he considers the distinguishing mark of Papadiamantis's work. Also, says Elytis, his diction, an unusual mixture of archaizing and colloquial speech, adds a richness and variety to his prose that is not found among his contemporaries.

Papadiamantis's novels and short stories made their first appearance in Greek newspapers and periodicals of the time. His longer works were serialized—a not infrequent practice in the nineteenth century—and almost all the earlier stories were written for special holiday issues. Between 1902 and 1908 two or three attempts were made by the author himself and by his friends to reissue some of his stories in a collection of one or more volumes. Nothing came of these efforts, mainly because of Papadiamantis's unwillingness or inability to act decisively in his own behalf. It was only in 1912, the year after his death, that the Athenian publishing house Fexis began to put out some of his work in a series of volumes. The first complete edition of Papadiamantis was that prepared by his biographer George Valetas (1954–55). Recently N. D. Triantafyllopoulos has undertaken the assembling of a new critical edition, of which four volumes (1981–1985) have appeared. In preparing these translations I have availed myself of all the published texts, following one or another as seemed most appropriate. For the benefit of the reader I have added explanatory notes dealing with Greek and Turkish expressions, local customs, religious rites, mythical and biblical references, and historical background.

The task of rendering Papadiamantis into another language presents difficulties because of his elaborate syntax and unusual diction, a diction so distinctive that a page of Papadiamantis could never be mistaken for anyone else's. The narrative portion of the stories is written in the archaizing form of Greek known as *katharevousa* ("puristic tongue"). This was an artificially modified form of the language introduced in the early nineteenth century that adhered more closely in vocabulary, morphology, and syntax to ancient classical Greek than did the current spoken (demotic) language. Until 1976 *katharevousa* was the official language of the Greek state, and during most of the nineteenth century it was the accepted literary language, at least for prose. The dialogue in the stories, on the other hand, is a faithful record of colloquial speech, often of the dialect spoken on the island of Skiathos. But even in the narrative sections Papadiamantis incorporates words and phrases from the spoken language, and at the same time he draws freely upon the vocabulary of ancient poets and Byzantine theological writers. The translator must thus deal with several forms of the Greek tongue: the ancient classical, the Byzantine ecclesiastical, the purist *katharevousa,* and more than one dialect of modern demotic Greek.

In the present translation I have rendered the original as exactly as possible without violating the demands of English idiom. For the dialogue I have adopted standard colloquial usage and try by varying the vocabulary and the level of the language to give some notion of the speech peculiarities of certain characters—for example, of the mother in "Fortune from America." I have not attempted to introduce either archaisms or English dialect forms, since these would bring associations and connotations that do not belong, I believe, in stories about a small Greek island at the turn of the century.

Elizabeth Constantinides

Tales from a Greek Island

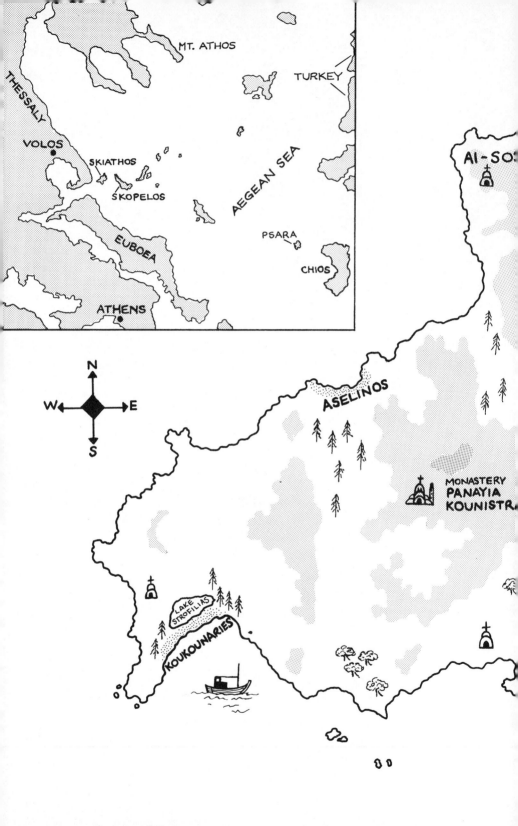

DESIGN: ANDREA GILBERT

Fortune from America

ASIMINA WAS A POOR woman, the wife of the town cooper. All her female relatives felt sorry for her and worried about how she would manage to marry off her four girls and get them settled in life. God had given her the four girls after bestowing two sons upon her. She reared these children with much toil and trouble, for her husband's work offered, to be exact, only two productive months out of each year. The rest of the time there was little to do, a few odd jobs, minor repairs. And even those two months brought more complaints and dissatisfied customers than income and profit.

All during August and September, the season when the grapes are harvested, the early muscat and the late black grape, the men and women that owned vineyards rolled kegs, drums, and barrels out of their houses and flocked to Master Stefanis so that he could repair them. Master Stefanis, who liked to jest, would say:

"What? All together in a bunch, good people? Why, the same thing happens to our confessor Father Makarios on the days before Christmas and Holy Week. No matter how powerful his blessing is, can one single priest forgive everyone's sins at one stroke? What can he do? He starts right in with his blessings and sacraments!"

In truth, how could Master Stefanis possibly please everybody, so many customers all at once? Not even with the best will in the world could he manage that. In his eagerness to please everyone, he pleased practically no one. Those whose casks he repaired first were dissatisfied, claiming that he was in such a hurry that he did a bad job. And those whose barrels were the last to be fixed complained even more loudly and sharply because their jobs were put off until the end. Each one had his particular complaint. Elderly widows would say, "Ah! It's because we're women, all alone, and have nobody to help us, that's why we're ignored. We're not human like other people." Some of the men would say, "Ah! If it's a pretty girl, really good-looking, then she gets her way . . . I know." Neighbors would say, "We have to put up with the bother and the noise you make all the time, but you don't fix *our* barrels. We don't count for anything; it's the other people that get the favors." Those who came from a distance would say, "We live in another neighborhood and have to make an effort to get our barrels here from 'way over there. But you don't pay any attention to us. Our money isn't as good as everybody else's."

In the end, most of the casks were repaired, though some people took them back before Stefanis got to them, and some tried to fix them on their own. For many years now a single cooper had held sway in that small town, yet no one else set about learning the craft. Only Uncle Dimitros Tsoumbos, sixty years old, presented himself as an apprentice. But he was so slow and sluggish, and had been from his youth onwards, that even if he did manage to learn something, he would forget it before he learned it, as the ancient comic poet says.

Master Stefanis was so busy during the two months of early autumn that from the crack of dawn until nightfall not even for a minute could he leave his workshop and the lean-to in front of it that he himself had built with logs and branches. His only other activity was to go to church on Sunday mornings and, as he was rushing by, to stop for a moment by the door of the small cafe of John the Vlach. He would call out to Andonis, the son of the owner: "Father Abraham! Send Lazarus!" "Send Lazarus" was the arranged signal for Andonis to bring him a small glass of raki if it was summer, or rum if it was winter. One glass a day was all Stefanis drank.

When Stathis, the firstborn, was twelve years old, his father took him out of school so that he could learn the cooper's craft. But scarcely had Stathis begun to learn a bit of the craft than he became infatuated with the sailor's life and went to sea. Three years later, when the second son, Thanasis, reached the same age, his father took him away from his books as well and put him to work in the shop. But this boy did not have the patience to learn even the rudiments. When he was thirteen he began to go out every day with the small fishing boats and ferries, and then when he was fourteen he sailed off on a schooner.

The people of our island had no bent for any occupations except seafaring. None of them ever became a land merchant or a factory owner or a manual laborer. Even if they were taught a trade, they abandoned it for their fickle mistress, the sea.

Nonetheless, the firstborn son of Master Stefanis never entirely ceased being a cooper, though he spent most of the time at sea. Stathis would always come back in July or August and stay for a few months to help his father. He grew to maturity, got married, and became a good, sober man.

As for the second son, he traveled a great deal, returning two or three times with long absences in between. Afterwards, when he was eighteen years old, he embarked on a large ship and went to America. From there he wrote two or three letters, with long periods of silence in between, promising that he would send them money soon. But he never did. Then he stopped writing and was not heard from any more.

Ten years went by. Thanasis gave no sign of existence. On two occasions Master Stefanis learned indirectly through a second party who had heard it from others, who had met the son, that he was living in one of the South American republics. Evidently there was plenty of gold there, but also plenty of disease, corruption, and crime.

During the first years of the young man's absence, neighbors and friends sometimes teased his father:

"Thanasis must have grown a mustache by now, Master Stefanis."

"What did you think he'd grow . . . spinach?"

"How is it," others would say, "that Thanasis has not sent any gold sovereigns yet?"

"The sovereigns have to get yellower. They're still not ripe."

One should note that "sovereign" was the term used in those parts for a type of squash that grew to a great size as it ripened.

If, however, Master Stefanis felt any longing for his absent son, he kept it to himself. In the past few years, as he grew older, he had begun to disobey his own rules and to stand two or three times a day outside John the Vlach's store calling out the password:

"Have mercy on me . . . and send Lazarus!"

During these years a different fate befell each of the four daughters, those daughters whose settlement was the anxious concern of Asimina's cousins.

The second daughter met her fate when she was only seven years old, before her elder sister did and before her brother left for America. One evening after a heavy rainfall had filled all the wells, holes, and depressions in the ground, little Rodavyi (that was her name) happened to be in the courtyard of a neighbor's house. She was bending over the edge of the deep well in her efforts to set a bird's feather afloat. Every day she used to see the boys floating objects in the nearby rivulet formed by rain in the low-lying center of the town, and she was now trying to imitate them. She bent a little too far over the side, lost her grip, and plunged headlong into the well. Her cries were stifled, and there was nobody nearby to see her. She tried in vain to reach up and grasp the partially covered mouth of the well. She thrashed about on the surface gasping. A few minutes later they brought her up dead.

Eleni, the eldest daughter, was the next to meet her fate, and this she did along with her younger sister, Margaro. Their fates were intertwined, yet paradoxically diverse. Eleni was betrothed to Panayis Nikoutsikos, a cabinetmaker by trade, who had been chosen for her by her mother's cousins as a fine, hardworking young man. When, however, the future bridegroom made his formal suit, as was the custom of that place, and entered the house of his father-in-law for the first time, he took his first look at the bride chosen for him and, at the same time, at her younger sister, Margaro. (Our women had, alas, discarded the veil a long time before.) Panayis did not want Eleni, he wanted Margaro: he did not want Leah, he

wanted Rachel. The next day he did not hesitate to express his preference to his future mother-in-law:

"Either you give me Margaro or I'll send the tokens back."

That the groom would toss away "the tokens"—that is, dissolve
the betrothal—was a chilling prospect. What could poor Asimina
and her husband, Master Stefanis, do? After much hesitation, inde-
cision, and quarreling, and after Asimina had heard her cousins'
opinion, the parents were forced to yield.

When Margaro heard that the bridegroom preferred her, she was
not slow to say that she wanted him too. She was indeed more
comely, more blooming than her sister, and she was just eighteen
years old. Eleni, poor thing, took it to heart that she was pushed
aside. Even before, she had always seemed somewhat pale, ill-
favored, and homely. No one knows whether she had been unwell
prior to these events, but what is certain is that soon afterwards, two
months after Margaro's wedding, Eleni died of consumption.

And that is how it came about that all at once, in one swoop, so
to speak, all the affectionate concerns of Asimina's cousins
evaporated.

The only daughter who now remained was Afendra, the young-
est, and she became the apple of her mother's eye. Her mother's
cousins were not very worried about her. Asimina had a mother's
ambition combined with a mother's longing for her absent son. In
her daydreams she would envision the triumph and splendor of his
future return from America. "My Afendra's fortune," she would say,
"will come from America."

And so the girl grew up with this idea in mind. In the meantime,
however, her fortune nearly came to her from more remote
horizons, from those regions, that is, whence it had come to the
unfortunate Eleni and to little Rodavyi.

A cousin of Master Stefanis's had married into a prominent family. She was now an elderly widow living on a pension. Because her
husband had been an administrative official, she was known as
Eparchina. She had lived in other towns of Greece and had acquired
foreign tastes and habits. One of her caprices, which seemed quite
odd to the local townspeople, was to arrange for her grave to be
constructed while she was still alive. It was dug in the grounds of
the public cemetery and had her name inscribed on a slab:

Here lies the late lamented P. H.
Widow of the late lamented sub-prefect S. H.

A few others before her, it is true, had done something similar. One old couple had dug twin graves and had left them gaping wide with their names inscribed on the tombstone. They were now of a ripe old age, he eighty-seven, she eighty-four. The graves yawned enticingly at visitors, but the husband and wife did not die. Some people said the two had constructed those open graves on purpose, in order to fool Death and to exorcise his power. And so the widow P. H. had followed their example.

One summer evening, a little after sundown, soon after her grave was dug and whitewashed and its shoring walls newly plastered, the old widow came by the cemetery. She was accompanied by her second cousin, the little Afendra, then twelve years old, for whom she seemed to have tender feelings. With baskets hanging from the crooks of their arms, they entered the cemetery grounds so that the widow could see her grave and point it out to her small cousin as a noteworthy sight.

"There, Afendra. Look where they'll put me."

The girl looked down with guileless curiosity and without fear.

"What a pretty little grave you'll have, auntie," she said, "a tiny little one."

"They measured me," said the old women, "but I don't know if I'll fit exactly. I'd like to go in just once and lie down to try it out . . . I'd have to stretch out well . . ."

The child laughed in spite of herself.

"How can you, auntie?" she said. "How can you lie down and try it out with that little hump on your back?"

The old woman grimaced.

"No!" she said. "I don't have a hump. How can I have a hump?" She lifted her hand to her back. "When we die," she continued peevishly, with some bitterness, "then the hump disappears from our backs, then all bodies become straight and we are all alike, all level to this plain where we will lie and to this earth that will cover us."

Suddenly the old woman had an idea. "Afendra dear, would you like to go in there and lie down nicely and feel proud of yourself so that I can see what I'll look like when they put me in? We're almost

6

the same height since you're growing so fast. If you stretched a little and if I stood a bit straighter, we'd be about the same height."

The little girl smiled guilelessly, without fear. She laid down her basket and descended into the open hole. She sat down, smoothed the hem of her dress, then stretched out, crossed her arms, closed her eyes, and felt proud of herself, as her elderly cousin had said.

"That's enough!" cried the widow of the sub-prefect. "Get up! People shouldn't see us. They'll think there's something wrong with us. How nicely you play dead! Come quickly! Let's go!"

That same evening Afendra narrated the event to two of her playmates. One of them, who was two years older, cried out in alarm and thoroughly frightened the girl.

"Oooh! You played at being dead? And you can even talk about it?"

"Why?"

"The ghosts will get you! They'll want to take you with them!"

Then Afendra really became frightened. That night she went to bed with a headache. She developed a fever. All night long in her troubled dreams she saw dead men and graves and ghosts. Her elderly cousin seemed to be dead and to have turned into a vampire that wanted to drink her blood. Afendra woke up ice cold and was overcome by deadly convulsions.

She had a bad case of the "frights," as her mother said. In the evening they called a priest and he began to read from the four Gospels over her head. The widow Eparchina was very distressed, and tried to placate the girl's mother, who, however, showed by her expression the ill will she bore her husband's cousin.

"Imagine Eparchina!" thought poor Asimina to herself. "Trying to drive my girl out of her wits, just like that! What business did she have going to the graveyard? What business, indeed? And she says she made her jump into the grave that she had dug to try it out for size! An innocent young girl, fresh as new wine! And she made her stretch out in the hole, just think! To scare away the dead . . . to keep Death away, that nasty miserable old woman, so he won't take her and save her from her sins! And she pushed her into the hole, just think! And she played at being dead, just think! Who knows if she didn't throw some earth on top of her and if she didn't wish evil on her? And now misfortune has touched my child. How can I bear having her crazy, frightened out of her wits, dear Lord! A precious daughter, fresh as a cool breeze. And I was counting on Thanasis to come from America and bring a heap of gold sovereigns. Then I would marry her off and set her up as mistress of her house, and I would be the happiest woman alive. Now Eparchina has done me a nice turn, indeed. May God give her what she deserves!"

When the priest had finished reading from the four Gospels over Afendra's head, she began to show signs of improvement. After three weeks the morbid fancies began to dissipate bit by bit from her mind. Her mother tried to cheer her up.

"There's nothing wrong with you, Afendra dear. You're fine now! And wait till our Thanasis comes from America to bring you all sorts of nice things and lots and lots of gold sovereigns. Then I'll deck you out and you'll be a bride, and on your wedding day I'll put a necklace of a hundred gold sovereigns around your neck, and you'll wear the wedding garland. You'll feel proud of yourself and everyone will envy you."

At that time a letter arrived from America. Thanasis wrote that he was well, and that his return would be delayed a little so that he could bring back many gold sovereigns.

YEARS went by. Thanasis had already been in America for seventeen years. He was more than thirty-five years old and his sister was over twenty. She was not too old, and her mother was confident that her daughter's fortune would not be long in coming. Only when Afendra quarreled with one of her companions did she hear the old refrain, the kind of remark that gives rise to derogatory epithets for every man and woman who lives in a small community. For there, nothing is hidden from anyone, and the passage from friendship to enmity is swift and easy. The old refrain would ring out again from the lips of her friend of yesterday, her enemy of today:

"Crazy . . . frightened out of her wits . . . that's her!"

This would reach the ears of all prospective suitors. But if Thanasis were to come from America and bring as much gold as his mother dreamed of, then that other difficulty would become a very small impediment for a prospective bridegroom.

At length, one fine morning, there came a letter in a large colored envelope with a whole array of seals and stamps.

"May it bring good news, neighbor!"

"May it bring good news, cousin!"

"Thank you, and good wishes to you too!"

Asimina was filled with joy, as was her daughter Afendra. The young woman considered the letter as indeed the bearer of the good fortune she had awaited for so long a time.

"Reverend," they called out, "come and read us the letter!"

The priest, who lived nearby, came up into Master Stefanis's house and read the letter. It was indeed from Thanasis. He wrote that he would come in one month. His health was not very good, he said, but he was convinced that the fresh air of his native island would make him well. He would also bring with him all his modest savings.

After so many years it was not only the sovereigns that had turned yellower in the South American climate, as Master Stefanis once said they would. His son's complexion had also grown yellower. In March he arrived in Piraeus and went up to Athens to consult some doctors. They found that he was consumptive. He appeared before the doctors with all his rings, chains, and tiepins. They took some of his sovereigns, gave him many prescriptions, various bottles with colored liquids, and powders smelling of the pharmacy, and advised him to go to his island, which was his destination anyway.

When it became known in the town that a ship was bringing Thanasis and that he had his gold sovereigns with him, his mother received five proposals of marriage for her daughter Afendra. An even greater number were ready to send proposals for Thanasis himself, but they knew that the young man would not marry before he had made arrangements for his sister. Therefore, all who were interested in him, male and female, vied in offering their services as go-betweens and brokers, thus helping to get his sister settled as quickly as possible. When Thanasis arrived, they took a good look at him and saw how thin and pale he was. They realized that he would not wed here on earth and dropped their projects.

Among the suitors asking for Afendra's hand, a young man who owned a small shop was considered the most desirable. He was commonly known as Grigoris the son of Monevaso. Grigoris reasoned that the money the sick man was bringing from America would be very handy for improving his business, paying off his debts, and getting more credit. Asimina's cousins, once again, thought of the advantages: it would be a good thing to have a relative in the mercantile class, which exercised considerable influence over the little town and ennobled it by providing it with its mayors and councillors. Finally, a match was agreed upon, and the pair was betrothed.

Stathis, the elder son of Stefanis, took the bank draft that his brother had brought from America, went to Volos, and got cash for it. The money amounted to five hundred British sovereigns. Stathis returned from Volos with eighteen or nineteen thousand paper drachmas. This was what the property of Thanasis came to.

After Easter the consumptive was taken to the small monastery of Saint Charalambos, located in a beautiful rural setting. The prospective groom, considering himself a civilized man, demanded that his betrothed set aside her native costume and adopt European dress. Afendra herself was especially eager to dress in the foreign manner, because out of superstition she did not wish to wear at her wedding any of the finery that had belonged to Eleni, her dead sister. Part of this garb had been buried with Eleni, but part of it was still stored in the chest. Afendra's other sister, Margaro, had been married very quickly. Her wedding dress had been gotten up on the spur of the moment, because at the time Eleni had no intention of handing over her own wedding finery to Margaro, nor for that matter would Margaro have accepted it. What was left of Eleni's costume in the chest was imposingly old-fashioned. It was in fact the wedding dress of her mother, somewhat altered to suit a later fashion. Afendra was much younger. Her fortune had come from America, and she wanted to adapt to the times.

The consumptive Thanasis was full of courage and hoped that he would regain his health now that he was back in his native land. He told his mother after his sister's betrothal:

"Just let me get well, mother, and then we'll have the wedding."

"Don't worry, my son, you'll get well, God willing. How can we have a wedding if you're not well? We'll have a lot of young girls to deal with, too. People will be sending us marriage proposals for you, dear Thanasis. They told me that five or six mothers are ready to send their proposals, just think! Lucky me! I'm the luckiest woman alive! They promise this, they promise that. But, don't worry, we're going to look carefully before we make our choice. They won't fool us . . . just take heart . . . you'll get well."

The delay did not please Grigoris the son of Monevaso, and evidently it did not please Afendra either. During those days the mother of the groom, old Monevaso, also happened to fall ill. On one occasion, as Grigoris was leaving his betrothed's house after a visit and was standing between the door and the staircase, Afendra whispered softly into his ear:

"Tell your mother that we're afraid Thanasis may die, and then because of mourning we'll be forced to put off the wedding. And I'll tell Thanasis that we're afraid your mother may die, and out of sorrow we'll be forced to put off the wedding until next year."

"Don't worry, I'll take care of it," said the groom with genuine admiration.

Thanasis gave in to his sister's request. But Monevaso would not think of letting her son go through with the wedding unless she could be there to give her blessing. Fortunately, her health improved, and she got out of bed in a few days. The preparations for the wedding were going on apace, and the invalid brother had been brought back to town from his rural retreat at Saint Charalambos, when the older brother Stathis and the groom had a disagreement about the money for the dowry.

The groom maintained that they had agreed on a sum of five thousand drachmas above and beyond the house, the vineyard, the small olive grove, and the bride's trousseau. Stathis on the other hand insisted that the sum was four and a half thousand, and included the value of the trousseau, the furniture, and the other household objects. Both were telling the truth, since each had mentioned a different amount as they were shaking hands over the agreement. And since, moreover, the groom insisted that his bride's clothes be in the Western style, her outfit would cost about a thousand drachmas. Stathis said he was prepared to be accommodating and to lay out four thousand for his sister with no argument.

When Afendra and her mother complained about Stathis to Thanasis, he agreed with them and told them to give the groom another thousand drachmas. But Stathis had assumed the power to bind and to loose, and could not be persuaded. The groom and Stathis exchanged sharp words.

"You seem to be playing the boss with another man's money. Somebody else earned this money."

"And do you think you're going to open up a big store with my brother's money—money that ruined his health? And where are your earnings?"

Just then old Stefanis happened to come in on his way back from the market, where he had stopped off at the tavern of John the Vlach. A proverb came into his mind:

"Well! Why don't you calm down? You're like the two men who were quarreling over somebody else's . . ."

Old Stefanis was not able to finish his sentence. Afendra, being well acquainted with his proverbs, turned toward her father, shook her head, and quickly brought her finger to her lips. She was afraid that her betrothed would take offense. Stathis knew his man, however, and was sure of the bridegroom's meek and conciliatory nature. As a matter of fact, even though he had insisted on a thousand more, Grigoris had already been given four thousand drachmas on the previous day and had already laid out a large part of this money for his business.

Upon his return to town the invalid Thanasis could no longer live in his father's house, whose ownership had now been transferred by written agreement to the groom as part of the dowry. It was there that the wedding banquet and celebration were to take place. To the west of the house there was a small square and beyond the square some other dwellings. One of these, a small house belonging to a poor woman, was rented for the invalid and his parents to move into.

Even though the consumptive was not strong enough to rise from his sickbed to attend the wedding, he would be able to look out the window and watch the dancing that would take place afterwards in the open square. It was already the beginning of summer. The young bridegroom evidently liked ostentation. He wished to invite a large number of guests, strangers as well as friends, to his wedding.

Meanwhile the demand for the additional thousand drachmas had still not been met. Thanasis told Stathis to pay it from the money that had been given to him for expenses. Stathis frowned, grumbled, and said, "All right!" However, he did not hand the money over to Grigoris. On the day before the wedding, the groom made his demand once more. Stathis then said that he had no more money, since everything he had been given had been spent on the wedding: let Thanasis give more money, if he wished. That is what Stathis said to the groom. To Thanasis he said:

"We'll give it to him after they're married, as a second dowry. What do you think?"

"Yes," said Thanasis, who was easily persuaded to everything he was told, especially by Stathis.

"Yes, of course," added Stathis, "That's how he'll show that he trusts us too, just as we trusted him."

When the older brother left, Afendra came in. She approached Thanasis's bed and began to fuss over him. She spoke in soothing tones:

"Well, you see, dear Thanasis, since that old mother-in-law of mine is afraid she'll die and insists on having her way and wants to have the wedding now . . . I told her you have to get well first and then we'll be married . . . no sooner did she get out of bed than she was in a hurry to give us her blessing. She's afraid she'll have a relapse . . . still, you're better now, Thanasis, aren't you?"

"Maybe I am better," said Thanasis, who was easily convinced that his health had improved when someone suggested it to him. In truth there were on occasion seeming improvements in his condition.

"God willing! May He restore you to good health. Maybe you'll get up, dear Thanasis? Maybe you'll gather your strength and come to the wedding and be proud of me when I'm wearing the wedding wreath?"

"We'll see . . . if I can . . . whatever the doctor says."

"If you don't come, they won't lay the wreaths on our heads," said Afendra. "You're a second father to us. We'll kiss your hand, Grigoris and I . . . meanwhile, won't you give the money yourself? They've promised him a thousand more drachmas. Won't you give it with your own dear hand? Do you have it under your pillow?"

As she spoke she looked covetously at the spot where the pillow lay, as if she wished to see what lay beneath the linen pillowcase and the woollen stuffing. She made a movement as if she were going to thrust her hand under the pillow. Thanasis did, in fact, have a wallet under his pillow that contained most of the money that Stathis had brought from Volos, about eleven thousand drachmas in all.

"Won't you give it," repeated the young woman, so that the groom won't find an excuse? At this point, dear Thanasis, we can't call it off. What would people say? If he does something to me, God forbid, and then says he won't marry me . . . I'd rather . . ." Tears choked her voice.

At that moment Stathis entered. Possibly he had been standing outside and had his ear cocked, or perhaps he just happened to overhear. Stathis changed the subject. He mentioned the details of the arrangements for the wedding, how there would be so many guests that they could not all fit in the house.

"This bridegroom has a swollen head," he said.

"Don't say that," said Thanasis smiling. "Our sister will be angry."

"I'm her brother," replied Stathis. "Grigoris is nothing to her yet."

Afendra had lowered her gaze and was silent. Asimina, who had been standing in the hallway, heard Stathis and came in.

"This is a joyful occasion. We're going to have a wedding that everyone will hear about. The mayor, the harbormaster, the telegraph man, the just-as-a-peace, the chiefest police, the customs officer . . . our groom has invited all of them! We'll have such a celebration tomorrow that it'll be heard far and wide, yes it will! They'll be having such a good time that it'll last for three weeks. Tell our cousin Kopsidakis to slaughter four lambs, three sheep, and two goats, a regular feast! And the *koumbaros,* too, will slaughter two goats and bring pies and baklava. And violins and lutes, just think! and all sorts of instruments, just think! and all the local violinists and three from somewhere else, and the gypsies with their clarinets, just think! Everyone will dance and they'll jump as high as the sky, just think! And that's not all. Girls will be coming for Thanasis, and their mothers will bring sugar cakes and *kourambiedes* and all sorts of good things. Yes, this winter we'll have another wedding. Is there any mother like me? It's a wonder I can still keep my head, don't you think?"

At that very moment a paroxysm of coughing and stomach pains seized the consumptive man. In all the confusion and noise, while the two women were trying to make the invalid comfortable, Stathis slid his hand under the pillow, snatched the billfold unobserved, and placed it calmly in his shirt. Soon Thanasis recovered from the seizure. His mother shut the bedroom door tightly, and as they were standing in the corridor said:

"Let him sleep. It's a sin in the eyes of God. He'll give the drachmas tomorrow. Blessings be on my boy! If only all of you could have someone to keep on providing for you. My boy has lost his youth, he is a sick man. For so many years he was deep in the earth where they get silver from, just think! Way down deep like a mole, just think, digging in the mines. Let him breathe; let him take in some air! He's wasting away in this world above, melting like a candle, my poor boy! Let him get a good night's sleep."

By the next day all the preparations for the wedding had been completed. The evening before, as Afendra's betrothed was saying good-night, she whispered a few words to him privately:

"He'll give me the thousand drachmas tomorrow. Mother gave her promise too."

The musicians went to escort the *koumbaros* to the groom's paternal home. Accompanying the *koumbaros* and the violin players were many of the guests, and also Stathis, dressed in all his finery. As the crowd was standing in front of his house, Grigoris, having no one else to ask, whispered to Stathis:

"What about the thousand drachmas?"

"I think Thanasis gave them to Afendra," answered Stathis hurriedly.

The procession of guests, violinists, and lute players that was escorting the bridegroom and the *koumbaros* arrived outside the bride's house. The groom, the *koumbaros,* and the relatives went up into the house while the others waited at the doorway. A few minutes later the bridal party came down leading the bride. She was decked out in a gown of last year's fashion and wore a hat trimmed with artificial orange blossoms. The bride was escorted by her mother and her cousins. Asimina was wearing the native costume, a silk overdress, a sleeved vest, and a jacket of black velvet, and the cousins were likewise arrayed in their finery. Old Stefanis was dressed in a pair of thirty-year-old island trousers of the baggy style, which, during the whole of his life, he had worn only five times before. He also wore a red fez with a blue tassel, brought to him from Tunisia at the time of the Crimean War. The fez was a gift from his own *koumbaros,* the captain of a merchant vessel, long since dead. From the pocket of his inner jacket, which came to his knees, Stefanis had hung a long red kerchief of flowered silk.

Before they descended, as the groom was approaching the bride, he asked in a very low voice, so that the *koumbaros* and the others would not hear:

"Did Thanasis give it to you?"

Afendra did not dare utter a word. Her head was already bent forward, and blushing she lowered it even further.

"Do you have it?" asked Grigoris again.

The young woman gave another, somewhat less noticeable, nod.

It was ten o'clock on Sunday morning, and the liturgy had ended. The procession headed for the church, where the marriage ceremony took place.

The wedding was a formal affair. After the dinner all the guests—the mayor, the harbormaster, the justice of the peace, the customs official, and the others Asimina had enumerated—all came with their wives for the dancing, some to dance, some as spectators only. The festivities took place in the small square beyond the house.

Many people participated in the dancing, almost everyone had a good time, and no one was disappointed. The unfortunate consumptive, Thanasis, had gotten out of his bed with difficulty and was seated on a sofa near the window. From there he could see the dancing, and as he watched he felt an inner satisfaction.

"If I hadn't come from America," he said to himself, "if I hadn't brought the money, none of this would be happening. Maybe there would have been a wedding, but it would have been a very shabby affair. And there wouldn't have been such dancing."

He felt the need at that moment to stroke the billfold he had placed under the pillow and had not looked at for three or four days. Being in the last stages of his illness, he could hardly stand on his feet. He pulled himself up and took three steps toward the bed. He lifted the pillow and saw that there was nothing underneath. The billfold was gone. He raised the other pillow and searched among the sheets. No trace of the billfold; it had disappeared.

He broke out into a cold sweat, and an agonizing cough choked off his breath.

"Mother! Mother!"

Little Anthousa, a poor girl who was a relative of the family, had been hired at the time to tend to the invalid, and she was standing at the door of the small house gazing enthralled at the dancing crowd, which took the shape of a long string of people, multicolored and perpetually in motion. In spite of the noise outside Anthousa heard Thanasis's cry and his coughing. She ran upstairs.

"Are you all right, Thanasis?"

"Anthousa! . . . Anthousa! . . . Run quickly, get my mother!"

"But she's in the dance."

"She's got to stop. Tell her to get here fast."

After a short time Asimina appeared. "Oh! I'm glad Anthousa came and made me leave the dance. I'm all dizzy, my child! What with the young women of today, the wife of the mayor, the wife of the just-as-a-peace, the wife of the harbormaster, the wife of the telegraph man—what do I know about dancing? That's enough for me. Well, good luck and happiness to the newlyweds! . . . Why did you call me, Anthousa? Do you want me for anything, Thanasis?"

"Mother, who took my billfold?"

"Your what? What did you say?"

"My billfold where the money was."

"Eh?"

"It's gone. They stole it from me, mother."

"What do you mean, my son?"

At that moment Stathis's voice was heard calling from outside the door. "Mother! Mother!"

"Who's calling? Is that you, Stathis?" Asimina leaned out the window.

"Tell Thanasis that I have the billfold. He shouldn't worry."

Thanasis was only partly soothed. "Why didn't he come in?"

"He's busy, my son. He's got all the bother of the dancing and the entertainment, and the refreshments. He's tending to all the guests."

Then the mother went down, crossed the square, and approached Stathis. She gave him an inquiring look.

"Go and tell Thanasis," said Stathis. "Tell him Stathis has the billfold and will give it back to him. I took it because I was afraid that your daughter would grab it when the coughing fit came over him. She was trying to persuade him to give her the thousand drachmas, the extra money the groom was asking for. That door is closed for good now. There won't be any second dowry."

The celebration lasted all day long and far into the night. The dancing stopped occasionally but soon started up again. Finally the guests scattered, one by one. Only the *koumbaros* and the relatives remained with the violinists and the lute players. After midnight they ate a second dinner. At dawn the *koumbaros* and the relatives promenaded to the music of the violins and the lutes. Then they returned and stood under the newlywed's window, where they sang the traditional nuptial song.

All that evening, that night, and the next morning Stathis did not approach the small house where his brother lay. The night before the wedding Thanasis had slept well despite his coughing fit and seemed to be resting quietly. On the night of the wedding, however, having discovered the loss of his billfold, he went sleepless and was wracked by violent fits of coughing.

It was during the midnight dinner, while the *koumbaros* and the close relatives were enjoying themselves, that the groom remembered to ask the bride:

"Where do you have the thousand? On you?"

Afendra nodded imperceptibly.

"And may I ask," continued Grigoris, "why your mother didn't put that necklace of gold sovereigns round your neck as you told me she said she would?"

"And where are we going to find the sovereigns?" asked Afendra, who now found her tongue. After all, the dressmaker had told her that brides who wear Western clothing were not obliged to keep quiet and merely look proud as in the old days when they wore embroidered caps and gold-woven skirts—in fact, said the dressmaker, they used to look like turtles. "And where are we going to find the sovereigns? Stathis only brought folding money from Volos. And anyway, the necklace my mother mentioned would only look good if I wore the local costume. It doesn't go with what I'm wearing now."

In the morning, when the last guests finally left to go home to bed, and Stathis returned to his own house, the old father came to get him.

"Go see your brother," he called out. "He wants you."

Stathis was in bed. He went back to sleep for a while and did nothing.

After a bit Asimina ran out and called Stathis's wife.

"Yerakina, where is Stathis? Is he still sleeping? Thanasis isn't well. Tell him to come quickly!"

A little later, Margaro, Stathis's other sister, came in.

"Hurry up, Stathis. Run! Thanasis is dying."

Stathis had gotten up. He washed, combed his hair, and kept delaying.

Soon afterwards an aunt appeared.

"Stathis! Come quickly! Thanasis is asking for you. He's breathing his last."

The last to appear was old Stefanis, once more.

"Run! Hurry! Your brother is receiving the last sacraments."

Finally Stathis set out. He encountered the priest, who was descending from the small house bareheaded and holding the sacred vessel. Stathis removed his cap, bowed low, and finally went up into the house.

Thanasis was at death's door. Stathis approached with a cheerful countenance and placed the billfold in his brother's hands. Thanasis took it and smiled.

"Forgive me, my brother," Stathis said. "I did it to be helpful. So they wouldn't strip you of everything. You need the money to look after yourself. To get well. To live a long, long time."

The consumptive said, "Thank you," grasped the billfold in his hand, and breathed his last. As soon as Thanasis gave up the ghost, Stathis took the billfold back and stuffed it in his shirt.

Asimina uttered a wail. Then, after the dead man was laid out, she forbade any lamentations. Her family had just celebrated a wedding, and the house of the new bride was nearby, a hundred feet away. It was not proper that the first day of her daughter's married life should be darkened by mournful sounds.

As soon as Master Stefanis heard that Thanasis was dead, he went off to the market, passed in front of the tavern, and called to Andonis, the son of the Vlach:

"Father Abraham! Have mercy on me and send Lazarus!"

Stefanis did not know that Stathis had taken the billfold with the money, nor that he had returned it to Thanasis, nor that he had taken it back again.

The couple's honeymoon was saddened by the death of their benefactor and the provider of their dowry. For a long time afterwards Grigoris kept on asking for the thousand drachmas and complaining to his wife that she had lied to him. Afendra, however, insisted that she had never told him with her own lips that she had received the money.

Stathis promised to take care of his parents in their old age, but he was never persuaded to give the second dowry to the groom. He had now found another argument: that the other brother-in-law, the husband of the older sister, Margaro, was now demanding a second dowry too, since the dowry he had originally received was much poorer than Afendra's.

"What will all these second dowries lead us to? What will become of us?" said Stathis.

Old Stefanis added sadly:

"What one man sows, another man reaps."

The Homesick Wife

THREE NIGHTS INTO ITS waning, the moon appeared over the mountain peak, and after many a mournful song and many a sigh, the young woman garbed in white finally exclaimed:

"If only I could climb into a little boat now . . . I think we could get to the other side." She pointed beyond the harbor.

Mathios did not notice that she had changed from "I" to "we" in the closing words of her wish. Impetuously, without thinking, he answered:

"I could lower that boat into the water . . . What do you say? Shall we try it?" He also used the plural as he ended his words. Without reflecting, as if he were only testing the strength of his muscles, he began to shove the boat.

The youth stood on the shoreline, where one after another the waves broke with a soft murmur and were swallowed by the sand.

The waves never grew weary of this eternal, monotonous game, and the sand never grew satiated with their everlasting salty wetness. The young woman was sitting on the balcony of the house her husband, an aging man of fifty-three, had rented for himself and his wife. The house stood by the shore. When the south wind brought in the flood tide, it was washed by the waves. When the north wind brought in the ebb tide, the waves did not reach it. The boat was partly drawn onto the land, partly bobbing in the sea, its prow buried in the sand, its stern moving in the waves. It was light, graceful, and slender of prow, and could carry four or five passengers.

A big local schooner had come into port three days earlier and was waiting for a favorable wind to sail off to her port of destination. This was the third day that the captain had been resting happily at home with his wife and children. The crew, all local men, were making the rounds of the taverns, seeking compensation in three nights for their forced temperance of many weeks and months. The only one left behind to guard the cargo and the ship's fittings was the cabin boy, and the only one to guard the cabin boy was the ship's dog. The cabin boy, a tall lad of eighteen, insisted, however, on all a sailor's prerogatives except the pay, and that evening he was whiling away his time at an out-of-the-way tavern on the street behind the waterfront market. A stranger in a strange land, he too was seeking solace. He had drawn the landing boat halfway onto the beach, with its prow buried in the sand and its stern floating in the waves. The oars lay in the stern, so light that a child could wield them with measureless delight, proud that his strength was multiplied by the yielding softness of the waves, waves that yield as a fond mother does to her pampered babe, who with his wails and demands makes her go where he wishes. Like a gull's wings that carry its white-feathered body over the sea's surface to the cavern of a rock washed by the water, so the oars would guide the little boat to an embracing sandy beach.

Mathios braced his arms against the prow, dug in with his legs stretched out behind him, and shoved with all his might. The boat surrendered and fell with a splash into the sea. It almost got away under the momentum of his vigorous push, because he did not have the foresight to hold on to the tow rope. Though he did not have time to roll up his trousers, he kicked off his light sandals and wading knee-deep grasped the boat by the prow and pulled it to the small dock nearby.

Meanwhile the young woman had disappeared from the balcony. In a few minutes she emerged from the northern corner of the house, her white waistcoat gleaming in the moonlight, and came to the edge of the water. The youth saw her and felt joy mixed with trepidation. He acted almost unconsciously. He did not think she was capable of doing it.

Unwilling to express her inner thoughts, the young woman said simply, "Oh well, let's just row around the harbor now that the moon is out." After a pause she added, "Just to see what it will be like when I set sail for over there." She always said "over there" when she referred to her native village.

The risen moon illuminated the mountain, green by day and black by night, and now turned its usual nocturnal darkness to a shadowy gray. Behind this mountain loomed the ridge of another, at times snow-covered, at times bare and rocky. There lay her native village, her birthplace. She sighed for it as deeply as if a great ocean separated them, yet it was a mere twelve miles distant, close enough that by day the low hump of the green mountain could not cover the towering ridge of the white one behind it. The young woman longed for her native village as if she had been separated from it for many years, though in fact she had been on this nearby island for only a few weeks.

She then innocently placed her soft white hand on the youth's shoulder—his whole being shuddered at her touch—and she stepped into the boat. He climbed in after her, took up the oars, and awkwardly began to turn about. Instead of pushing against the dock, however, he rammed the left oar against the seabed, so that the boat came alongside and bumped against one of the stones of the dock.

"Look out! We're going to damage somebody's boat!" she called out. At this she began to consider the whole matter more soberly and added, "Won't they be looking for their boat? Won't they need it? Whose is it, I wonder."

The youth, somewhat flustered, answered, "We're only going around the harbor, then we're coming back, and I don't think they'll be looking for it before then . . . whoever it is that it belongs to."

He sat at the oars and began to row. She sat in the stern, her beautiful face turned toward the pale light of the moon, which sprinkled silver dust over her delicate features. The youth looked at her shyly.

He was not a sailor, but, raised near the sea, he knew how to row. He had abandoned his studies at the school in the provincial capital and had come back home in the middle of the term after refusing to submit to the punishment imposed on him when he had words with one of his teachers, who seemed to him more ignorant than could be tolerated. He was barely eighteen, but looked more like nineteen or twenty with his thick, dark, curly beard and mustache.

After the young woman settled down in the boat, another worry entered her mind, a sequel to the one she had voiced about the owner's search for his boat, and she cheerily added, "The boat owner will look for his boat and Uncle Monahakis will look for his Lialio."

The youth smiled. Uncle Monahakis was her husband's name, and Lialio was hers.

At that moment the loud barking of a dog was heard from a ship's deck. It was the mascot of the loaded schooner, whose boat they were in. The dog had jumped onto the tip of the schooner's prow, next to the carved figurehead, a crude helmeted female. Upon seeing the boat the dog at first wagged his tail, but when it drew closer and the dog did not recognize the cabin boy or any other crew member in the two passengers, he began to howl and wail excitedly.

The youth veered away from the schooner, but when the dog saw the boat withdrawing, he howled even more excitedly.

"What's wrong? Why doesn't he keep quiet?" asked Lialio.

"He probably recognized the boat."

"Does this little boat belong to the schooner?"

"Probably."

The youth offered this conjecture with some regret, for if this was the case it would necessarily cut short his dreamlike excursion. But contrary to his expectation Lialio clapped her hands like a naughty child that finds pleasure in what others insist on forbidding.

"Then I'm happy," she said. "Let the dog bark for his boat, and let them search for me at home."

The youth screwed up his courage and asked, "Where was Mr. Monahakis when you left the house?"

Lialio answered, "He spends all his time at the cafe, doesn't budge from there till midnight. He always leaves me alone." She seemed on the verge of tears, but with a great effort controlled herself.

The youth kept on rowing. After a while they came to the

eastern mouth of the harbor. From there against the horizon one could see the long island where the white mountain arose, at times snowy, at times bare and rocky. They approached the promontory that formed one side of the harbor's mouth, which was sheltered at the southwest by two or three islets, and the young woman fixed her gaze on the horizon, as if she wanted to peer farther and see more distinctly than the pale moonlight permitted.

"Let me take a look over there and then we can go back," she said. Then she sighed.

The youth again took courage and asked, "How does that song go, the one you sing sometimes?"

"What song?"

"The one that mentions helm, sail, distant peaks," said the youth hesitantly.

"Ah." Thereupon she began to half-recite, half-sing, in tender whispering tones filled with sentiment:

Ah, when shall I grasp the helm,
Ah, when shall we hoist the sail,
To look on those distant peaks,
So my heart no more may ail!

Two or three times she repeated this quatrain, set to an old melody she knew.

"There, now you can see those distant peaks," said Mathios, "except that we have no helm, and instead of sails we have oars."

The young woman sighed again.

"Is it time to go back?" asked the youth. He said this sadly. His words seemed wilted when they left his lips.

"A little farther, a little farther still," answered Lialio. "The shadows those islands cast keep us from seeing clearly over there. I can only see Derfi."

"Derfi is the other way," said the youth, pointing southward towards Euboea.

"Derfi is what we call that tall mountain in my native village," Lialio corrected, pointing eastward. She sang her song again, with one small change:

Ah, when shall I grasp the helm,
Ah, when shall we hoist the sail,

To look on Mount Derfi's peak,
So my heart no more may ail!

The youth let out a deep breath like a sigh.

"Oh, but I'm forgetting that I'm wearing you out with this row-ing," said Lialio. "Really, how crazy of me . . . your delicate hands are not meant for oars, Mr. Mathios."

The youth protested. "No, no, I'm not tired. The oars are very light. These little oars can't tire me."

Lialio insisted on taking one of the oars, and bending began to dislodge one of the tholepins to bring it nearer to the stern where she was sitting. The youth tried to prevent her and their hands met in a warm touch.

"And you said that my hands were delicate!" protested Mathios with a diffident air.

"Well, then, shall we go ahead and hoist the sail, as the song says?" playfully suggested the young woman.

"With what?" Unwittingly, he glanced at her white overdress. Lialio laughed and once more leaned back against the stern.

They had already reached the mouth of the harbor. On one side of the boat was the steep promontory that apparently had been formed by an earthquake or a sinking of the land and interrupted the verdant harmony of the mountain. On the other side were the two or three small islets to the southwest that ran across the mouth of the harbor. The moon rose steadily into the firmament, blotting out even the outermost stars, which earlier were timorously shining in the corners of the heavens. The sea bristled gently under the slight, steady breeze, a remnant of the stronger wind that had fur-rowed the surface all day. It was a warm night in May, but the breeze grew cooler as it moved across the water at the mouth of the harbor. Two dark masses, reflecting a faint silver in the melancholy light of the moon, were outlined against the horizon, one to the east, one to the west, but the details of the landscape remained blurred in the alternating light and shadow. These masses were the two neighbor-ing islands. The moonlit night cast a mysterious charm over all things. The little boat sailed close to one of the islets, on which they could see some forms illumined, others in shadow: rocks gleaming in the moonlight, dark bushes gently rustling in the breath of the night air, and caverns battered by the shuddering waves, where one might assume the presence of seabirds and where one could hear the excited flutterings of the wings of wild doves put to flight by the splashing of the oars and the approach of the boat. On a mountain slope off to the northeast appeared flickering lights, indicating places where in daytime could be seen the white houses of a village high above the sea. Against a small, hollowed-out rock near the islet the waves beat with a roaring din. In the general harmony of the moonlit sea it was as if there were a separate orchestra playing sounds louder than all the coves, inlets, and beaches, all the shores and cliffs beaten by the waves. Spontaneously Mathios lifted the oars and held them for a long while against the gunwale without moving, like a white seabird that gracefully glides over the water and hangs motionless for a few seconds, one wing up, the other down, just before it swoops down, catches a swimming fish and lifts it writhing and wriggling in the air. He felt an indescribable enchantment. Lialio also came under this peculiar spell, and their glances met.

"Shall we hoist the sail?" repeated the young woman. Evidently she had not ceased to think about that since first mentioning it. She spoke simply and naturally, as if she were voicing the thoughts of them both.

"Let's," answered Mathios unthinkingly, and since he scarcely realized what he was saying, this time he did not even ask what sail.

Lialio spared him the trouble of searching. She got up, bent gracefully, and with a quick movement took off her white pleated overdress and held it out to Mathios. "You set up the mast," she said.

Surprised, but smiling and utterly charmed, the youth took one of the oars, lifted it up and placed it perpendicularly against the seat he was on. He next took one end of the tow rope and with it lashed the oar to the seat. Then he took the second oar, untied the other end of the tow rope from its notch in the stern, and bound the second oar horizontally to the first as a sailyard. Finally he took up Lialio's pure white overdress and attached it to the second oar as a sail.

Lialio now sat in her shirtwaist and her skirt, which reached below her knees and was as white as her overdress. Her stockings were white too, and beneath them one could imagine her slender, rounded legs that were whiter still. Her neck, fair as a lily, was imperfectly covered by her red silk embroidered collar. She sat by the stern, drawing herself together, making herself smaller than her well-proportioned, graceful carriage usually showed her.

The breeze grew stronger, the improvised sail billowed out, and the little boat picked up speed. No longer was any mention made of returning to the harbor. Why should there be? It was clear from that moment on that they were sailing toward those distant peaks.

Mathios sat in the stern, but not too near Lialio, and looked out over the sea so as not to gaze overlong at his fellow voyager and disconcert her. At that moment there came into his mind the song of a Heptanesian poet, which played so important a part in the romantic loves of so many in those days, "Awake, sweet love." He remembered the verses that begin "The pale moon only . . . ," and he also thought of these lines:

Farewell, you shady glen,
You waters from cool spring;
Forever more, farewell,
Sweet dawns and birds that sing.

He remembered these lines, but did not wish to sing them. They hardly seemed appropriate now. Indeed, the song that seemed to him the most appropriate for that night was Lialio's favorite:

Ah, when shall I grasp the helm,
Ah, when shall we hoist the sail,
To look on those distant peaks,
So my heart no more may ail!

He sat beside Lialio, but not too far, so near that he could not easily look at her, yet so far that he could not feel the closeness of her warm body and breath. He longed to gaze at her, but kept his glance averted until he grew dizzy from looking at the waves. He doffed his short light jacket and asked her to put it on so she would not catch cold, for as the night progressed a land breeze had begun to blow down from the mountain. Lialio refused the garment, saying she was not at all cold: she felt in fact quite warm.

Mathios did not insist. He began to think about her circumstances, that portion of her life and situation he was acquainted with. During the short time she had spent on their island, the young woman had become quite friendly with his family. Though she still retained most of her virginal freshness, Lialio was not in her earliest youth. Nor was she a new bride; she was twenty-five years old and had been married to Mr. Monahakis for five years. He had taken her as his second wife after the death of the first, and after the marriage of his daughter, who was one year older than Lialio. He felt that marrying this twenty-year-old girl made him a full twenty years younger. For some time afterwards, however, he lived away from their native island as a civil servant in the financial administration, moving wherever the government wished to transfer him. Lialio was not unhappy. She remained with her parents, unable to follow Mr. Monahakis in his nomadic wanderings up and down Greece, wherever they pitched him, "like an old boat, blown here, blown there," as he himself used to say. Alas, the wind in those places was not propitious to delicate flowers, and Lialio would have wilted in a month if sacrilegious hands had tried to transplant her. The vase was of alabaster, the plant was easily broken, its blossom gave forth a subtle fragrance that was not meant for coarse nostrils. When after many efforts Mr. Monahakis finally got himself transferred to the island next to his own, he persuaded his father-in-law, who held him in the highest esteem among all their coevals, to send Lialio to him at his new post so that they could live together under the same roof. Lialio wept the day she took leave of her stepdaughter, for whom she felt the affection of a sister. The stepdaughter had just given birth; she no longer had any fears that she would acquire a small stepbrother that would be an uncle to her newborn child. Lialio went aboard ship and crossed, or rather was transported, to the nearby island.

The joyous day of her arrival was celebrated by a gathering of Mr. Monohakis's friends. From the next day onwards, however, he stopped receiving at home, and this was not at all strange, for he himself was never there. He was either at his office or at the cafe, where, ever jovial, talkative, and laughing loudly, he would light his four-foot pipe, which ran the length of his blue baggy trousers. His cheeks were as red as the tall fez he wore, which drooped along a crease toward his right ear under the weight of a long, twisted tassel that spread over his shoulder.

After the second week from Lialio's arrival, whenever she was awake as her husband came home at midnight, she would complain bitterly and demand that he send her back to her native village. She could not live, she declared, so far from her parents. Indeed her heart had begun to ache a few days after she left home. She had no appetite and her face grew pale. Uncle Monahakis, however, informed her that once she had come, it was not fitting for her to leave so soon. He expounded at length his view that a wife is obliged to go wherever her husband goes, for otherwise the purpose of a Christian marriage would be thwarted, the purpose being, according to the weightiest Orthodox tenets, not the propagation of the species but the exhibition of restraint and sobriety between man and woman, for otherwise, said he, in cases of childlessness divorce would be sanctioned as a matter of course. As far as the propagation of the species is concerned, a natural union would suffice, and that is a very different thing from a religious and civil marriage. He lined up a whole series of quotations from both Testaments, such as "This is now bone of my bones, and flesh of my flesh," "What therefore God hath joined together, let not man put asunder," and "The head of the woman is the man." Pressing her braids against her face with her hands, Lialio stifled her sobs and wiped the traces of her tears with the two ends of her white veil.

As a neighbor Mathios learned about this situation and secretly fell in love with Lialio. The grace of her slender body was not lost even in her loose-fitting costume, and the curls of her hair, bestowed not by art but by nature, framed her captivating forehead. The glow of her deep black eyes shone darkly under her arched eyebrows, and the crimson of her lips was set off against her pale transparent cheeks, which turned a delicate rosy hue at the slightest effort or emotion. But it was the calm, thin flame in her eyes that seared the youth's heart.

In a word, he was in love with her. She would often come out on the balcony, look at him reflectively for a minute, her thoughts far off. Then, glancing away, she would turn her eyes towards a point on the western horizon formed by the distant mountains. On the evening in question, Lialio's husband being away, she saw Mathios as the moon was rising. He had stepped out after dinner for a breath of sea air and was standing by the shore. He saw her on the balcony, greeted her, and they exchanged a few words. Then, casually, and without much thought, she made the unexpected suggestion of an outing in the boat, and that is how this strange little voyage had come about. The young woman seemed to live a dream life, to dwell in a reverie. From time to time she would suddenly awaken from her prolonged dream and seemingly become aware of the real world, but after a few minutes passed she would fall again into somnolent lethargy and sink even deeper into her fond reverie.

It was already midnight. Since they had no rudder, the sea current and the land breeze pushed them little by little in a more northerly direction toward the flickering lights of the village high on the mountain, which now seemed closer to them. They were now alongside a rocky islet standing by itself off the northeast coast. It was called Aspronisos, the White Isle, and was used as a warren for rabbits put there by the islanders, as well as being the realm of all sorts of gulls and other seabirds.

Only then did Mathios take in hand one of the oars—he had previously been obliged to take down the mast, furl the improvised sail, and return Lialio's overdress to her, since she had begun to feel cold, though she did not want to admit it. Using the oar as a rudder he tried to direct the prow to the right, towards the westernmost part of the opposite shore, called Trahili. But the makeshift rudder was of no use, since he could not find a favoring current, and once more he was forced to begin rowing.

However, the nymphs of the night breezes beginning to blow from the land and the nymphs of the sea currents furrowing the narrow body of water between the two islands were favorable to Lialio. The two voyagers had scarcely put a few yards between themselves and the White Isle when there appeared by the three islets to the southwest a large launch moving at full speed from the mouth of the harbor headed for the promontory of Trahili. Its six oars beat the waves as it skimmed across the sea like a runaway racehorse galloping through the meadow.

Lialio started, and the youth looked behind. Immediately he stopped rowing, uncertain what to do.

"Quick, quick," said Lialio in a whisper, as if afraid that her voice would be heard far beyond the White Isle.

The youth quickly began to put about. They were in the shadows along the shoreline, with no moonlight. They rounded a jutting rock and were concealed behind the little island.

"What do you think that means?" asked Lialio anxiously.

"No doubt it's for us," answered the youth.

"Are they out chasing after us?"

"It's us they're looking for, I'm sure."

"What is that big boat?"

"It's a launch with many oars, and it's fast."

"So if we were out there they would catch us?"

"They're heading for Trahili. They'd soon have caught up with us if we'd gone in that direction."

"So we did well to come this way."

"We didn't intend to come; the currents carried us."

"The currents know what they're doing," pronounced Lialio solemnly. She spoke like one of those who have significant dreams and improvise an interpretation for each one. As she spoke she persuaded herself that inanimate things possess a mind and that everything is subject to the command of some deity. Indeed, it almost seemed as if some Nereid of the sea currents or some zephyr from the land had purposefully directed the little boat with its charming cargo to this place.

"What shall we do now?" asked Mathios, who inside himself felt powerless without the help of some beneficent nymph. And then he realized why it was that from the day the world was created, female rule has never ceased.

"Now," said Lialio, speaking with mathematical precision, as if she had foreseen everything, "we'll wait for half an hour, and if they don't suspect we're here and don't head in this direction to look around, we'll go over there, to St. Nicholas—you know—while they're headed that way, to Trahili. From there, from St. Nicholas, we'll climb up on foot for half an hour to Platana, the village high up, and from there, when God sends the daylight, we'll continue on foot for three hours until we reach my village, the big one. If only I could set foot once more on that sacred soil! But—if they suspect we're here and head in this direction, then quick as a wink on to Xanemo, as you call it, back on your island, near Kefala, and there we'll toss the boat on the shore and go back to your village by land. 'Where were you, Lialio?' 'I went for a walk, Uncle Monahakis, and here I am, back again.'"

She laughed to herself as she said this. Then, since Mathios still seemed uneasy, she added, "As long as they don't catch up with us . . . I don't care what people will say. I don't give a hoot! As long as we don't do anything wrong, let foolish people blame us."

The youth, overcome with emotion, bent over and kissed her finger tips. Yes, he thought, he wasn't doing anything wrong, any more than many another who was, as history tells us, unjustly sentenced to die slowly on the pyre.

"If I wanted to have love affairs," she went on, in a severe tone, "it would be very easy if I stayed with Uncle Monahakis. The proof that I don't want to is that I'm on my way back to my parents. My parents won't be able to act as a cover for love affairs, but Uncle Monahakis would, he certainly would!"

A sharp knife tore into the youth's heart. He thought that the young woman undoubtedly had a lover in her native village. So, then, she was running after him! It was for him that she had undertaken this strange sea voyage. If so, what was his own position? What role did he, Mathios, play in such a situation? A bridge two lovers walked across so they could meet, the ferryman Charon in the service of infernal loves. What a great fire was burning inside him! He felt all of the primitive surges of the tragic hero raging and boiling within.

How easy it would be to change this romance to high drama, if only the literary conscience of this author would allow it. Imagine the launch pursuing the two fugitives in the small boat. Imagine Mathios escaping the pursuers by a remarkable display of rowing. Imagine him discovering at the last moment that the homesick wife has a lover over there. Imagine him plunging a dagger into her breast or sinking the boat and drowning them both at the same time. Finally, imagine the launch in the moonlight searching the depths of the sea for the two bodies. What a marvelously romantic story! What tears, what sensibilities!

Nonetheless, Mathios controlled himself with great difficulty and, looking at the young woman, merely asked, "Wasn't there anyone in love with you over there, before Mr. Monahakis married you?"

"Oh, many were, of course," Lialio declared blithely. "But this is the way it is: they don't fall in love with poor girls, except in the way they love flowers, just to enjoy their fragrance one time and then leave them to wither away or pluck their leaves. And then, I wasn't one of those that have a large dowry, you know, so that they could fall in love with me and marry me with all pomp and circumstance, or even abduct me and marry me secretly before a priest, and in that way be sure that later my parents would be obliged to provide a dowry even though they were boiling mad. That's why there was no one else to ask for my hand except Uncle Monahakis. At least there was him." Then in a low voice she quoted the folk song:

My parents gave me away,
In marriage was I given,
But never did I say,
That it was my free will.

"Then why are you running away from Mr. Monahakis?" asked
Mathios, referring to the final words of her explanation.

"I'm not running away from him; I'm returning to my native
island. I'm going to join my parents. If Uncle Monahakis comes to
my village to find me, he'll be very welcome. He knows very well
that I'm not the sort ever to dishonor him. But he also knows that
I can't live in a strange place."

The youth's anxiety was not allayed. He suspected the young
woman was playing tricks and that he was her victim. Abruptly he
asked, "Can it be that there was no one man that loved you more
than the others? And that you loved him too before you were married? Or after you were married?"

Lialio sighed deeply and said, "Ah yes, to be honest with you the
man that would have married me, whom I too wanted to marry
. . . it's now six years since the Black Sea swallowed him up. The
ship was lost with all aboard. But if you have any pity, why do you
insist on asking me about that?"

All this time the two fugitives had not ceased to observe the
launch. After it had gone a considerable way with its prow pointing
east, it suddenly stopped moving as it reached the tip of the third
and easternmost islet and remained there for a few minutes.
Mathios pointed this out to his fellow voyager.

"I know what's going on," she said.

"What?"

"You'll see now."

The youth looked straight into her eyes. She said, "Be patient. I'll
relieve you of all your doubts. In a minute you'll see the launch heading for Trahili."

"How do you know? Are you a sorceress?"

"Yes, I am . . . I am a sorceress," she said with conviction.
Mathios felt an undefined fear before her flashing glance.

At that moment the launch turned decidedly eastward and went
on its course at full speed. Mathios uttered a cry of admiration.

"This is how it is," continued Lialio. "I'll wager ten to one Uncle
Monahakis is in the launch."

"What then?"

"The other men—those at the oars—must have suggested that they look around the islets, where they might find us hiding somewhere. That's because they want to avoid the backbreaking effort of a long trip, or maybe because they think that's more likely. But Uncle Monahakis knows very well that I've no reason to be by the islets and that I only wanted to go to my native village. He's sure that I'm headed straight for Trahili. He hopes to catch up with me before I step ashore at Agnontas, the little harbor on our island over there, and convince me to go back with him to your village. That's why he didn't want to waste time looking around the islets—so that I wouldn't get away from him once I've landed over there. And so he has persuaded the oarsmen to keep straight to their course, even though they're cursing under their breath. Well, that's how it is."

"What then?"

"Well, when they've gone on ahead for quite a ways, then we'll cross over. Give me one of the oars."

Mathios did not object. He shifted one of the oars towards the stern. After a short time the launch moved off into the distance, so that it could scarcely be seen against the vast horizon. It was like a dark bobbing mark, a black dot on the silvery surface of the sea.

"Now let's set to rowing," cried the graceful Lialio cheerily.

Mr. Monahakis was indeed in the launch. The homesick wife was not mistaken. Half an hour after the two fugitives had embarked he was presented with the unpleasant news that "his Lialio" was no longer at home. He was sitting in the cafe engaged in a lively political discussion, with his long pipe ever burning, extending beyond his baggy trousers, when a ten-year-old barefoot boy, dressed in striped shirt and striped pants, came in and said, "Uncle, your wife's gone!"

"She's gone? Where did she go?" the good man said in amazement.

"Don't know."

"You don't know? Who told you then?"

"Markina's Vasilis was over there, by the shore, 'n he saw her."

"And who is this Markina's Vasilis?"

The boy turned toward the door and said, "There he is! He's standing outside the door."

Mr. Monahakis and his erstwhile interlocutors, whose curiosity was now greatly aroused, all turned toward the door. Another barefoot boy, an eight-year-old, stood outside. He was bareheaded, with one trouser leg raised to his calf, and his feet were wet from the sea. He kept his face half hidden behind the doorpost and his body half hidden behind the wall, and peeked with one eye into the cafe.

"Hey, you," Mr. Monahakis called to him, "did you see my wife leave?"

"Sure did," answered the boy.

"And where was she going?"

"Don't know."

Mr. Monahakis got up with vexation and angrily gestured as if he were about to hurl his pipe to the floor. The first boy, who stood five feet away, was startled and began to run off, fearing that he would get a beating with the pipe. The boy outside the door disappeared behind the wall.

"Don't be afraid," said Mr. Monahakis. "If you're telling the truth, you won't get a thrashing. Come here. Tell me what you know . . . because . . ." That "because" was the only word he spoke that indicated his sorrow, his anger, and his shame.

"Well, Uncle," said the boy, regaining his courage but staying near the door, "Vasilis saw the boat your wife got into with Kalioris's son. They headed for Daskalio for a ride. Vasilis called me an' showed me the boat way out there, but I didn't see the people. We kind'a thought they'd come back quick—then we saw them go out beyond Pounta an' they went outta the harbor. We waited for them to come back an' they didn't come back."

"How long is it since you saw them?"

"Well, about two hours—maybe more."

"And why didn't you come to tell me sooner?"

"Well, it wasn't that long. Just an hour . . . maybe an hour . . . maybe less . . . just a little while . . . a little bitty while."

Mr. Monahakis once again made a threatening gesture as he laid his pipe in the corner. The boy quickly dashed off.

Meanwhile Markina's Vasilis had run a hundred yards ahead, with the eagerness of children to announce either good or bad news, as the case may be, in the first instance to get a reward from the interested party, in the second to enjoy that party's consternation. Out of breath, Vasilis reached the house of the schooner's captain. Standing under the balcony he saw an open door leading from it into a room flooded with light. As loud as his lungs permitted, he began to call out, "Uncle! They took the little boat!" Earlier Vasilis had not been brave enough to enter the cafe and bring the news to Mr. Monahakis, but now, after seeing his friend tell the news without getting a beating, he had screwed up his courage and hurried ahead to get to the captain's first. Thus he would be the one to enjoy the moment. Besides, he knew that the captains' thick cane could not reach him from the balcony.

Captain Kyriakos was still sitting at the table. He had not yet left off the nibbling and sipping enjoyed by seamen who return home for a number of days and wish to protract this rare pleasure as long as they can. He got up and came out onto the balcony. "What do you want?" he asked.

"Well, they took your little boat."

"Who did?"

"Mathios—Mathios of Malamos."

"Who's this Mathios of Malamos?"

"Well, the son of Kaliorina—isn't that her name?"

"And where is he taking it?"

"Well, out of the harbor."

"By himself?"

"With a woman."

"With a woman!" repeated the captain in astonishment. "What woman?" He did not hear the boy's answer, since for better or worse Vasilis was standing beneath the protective cover of the balcony. "And why didn't you come to tell me?" shouted Captain Kyriakos. But the boy had disappeared around the corner, and as he ran off nothing could be heard but his running footsteps on the flagstones.

"That devil's son the cabin boy is probably drinking it up somewhere," muttered Captain Kyriakos, "and he's left the boat to shift for itself." Immediately he sent some men out to look for the cabin boy, and after a long futile search in the waterfront taverns they finally found him in a bar on the inside street. The captain ordered two members of his crew, who were resting at home, to borrow a small craft, board the schooner, and lower the big launch with six oars from its deck. He did not care so much about the woman who was apparently being abducted, nor about the fortunate youth accompanying her, as he did about his slender, sturdy new boat. He also ordered his sailors to enlist two or three ferrymen from the harborside to man the oars of the launch and to set out in pursuit of the little boat.

Meanwhile Mr. Monahakis found out whom the stolen boat belonged to and made a crestfallen appearance at the captain's home.

"You can come along on the launch too," said Captain Kyriakos, who had finally discovered whom the stolen wife belonged to (for "stolen" was naturally enough everyone's interpretation of the event).

To be aboard the launch was precisely what Mr. Monahakis desired, for he was afraid to remain in the village in a state of anguish and expectation. He felt that if he participated in the pursuit the distraction would make his pain seem milder. He trusted Lialio and was confident that she would not betray his honor—as she had told Mathios—but then again, he thought, who could know? Who can unravel the mysteries of woman's nature? He knew of Lialio's propensity for melancholy and daydreaming and of her profound homesickness. But how could he make others understand these things? Woe to him who falls into a ditch filled with water, even if the water is clear. Probably people will stretch out a helping hand, but they will never stop making fun of you. But he was nevertheless sure of his Lialio—as sure, that is, as any man can be of a woman. A close friend of her family's, he used to kiss her and dandle her on his knee when he was thirty years old and she was three. When she was five, he used to bring her sweets as a matter of course, not knowing what the future held. From the days when she lispingly called him Unky Monahakis to the day she became his wife—still calling him Uncle Monahakis—he had studied her carefully, observing her development as child, girl, and woman, and he knew that more than all other women she relied on her wits and her nerve.

Half an hour went by before Captain Kyriakos's two crewmen could be persuaded to detach themselves from their homes, another half hour before they could find a small craft, board the schooner, and lower the launch, and yet a third half hour before they could impress as rowers several ferrymen and fishermen of the harbor—whose own two- and four-oared boats were too heavy for the pursuit—and could talk over the matter with these ferrymen and fishermen and reach an agreement to put out. Finally, they boarded the launch and set out, with Mr. Monahakis as the seventh man sitting at the rudder.

Rowing in unison they quickly left the harbor. But where were they to search for the little boat? The sea, though talkative as a woman, can be just as reticent and never reveal her secrets. Finding the trace of one little boat on the vast blue expanse is as likely as finding the trace of another's kiss on a woman's lips. After all, thought Mr. Monahakis, she was a woman. Love is a deceiver, and youth is easily deceived. Who could say that she had not already sinned? Oh, how right he was when he told her that she would be safe with him because an elderly husband, besides everything else, also acts as a father to a young woman. (And how right she too was when she remarked that she was safe with him even if she wished to go astray.) Even if she were a thousand times innocent, the world would condemn her, but with him, even if she were a thousand times a sinner, in the eyes of the world she would be an honest woman. Alas, if she had to endure an ordeal by arrow like the princess of the fairy tale, the arrow would only brush the tips of the soft fingers of one hand.

The little boat floated over the surface of the sea between the two islands. The kindly naiad of the sea currents sent a favorable current under its keel and the propitious zephyr of the land breezes dispatched a soft wind against its stern, strengthening the youth's arms and shoulders and tightening the young woman's soft muscles. They rowed like two trained sailors. The light oars did not tire them, and they had completed more than half of their watery journey. Only when the launch, racing like a mare let loose, drew near to Cape Trahili, did its crew catch sight of the little boat.

"What's that over there?"

"The boat."

Mr. Monahakis turned his head to the left. "Ah—that's it."

"How can we tell? I don't think that's it," said one of the sailors, who wanted it not to be, so that he could avoid further exertion.

"That's it—no doubt about it," said another seaman, who very much wanted it to be the boat because this strange sea-drama greatly piqued his curiosity about the outcome—if, that is, they managed to overtake the boat with the woman and her lover.

"That's it!" pronounced Mr. Monahakis. "Let's swing in that direction, men. I'll luff round."

"Where's it headed for?" asked one of the sailors.

"For Ai-Nikolas. You see, they chose the shortest route. We've been breaking our backs all this time for no reason."

"Let's change our course," cried out Mr. Monahakis, "please

. . . let's change direction right away. Somebody backwater, so I can luff round."

The six oarsmen had stopped rowing, but the launch kept its forward momentum. Mr. Monahakis, however, anxious to waste no more time, cried out, "Backwater, men, backwater. Turn thataway. Luff round."

But no one was paying attention to him. They were holding council in the middle of the sea. Some maintained that they should hold to their present course, the others that they should turn northwards in the direction of the little boat. In the end the opinion of the majority prevailed, those who were aroused by the prospect of an enjoyable spectacle. They turned the prow to the left, taking up their oars with renewed vigor, the kind that comes from man's natural striving for victory and his hope of unusual quarry. But the launch was three times as far from the desired harbor as the boat, and even though the launch had triple the oar power, it had five times the weight and three times the displacement.

Mathios was quick to note the sudden change in the launch's course and pointed it out to his companion. "Look!" he said. "They're after us."

"Let them try and catch us now," cried out Lialio cheerily. "They seem to be much farther away than we are."

"Oh yes, much farther away, but they have many oars."

"And we have lots of strength." And she redoubled her efforts at the oar.

For more than an hour a game was played along the length of the shore as the pale moon sank peacefully in the west and the voice of the rooster rang out for a second time over the farmhouses scattered on the hillsides and in the valleys. It was the game of the fearsome octopus with its long tentacles chasing the sprat, of the diving, playful dolphin hunting down the garfish. The launch sped forward to the rhythmical beat of its oars against the forked iron tholepins, like a dread shark, ceremonious, unswerving. The little boat moved like a cork over the waves with a gentle plash as soft as the sound of a kiss. With its small, toylike oars it pushed aside the caressing waters, which escorted it on its way like an honor guard preceding and following a royal carriage. It seemed as if invisible Tritons were carrying it over the surface so that its deep keel would not hinder its speed.

It was obvious, however, that the launch was catching up with the little boat. The two vessels continued on and on, the launch gaining and appearing ever closer, but now only a short distance, a very short distance, separated the little boat from the shore. Though the launch was moving very fast, Mathios was still able to thrust the little boat vehemently onto the sand from the shallow water.

"May we always have such a fair voyage!" exclaimed Lialio joyfully. She stood up, glanced at the white wall of the chapel of Saint Nicholas gleaming in the moonlight, made the sign of the cross, and was the first to jump out onto the beach, splashing her heels in the water.

Mathios jumped out after her and tried to pull in the boat. The launch was now no more than forty yards from the inlet. He labored to drag the boat onto the sand, since he was eager to escort Lialio up to her village. He suspected that the men in the launch would pursue them on land also and, without knowing why, he was happy at this prospect. Lialio's last revelation about her suitor being drowned in the Black Sea had not sufficed to put his mind at ease. An unwholesome thought led him to reflect that a woman who could forget a luckless youth and marry an old man was capable of abandoning the old man for yet another, someone living in her village. But if the men from the launch pursued the two of them on land, and she entrusted herself to him, and together they reached her village, then indeed would his love be sanctified on land as well as on the sea.

Suddenly through the silence of the night there came the voice of Mr. Monahakis, who could be seen by the light of the moon standing in the stern of the launch. "Lialio! Say, Lialio!"

Lialio stood still, her head bent in thought. Then she called out in response, "Yes, Uncle Monahakis?"

"Do you want to go to your parents, sweetest? That's just fine. Wait for me. I'll go along too and escort you there, my love, so you won't meet any danger, all by yourself."

"You're welcome to come along, Uncle Monahakis," answered Lialio without hesitation.

Fearful and uncomprehending, Mathios stood near and looked shyly at her. "Go back on the launch, and Godspeed, Mathios, my pet," said Lialio in a voice filled with sincere emotion. "It's a shame I'm older than you. If Uncle Monahakis died, I would marry you."

The Haunted Bridge

ORGIVE ME, ARETO, FOR-
give me!"

"You are forgiven, father! You are forgiven!"

"With all your heart! Areto, my child!"

"With all my heart, father, I pray for your forgiveness!"

For days and weeks on end old Koumenis lay on his deathbed. He was suffering horribly as he departed from this world and entered the next. Powerless to step over the threshold of gloomy Hades, he was wasting away in his agony, unable to disappear. He was choking but could not stop breathing. He appealed to his daughter Areti, the child of his first marriage, for her blessing and forgiveness, because he had abandoned hopes of rising in health from his sick bed, and his only desire was to fall into the pit, into the dark abyss.

Many years later, when Areti, then the wife of Bozas, was my mother's age, and I was still a child, she would relate all these things to my mother and me. I would hear her recite in a direct, impassioned way a folk song that seemed to her to have a clear allegorical meaning and to be directly connected to her own fate:

A bridge they were building by the strand
But never could they make it stand.
Each night they finished its sturdy frame—
Upon the morrow down it came.
A little bird arrived in flight
And perched upon the bridge's right.
With manlike voice, not like a bird's,
It spake these dire and dismal words:
"A human life is the demand
Or else this arch it shall not stand.
A human life must be the price,
And the one that you will sacrifice
Will be no stranger, nor simple churl,
Nor passerby, nor orphan girl;
The one who must surrender life
Is the master builder's own dear wife!"
The master builder, when he heard,
His 'prentice sent t'obey the bird.
"Oh, come, my lady Areti,
The master calls, oh, come with me!"
"If it's for weal, bedecked I'll go,
But as I am if it's for woe."
"Oh, come milady, he awaits."
"Three sisters we, with wretched fates:
We're haunting spirits where men cross;
Evdokia dwells at Tyrnavos,
Another arch meant Maro's loss,
And I, the lady Areti,
This bridge must haunt eternally."

Perhaps because of the identity of their Christian names, the long-suffering Areti, wife of Bozas, found an uncanny similarity between the fate of the song's heroine and her own bitter lot. She suffered much from her husband's indifference. Bozas, or Patsostathis, as he was also known, was a farmer with fields and other property but was not much inclined to work. He preferred to practice the butcher's trade in the marketplace and to spend his time with the other animal traders. He liked to hang about the slaughter-houses, a true "butcher's dog," to eat stews every day, and to have his fill of wine and sleep. At home his wife and five children usually went hungry. Areti, being a good, dutiful woman, endured all this with the patience of a saint and lived like so many other women by doing housework for others and practicing frugality at home.

Together with the song of the Haunted Bridge, Areti told my mother the brief, simple story of her insignificant life.

SHE was five years old when her mother's death made her a lone-some orphan. After a year had passed, her father remarried. Her stepmother was "from the lineage of the Karamousalis." From the very beginning she hated her stepdaughter, but for the time being she put up with her. When a year later the woman gave birth to the first of her three children, her resentment toward Areti increased threefold. It was Areti's bad luck that the newborn child was a girl. Ah, of course, Areti, that little crow, that little owl, was to blame! If she had been the sort to bring good luck, the child that came after her would have been a boy! Then the stepchild's position in the family would have been more bearable. But because she was such a "jinx," she brought another girl after her. Not surprisingly, the stepmother took this event as a bad omen. During that year Kara-mousalina carefully tended her infant. All the while she cursed, reviled, and beat her unfortunate stepdaughter, sometimes with the sole and heel of her wooden shoe, sometimes with a rope folded in four, which she used to hang the baby's swaddling clothes by the fireplace each day, for that winter it never ceased raining and snow-ing. Before her little Maria was weaned, the stepmother was again pregnant, and when the first baby was nineteen months old, another girl, Eleni, issued from her mother's womb into the bright light of day. Ah, then Areti's position was indeed unbearable. Just think of it, in less than three years that jinx of a girl had brought after her two new sisters by the very same father!

One fine autumn morning, almost as fine as if it had been spring, Koumenis took one of his neighbor's boats and set off alone without sailor or oarsman. He intended to cross over to Kanapitsa, the beach that lay across the large southern harbor of their island and to the west of their village. He took along an axe, a fishing net, and a grappling hook, with the intention, so it seemed, of cutting wood and loading his boat rather than fishing in the shallows. He also took along the eight-year-old Areto, evidently to carry wood as best she might from the thicket closest to the seashore.

Koumenis seated his daughter in the prow and began to row. The boat glided out into the harbor, some distance from the village so that the houses appeared like small chicken coops and the people walking up the western side to the plateau looked like mice scampering about. The women washing clothes under the elm tree by the seashore down below the cemetery resembled bobbing wagtails. The boat approached the opposite shore of Kapanitsa, leaving behind the dark blue waters of the deep and drawing into the azure shallows, where sea nymphs and mermaids would have delighted to swim and dive down to the magical seabed. There they would have found caverns and seaweed, pearly shells and innumerable lovely little fish playing in schools.

Nicholas Koumenis caressed his little daughter tenderly and pointed to the beautiful sights in the shallows and in the deeper waters. "Look, my little Areti, look down there. Do you see how they shine, all red and blue?"

"I see them, father!"

"Look at the green sea-moss, look at the seaweed! Look at the little oysters and the pebbles. How pretty they are, Aretaki!"

"Pretty, father."

"Look at that little thing down there! What do you see, my little Aretaki? Bend over to look at it, bend over!"

Koumenis leaned toward the side where Areti was sitting, and the boat listed dangerously. By exhortation and gestures he compelled the little girl to bend over and look down into the water. She began to sense an undefined fear and clasped the gunwale tightly. Her father continued to urge her with vehemence to lean over to see the "pretty little things" down at the bottom of the sea.

At a certain moment, as he was facing forward and gesturing toward the prow, his right hand released the oar and he grasped little Areti by the shoulder. But no sooner had he touched her than he removed his hand, as if he were frightened at his own thoughts.

"Oh, naughty girl! You don't want to bend over to see how pretty it is down there."

Aretoula began to cry.

Her father set about rowing furiously with all his might and main, as if he did not know what he was doing, as if he were angry

44

with himself. The poor child, her eyes blurred by tears, stopped looking about her and wept without knowing why. Then she felt a slight jar. The boat had reached Kapanitsa, the shore of the small cove, and its prow slid gently over the sand. Aretoula lifted her tousled blond head, saw that they had arrived, and was about to get up and jump out. Her father, however, acted first. He grasped her roughly by the armpit, lifted her up in the air for a minute and then threw her down onto the sand as if she were a bag of hardtack. He alone heard the thud of her fall; it vibrated deep within his entrails.

Then he lifted one of the oars, pushed against the sand, and, as if he had changed his mind, put out to sea again. It appeared that he no longer wished to chop wood. When he was many yards distant, he took up his fishing net and stood up. Leaning over the prow, he began to watch for fish.

Aretoula stopped crying. She did not call to her father to come and take her back on the boat. She instinctively felt that the boat was not a good place to be. She took a few steps and sat down behind some tall bushes near the ruins of an old hut, where she was concealed by a hill. She gave no sign of life to the infrequent passersby who were going to and from their fields, and no one discovered her presence. Water trickled down a small gully near the ruin, and Aretoula bent over and took a drink. Then she ate some *trefla,* a sort of wild clover, that she found growing near the streamlet. She remained there in hiding all day long.

Night began to fall. Miserable and hungry, the little girl turned toward the east, where she saw the houses of the village. She found a road and began to walk, or rather to drag her feet, in the direction of the houses. Two kindly plowmen, a father and son, were returning from the fields. The last of those who had gone out, they had been overtaken by night. They saw her dark little figure creeping by the edge of the road and took her with them to Geladadika, the small outlying settlement on the western edge of the village. When they questioned her, she answered that her father had brought her there in the morning by boat and had left her for a while on the beach. She hoped he would return to pick her up, but he had not come. She said no more.

ARETOULA did not want to enter her stepmother's house again. When her own mother's relatives scolded her, she answered that her "mother Karamsalina" did not want her, and that she encouraged little Maria to pinch her and pull her hair. Her mother's relatives, poor like her, willy-nilly took her in and, as she grew up, taught her to wash clothes, scrub floors, whitewash houses, and also, according to the season, to pick herbs, thresh grain, gather olives, and, in the summer, to raise silkworms. When she was thirteen, they married her off. In those days the daughters of poor families were married sooner and more easily than they are now.

Nonetheless her stepmother continued to persecute her. A little before Areti was to be married, her father slandered her one day, hard though it may be to believe this. Clearly her "mother Karamsalina had gotten to him again."

How this happened we do not know. Evidently her stepmother calculated that if her stepdaughter were out of the way, the cottage, vineyard, and small olive grove that had belonged to the girl's dead mother would be legally inherited by Koumenis, and in time would come into the possession of her two daughters, Mario and Lenio, who otherwise would receive only small dowries. And so her father, alas, slandered her. He implicated her with a man, a mere passerby, a stranger, a peddlar who happened to be passing through the neighborhood. For a while the women of the neighborhood believed the story, but after a while her "righteousness was as the light and her judgment as the noonday," and her innocence was made clear. Areto's marriage took place as scheduled.

More than twenty years had gone by since then. Old Nicholas Koumenis howled like a dog in his death agony, for his soul could not find its release.

"Forgive me, Areto, forgive me!"

"You are forgiven, my father!" answered the weeping Areto.

"With all your heart, Areto!"

"With all my heart, father!" cried out the meek, long-suffering woman.

Finally, after many days and nights of indescribable torture, the wretched father gave up the ghost—the father who once had wanted to hurl his daughter into the depths of the sea, as if to make her a haunting spirit.

"And I, the lady Areti,
This bridge must haunt eternally."

The Matchmaker

Near the column in the square, where the islanders tied the cables of ships wintering in the harbor, stood the grocery store of Zagarianos. There one morning Captain Savas, the owner of a freighter moored in the harbor, sat cross-legged on a bare, greasy bench. He called over Captain Stelios, a highly respected seaman known to all as a skilled boatswain, and ordered two *mastihas*. Over the toasts and the clinking of glasses, "between the cup and the lip," Captain Savas said: "I'd like to tell you something, Captain Stelios. I'm going to speak from my heart."

"Say on, Captain Savas," said Stelios, his curiosity aroused.

"If you'd like to do me a favor and go to the woman that used to be your neighbor . . ." Savas looked at Stelios and stopped speaking.

"Who is that?" asked Stelios.

"I thought of sending a matchmaker," Savas continued, without answering directly, "but I don't place much faith in those gossiping women. I prefer to open my heart to you."

"What neighbor?" asked Stelios again.

Savas lowered his voice. "That good-looking widow, Kratira, the daughter of Andreola," he said with an amorous smack of his lips that reverberated as far as Stelios.

"Ah!" said Stelios.

"Go and tell her," continued Savas, ". . . well, here's what you should tell her. You tell her, 'Captain Savas sent me,' that's what you'll say. 'He wants to make you the mistress of his house. He would be very pleased,' tell her, 'if you're willing too, to welcome you to his home, his hearth, his possessions.' She'll be, tell her, a lady of property. She'll have beans and chick-peas and coffee and sugar and oil and honey—everything she needs or wants. Now, at our age, tell her, we're not interested in matters of the flesh, only in shelter over our heads and a little consolation. She'll take care of the two children that my wife, God rest her soul, left me, and I'll be traveling summer and winter, risking my life at sea to bring her back goods and provisions, everything she needs or wants. If she wants to enter life's stream once more, to be the mistress of a house—she's been discreet and proper, though she married young, since the time she lost her first husband, she was a young girl, and doesn't have any children of her own—let her think of my children as hers, and I'll make her a grand lady and bring things in for her by the barrelful so that she'll have everything she needs or wants. At our age we don't need anything else, only shelter and consolation."

Captain Stelios, who was listening carefully, smiled in spite of himself. He thought for a minute and then said:

"All right, Captain Savas, we'll see. I don't have much confidence. But since that's my old neighborhood, and since I often go to my storehouse that's over that way and . . . say good day to her sometimes . . . I'll tell her if the occasion seems right."

They drank a second glass of *mastiha*. Savas repeated two or three times what he had said, added a few more points, and again concluded with the phrase "only shelter, consolation, and care in old age."

Finally Stelios said again:

"All right. I'll mention it to her if I can," and got up to leave.

Before he stepped over the threshold of the shop, Savas called him back and said:

"Listen, Captain Stelios. Tell her this too. She mustn't think I'm too old . . . well, you know . . . I'm still able."

Stelios gave a loud laugh.

"Yes, tell her this too. She mustn't think I'm an old fogey, an old wreck. I'm still able."

"All right, Captain Savas."

And Stelios went away.

CAPTAIN Stelios was no longer a neighbor of the aforementioned young widow, but he had lived in her neighborhood in the past. He had formerly had a house there, which he now used as a storage place for various nautical gear, rigging, ropes, and sails. As an old friend of her late husband he often visited her and felt bold enough to greet her in all innocence and exchange with her the usual commonplaces. Kratira, daughter of Andreola, had been widowed six years earlier, but it happened that recently, about a year and a half ago, Stelios himself had become a widower, and since that time he had felt much less free in addressing the widow.

Nevertheless, spurred on by his friend's request, Stelios set out for his storehouse, where he usually busied himself with the repair of nautical gear; some was salvage from shipwrecks and intended for sale, and the rest belonged to the brig he would sail in spring. On the way, as he was walking along, he said to himself:

"Well, now! I'd need a lot of cheek to go to Kratira and talk about such things. To ask her if she wants Savas as her husband! Why, I don't have the courage to ask her . . . if she wants *me* as a husband. I'm surprised old man Savas didn't think of that. Maybe, in this case, there's truth in the saying 'Proposal through a bachelor, proposal from a bachelor.'"

Then, gradually, the temptation of self-interest took hold of him, and he thought:

"I wonder whether it was God or the devil that prompted him to tell me. I could never ask Kratira directly if she wanted me, but I can talk to her about a third party, if she wants to marry so-and-so. This way I can start up a friendly conversation and take some soundings."

He began to compare his qualities to Savas's, what advantages, more or less, each might bring:

"He's a widower; so am I. He's about fifty years old; I'm forty-five. He has two children; I have one. He has his own ship; I don't. But I'm a boatswain and a pilot with an excellent reputation and a captain's license, whereas he has only a steersman's license. And along with everything else, I'm better looking than he is. I'm also an old friend of her late husband's, and I think she prefers me to all the others." He continued his train of thought: "I'm not only better looking, I don't need to pretend: I am what I appear to be. But he, hypocrite that he is, after mentioning shelter and consolation again and again, finally comes out into the open and starts crowing: 'She mustn't think I'm too old. I'm still able.' By saying that, he himself shows he's afraid that things aren't the way he says they are. He's afraid he appears otherwise. But I, I've no need to crow like a rooster."

As he was saying these things to himself Stelios reached the entrance of the one-story building that was his storehouse. It lay right opposite the door to Kratira's ground floor. From inside her house one could hear the cheerful, lively sounds of the shuttle and comb of her loom, where like another Penelope she sat all day and wove. The storehouse was not only opposite her door but in full view of the loom itself, which stood in the back of the room. Her door, facing west, was wide open to let the winter sun penetrate deep into the stone-paved room.

Kratira, noticing Captain Stelios, lifted her head for a moment. Stelios saw her brief glance and called out a hearty good morning. This greeting served as a precursor, a harbinger of the closer encounter about to come. The widow's look drew him on. He took a few steps, reached her door, and stood on the threshold.

"Well, neighbor, how are things with you?" he asked.

"They're as you see. I'm here, working away, toiling over the loom."

"It's the same with me. I'm toiling over ship's gear," answered Stelios, "trying to make old things new again. Anyhow, it's a useful way to make old neighbors like new again."

The widow gave an unrestrained smile.

"Everything that's old can become new again"—Stelios's tongue was loosening up—"there's nothing old that can't be renewed. Lord knows, if love too . . ." He bit his lip and kept quiet. But in an apparent state of perplexity whether he should go forward or retreat, he nevertheless took two steps in from the threshold, as if he felt a need to explain his boldness, and approached Kratira's loom.

"Come and sit down for a little, Captain Stelios," said the widow.

Stelios sat down on an old bench in the room.

THE widow's ground floor had once been a shop and had known days of glory. It used to be called by these names: cafe, barbershop, and fiddler's shop. In days gone by it was run by Kratira's mother, Andreola, and her husband, old Nikolas, who became blind in his later years. Nikolas was a barber and surgeon, skilled at incising veins. Andreola, for her part, had knowledge of all kinds of herbs and ointments. They raised three children, Filaretos, Mitros, and Kratira, and then the old couple passed into decline. Their eldest son, Filaretos, became a renowned fiddler; the second son, Mitros, sometimes played the bouzouki and sometimes the *laouto*, but mainly he practiced the calling of a barber. Filaretos married, had two children, was struck by disease, and died young. Mitros left his country, sailed the seven seas, and did not return. Of the whole family, only Kratira and the young children of Filaretos survived.

Kratira married young, had no children, and was widowed after two years. She was now in the seventh year of her widowhood and about thirty years old. Just as her brother Filaretos had been passionately dedicated to his music, so, too, her husband, Yiannis Varnalis, had been devoted to song. But he died young, a consumptive, enjoying for only a brief two years the woman he had married for love. For the whole town his death and funeral were a scene out of tragedy. Even years later the people in the neighborhood, the marketplace, and all quarters of the town still remembered Kratira's impassioned songs of lamentation.

Shortly afterwards her brother Filaretos also died of the disease of the lungs. But it happened that he died in Athens, where he had gone for medical treatment. And now he lies buried in a small corner of the First Cemetery, unknown like all the others there— even more unknown than the others. They said the fiddle had affected his chest, and that this was the reason he had become a consumptive.

When Filaretos was invited to play at a wedding or a celebration or a feast, he was hardly ever in a pleasant disposition. Whether they paid him well or not, whether they stuck valuable Austrian coins or modest Turkish pieces on his forehead, was a matter of indifference to him. He was not much concerned with pleasing others. He himself had to be "in the mood." And that mood was an imperious thing: Filaretos did not control it; it controlled him. No matter what his pay had been, he would return in a state of nervous agitation, weary yet not aware of his weariness. Arriving home at midnight from a feast, or in the small hours from a wedding, or in the morning from serenading a bride and her groom, he would open the store and summon his mother. She slept on one ear and kept the other cocked to listen for him. He would call her, or rather she would come down before he called her, to light the fire and brew him some coffee.

Afterwards, instead of wrapping his fiddle in its covering and hanging it on the wall, he would hold it against his breast and embrace it, draw the bow across the strings two or three times, and for his own pleasure begin playing a poignant melody. Any groom or godparent or guest would have gladly given all his Austrian coins to persuade Filaretos to play him such a melody. For this was not the mere sound of a fiddle or any other stringed instrument; it was the human soul the bow was stroking, and that indeed is an entirely different matter. He made his instrument sing and speak and trill as no one else could, so that it aroused the whole neighborhood from its early morning sleep.

"You're wearing yourself out, my child, tired the way you are. You're doing harm to yourself. And you'll wake all the neighbors at this early hour."

"Let them sleep," was Filaretos's reply.

"How can they sleep when you don't let them?"

"Let them take a sleeping potion."

Such was Filaretos, the perfervid musician, whose fate it was to lie unknown in a hidden corner of the most famous cemetery of modern Greece.

His younger brother Mitros often accompanied him on his own instrument. Mitros also had a large pair of scissors that he used to cut hair and a razor that devastated the beards of all the town's male population. Scissors, yes, and a brush, a comb, a dark towel, and a small hand mirror—a monstrous mirror that showed two faces, the one human, the other bestial. If a boy of eight was taken by his father to Mitros's shop for a haircut (as happened to this writer), how frightened he was when Mitros showed him the back of the mirror, terrifying the child with its horrible ogre's head. This was assuredly a mirror that looked into the future, where all the young could see their ugliness to come, the face they would have if they managed to grow up and become men. A boy might hope, if he were not in ignorance and woeful error concerning his fortune and the way of the world, that the gods would love him enough to allow him to die young. Then he would not live to produce such ugliness in body and soul.

That same stone-paved store was now the widow Kratira's ground floor, where she had set up her loom and did her weaving, where Captain Stelios had now entered. Stelios noticed that his initial indiscretion had not been greeted with coldness. On the contrary, Kratira seemed pleased enough to invite him in, as an old neighbor and friend of her late husband, to sit for a while by her loom.

The words "good-looking widow" that Captain Savas had spoken with a smacking of his tongue and lips affected Stelios like a contagious disease. Though he had often looked at Kratira in recent years, he had never taken the opportunity to observe her face closely. She had "dainty looks," to use the description old women give of fine-featured women. She was rather pale, with a delicate skin, a slight rosiness in the cheeks, and a white forehead. The lower part of her face, below the nose, around the mouth and chin, the "love philtre" where they say Eros has his dwelling, was finely and harmoniously molded. (Old crones, when favorably describing some woman's features, make an appropriate gesture and call this portion, for want of an exact word, "this here part of her.") In short, this thirty-year-old widow was endowed with comeliness and grace.

"It's almost March," Kratira said, opening the conversation. "Are you going to sea again this year, Captain Stelios?"

"Yes, of course. What else can I do? As long as we've got the stamina, we'll plow the thankless sea."

"Ah! Who knows what happened to my brother Dimitrakis, who went off to sea! It's been ten years since we've heard anything from him. They say he's gone to Australia," continued the widow. "My parents, too, they're gone. So is Filaretos. All of them. I did have my nephews, my brother's children, may he rest in peace. From time to time they used to pay me a family visit, but now, it seems, their mother doesn't let them come to see me. They say she wants to get married again. Maybe somebody whispered words in her ear that I supposedly said this and that. How mean people are, Captain Stelios! I haven't said a word. Only, when I heard about it, I thought of Filaretos, who lies buried far away, and I wept. Let her get married! Why doesn't she? I won't object. I wasn't asked, and I won't say anything. She'd do well to get married. She's still a young woman, a lot younger than I am. Only I've taken it to heart that she won't let her two children come here so I can see them. From the day my departed"–she meant her husband–"shut his eyes, Captain Stelios, my house is a house that's closed."

She said all of this ingenuously and confidentially, as if she were speaking to an older relative, the sort she did not have and missed having. Stelios listened with rapt attention. He decided it was time to bring up the subject:

"Yes, indeed," he said, "all of us are in the same situation. Men fall apart when they're widowed, and women feel their house is closed up. That's what we were saying, my friend Captain Savas Apanomitis and I, this morning. He, too, is a widower, like me. He has two children. All year long, summer and winter, he sails on his freighter and risks his life at sea, and who is looking after his children in his empty house? That house with no mistress, like a nest without a mother bird in winter . . ."

On hearing these words the widow suppressed a laugh and bit her lip. Stelios's flow of words was interrupted. He looked at her with curiosity.

"That's why he's sent me two matchmakers already," said Kratira.

"He has?"

"Yes. He's sent me two matchmakers, old Maherina and also Thasitsa."

"Really? But he told me that he doesn't have any confidence in gossiping old women."

"What harm have gossiping old women done him? It's I who answered that I don't intend to get married. I'm not for Captain Savas."

"Is that so?" Stelios also laughed, relieved in his conscience as well as his heart. Then he went on:

"It would be his pleasure, he says, to make you a grand lady, with beans, and with chick-peas . . ."

"Oh! He's always mentioning beans and chick-peas. It looks as if he wants me to observe a Lenten abstinence for the whole year!"

Stelios laughed loudly.

"That's exactly what Maherina and Thasitsa were telling me the other day," she said, and her laughter united with Stelios's guffaws.

"Tell me, Kratira, honestly, why don't you want him?" asked Stelios.

"I don't want him, first of all because . . . I haven't yet decided to get married,"—Stelios noted the adverb *yet*—"and second because even if I did decide to get married, I'm not for Captain Savas. There's nothing wrong with him, but as far as beans and chick-peas go, I've got enough, praise be to God. It's my hands and arms I've got to thank for that."

Saying this, she pulled the comb of her loom, which she had let go for a minute, toward her. Her shuttle sounded as it sped like an arrow through the space between the threads of the warp and sprang out from the other end. The two foot pedals creaked as they were set in motion, one up, the other down, by her delicate feet in their embroidered slippers.

"So you haven't yet decided to remarry," said Stelios.

"No, I haven't."

"What if it's a question of someone else, not Captain Savas?"

"Then I'll see," said Kratira.

"And what if he happens to be somebody you know, sober, right-thinking—if that person is an old acquaintance. In fact . . ."

Kratira scarcely seemed to hear as she looked off in another direction.

"If he is an old neighbor, a good neighbor, and a friend of your brothers, of Filaretos's—may God rest his soul—and of Dimitrakis's—may he be well, wherever he is."

Kratira was silent.

"And, Kratira, if he was an old acquaintance and friend, faithful and sincere, of your husband's?"

The widow blushed from the roots of her curls to the edge of her collar.

"In a word, if I asked you, Kratira, to accept my proposal and to take on, once again, life's burden, what would you say?"

Kratira recovered, thought for a moment, and took command of herself, resuming her normal coloring. She said:

"It's now almost March, Captain Stelios. With God's blessing you'll go on your voyage, and when . . . and when . . . it's still not two years since your wife died, may she rest in peace. When you return, with God's blessing, we'll see."

The succession of events described by the widow in those few words came to pass. In March Stelios took ship and sailed away. He was at sea for eight months. In autumn he came back. The ship had returned to its native shore.

The wedding was celebrated at Christmastime.

The Bewitching of the Aga

B ARE AND FRIGID, THE small mosque of the deserted town gleams from afar like the skull of a recently exhumed skeleton, a frightening sight with its empty eye sockets and wasted nose. The skeletal mosque has only one low entrance in the middle, half-buried, without door leaves, and two ruined windows on either side. Above it stands Barberaki, a proud peak whose countenance is sheared on all sides by the winds that blow from east and north and west. A vast panorama stretches out below across the glittering blue sea towards liberated Thessaly and the enslaved soil of Kassandra. From Barberaki one can see the deserted town, built long ago on a cliff whose base is washed by waves, and the unsightly mosque with its two round cavities on either side and its oblong hollow in the middle. Over the mosque looms the *konak,* three of its four walls still standing, its roof fallen to ruins, a ruin of centuries past. In that deserted place shadows still flit about, old memories come alive, and phantoms sing lamentations. The north wind whistles pitilessly through the blackened ruins and the trees that lean against the mountainside like wayfarers bent and panting as they climb the slope.

Two or three times a year visitors from the other, southern, end of the island come to see the deserted town. The women scattering about the ruins go from one wild fig tree to another in search of ripe fruit to place as fertilizer on the cultivated fig trees of the plain. The children, urchins of today's world who have come along for the outing, scurry about everywhere among the ruins. They climb the wild mulberry trees and bedaub their hands and lips with the red fruit. When they have glutted their stomachs with berries and hidden some in the folds of their shirts, they disperse in all directions and amuse themselves with jumping about, sliding down hills, and listening to the echoes of their voices mocking the deserted landscape and its phantoms. Many climb recklessly onto the roof and over the dome of the humble mosque and parody with uncouth sounds the call of the muezzin, a call it is their good fortune never to have heard.

Then the phantoms turn to flight, the shades wander off, and the plaint of the desolate land fades away to a final muffled sigh that sinks far off into the waves. The birds of the sea and the birds of prey soar into flight from their rocky perches, plunge down toward the sea-cave, or disappear into the vastness of the open sky.

AND yet this *konak* was once inhabited, and that mosque once echoed with prayers to Allah and with obeisance frequently performed, as custom prescribed. Actually there was only one aga in the whole village, which each year paid a stipulated tax of two or three hundred gold coins to the sultan. The last aga, who came a few years before the Revolution, brought with him a harem consisting of a wife and a slave. After him, about the time of the national uprising, there came only one tax collector, and after him no one else.

And so, this aga, the next-to-last Ottoman to come to the island, arrived from Thessaly. He was a quiet, mild-tempered man. He spoke Greek. He accepted whatever gifts were offered him and frequently asked the inhabitants for more. He was a grave man with the disposition of a guardian who is favorable but aloof. He had the look of a charmed serpent whose teeth had been removed. He and his harem lived peacefully among his fellow men.

Every morning he would come down from his *konak* wearing his long coat and felt slippers, would open the door of the mosque, enter, climb onto a table near the window, stick his neck out of the window and softly chant the morning call to prayer, *Lā Allah, ilā Allah.* He would turn toward the sea as if entrusting his words to the winds for them to carry to Stamboul or Mecca or anywhere else they might wish. There had never been a muezzin there; each successive aga had acted as muezzin to his own self. Nor had there ever been a minaret; the mosque's high window had substituted for the lack. Almost immediately after the *Lā Allah* the aga would leave and lock the door — though whether he had made his obeisance or not and whether he had touched his head two or more times to the marble floor or not were facts that could not be ascertained. He would then go back up to his *konak,* light his long pipe and smoke for a long time. When he had dispelled his drowsiness, he would put on his white turban, his broad sash, his overcoat, and his leather shoes, and, still holding his pipe, would descend and make his way to the *kiosk.* There he knew he would meet two or three others who were whiling away the time as he was, notables of the village who wore shirts with wide, open sleeves and long embroidered sashes and who would converse with him. *Lakirdi soilé.*

The priests of the area, who officiated at one of the two parish churches of the town and took turns at holding liturgies in the forty chapels scattered about, would see the aga passing by as they sipped their morning *raki* after church outside the small shop of Uncle Anagnostis Tsipotos. The aga would greet them with respectful disdain and pass on. The good housewives would also see him when of a morning they brought their unleavened *pitas* to the baking oven that lay a little beyond the mosque and was tended by Garoufalia Xinou. Auntie Siraino Pantousa, a good Christian soul, would see him, too — she who inspired fear in all the other women on two accounts, her tongue and her eye. People said that on one occasion she had succeeded in separating a couple on the very day of their wedding. The wedding wreaths were prepared, the bride was gotten up in her finery, the guests were present, and the priests were about ready to put on their stoles. But with a word that Siraino whispered into the ear of the mother-in-law (the groom's mother, that is)—a slanderous word, no doubt, against the bride—she managed to have the marriage called off. On another occasion, when a small two-masted ship, newly built and freshly painted, was sailing along in the distance, Auntie Siraino Pantousa and some other women were gazing out to sea from the top of the rock. Unable to bring herself to express admiration, she cried out:

"Well? What about that sailboat? What's fine about it?"

No sooner had she spoken than the rigging of the ship, unbelievable as it may seem—yet eyewitnesses tell the story—the rigging of the ship collapsed with a crash and the ship became a raft, mutilated, tossed hither and thither by the waves. This whole matter, however, seemed more in the nature of an apocryphal tale than a credible report.

As the aga was passing by the oven with his turban and his long pipe, the women, whiling away an hour or so in the small courtyard until it was time to place their bread in the oven, saw him and murmured a few idle words to one another:

"A handsome aga."

"Our town's been good for him."

"It's the fresh air."

"The brisk north wind."

"Have you seen his harem?"

"No."

"She's wrapped up to the eyes."

"His *hanum,* you mean."

"His wife! Oh, my!"

"And his slave."

"She never leaves the house."

"His slave, Fatimeh, comes out sometimes."

"Have you seen her face? She's black, devil take her!"

"Black—black as can be."

"And her teeth glitter."

"Anyway, he seems to be a good man."

"A mean and nasty one."

"As mean as his smile is nice."

"No matter what you say, he's a Turk."

"The dog!"

"But he's good-looking, my dear."

"Handsome man."

"Our town's been good for him."

"It's the fresh air."

"D'you want," suddenly called out Auntie Siraino Pantousa, "d'you want me to do him in within a month's time?"

The women stood silent for a moment. Garoufalia, the oven-tender, who was at that minute sweeping her oven, heard this and stopped her work. She turned around and said:

"Well, now! What spells will you cast on him?"

"Oh, what nonsense!" said another.

"That's a bad thing, Auntie Siraino."

"What's that to all of you? Spells . . . yes . . . no. I know what I'm talking about." The women did not know what to say.

"I don't believe it," said one of them.

"We're better off without such things."

"What do we care?"

"And even if we get rid of one or two Turks, Turkey can't be done in so easily," said an old woman with a sigh.

"You'll see," was Auntie Siraino's only response.

In the evening of the same day, around the hour of sunset, Auntie Siraino lay in wait by the narrow street between the oven and the small workshop of Uncle Anagnostis Tsipotis. At that moment the aga, with his unlit pipe under his arm, was returning from a walk along a lane near the low walls of the town, heading home for supper.

"*Axám hairolsoún,* Aga," said Auntie Siraino Pantousa boldly. She had heard in days gone by a few Turkish words from the lips of her late husband, a traveler to Turkish lands, and she recalled them to mind.

"Good evening," answered the aga in Greek, looking at her with surprise. "What do you want? Do you have some complaint to bring before me?"

"Me? A complaint? Neither a complaint nor a gift, Aga." She muttered the word "gift" inaudibly so that her interlocutor would not hear. "I just wanted to bid you good evening. It's been a while since I've seen you."

"Kind of you," said the aga smiling.

"I see that you look peaked."

"What?"

"You've grown very thin—preserve us from the evil eye, Aga! Our town hasn't been good for you."

"Really?"

"Thin. Very pale. May the evil eye not catch you. Pale as wax. You're wasting away in this land of the living."

"*Astaghfir-u-llah!*" exclaimed the aga.

"Yellow as a florin, Aga. Your dear face is sickly bright."

"*Allah! Allah!*"

"Look after yourself, Aga. The air in these parts doesn't agree with you. Be careful that you're not done in, poor soul, far from your homeland."

The Turk instinctively raised his pipe, feeling the need to bring it down on the back of this prophetess of evil. But Auntie Siraino had retreated ten steps and slipped out of sight around the first corner of the narrow street.

That evening after it was dark the aga looked at himself in the mirror again and again. The light of the candles in the upper chamber as well as his own agitation at the soothsayer's prophecy made him appear pale to his own eyes. He stretched his hand over the table but had no appetite for food. He filled his pipe but had no desire to smoke. He turned to his wife, the *hanum*.

"*Hanum,* is it true that I've grown pale and thin in recent days?"

The *hanum* looked at him for a long while.

"Pale? You're fine. Have a couple of glasses of sweet sherbet. I'll make some halvah and a cheese pie for you tomorrow. I'll hang an amulet around your neck so that the evil eye won't harm you."

Fatimeh, the slave, was moving in and out of the room at her various tasks, lighting her master's pipe, removing his slippers, straightening the pillow on the sofa for him. She heard this conversation and without thinking turned around.

"And what do you say, Fatimeh?" the aga could not help asking. "Is it true that I've grown pale? Does my face appear changed?"

Perhaps in revenge for the many beatings she had endured, Fatimeh took advantage of the situation and said:

"My master pale . . . get black . . . black like my hide!"

The *hanum* snatched up her slipper and hurled it at the slave's head, but she had already turned away and slipped out of the room.

From that day on the aga grew pale and had no appetite. He became melancholy, grim, and forbidding. He would carry his unlit pipe under his arm, ready to use it on the back of anyone who contradicted him or asked him an idle question.

Auntie Siraino Pantousa had disappeared from the village. She herself grew frightened at what she had undertaken. She grew frightened of her own tongue and eye. Other people evidently fed her fears too. The old woman who had pronounced a few days earlier that Turkey could not be done in said to Siraino:

"They'll hang you, my child. Who will stand up for you? Do you think they'll forgive you because you're a woman? All he has to do is blow a whistle—you'll see—and thousands of Turks will descend on us from up there"—she pointed northward and eastward towards the mainland—"and our poor island will run red with blood."

Auntie Siraino got up and fled from the village that night. They say she hid in a safe place, a cave that had another way out, a secret way that no one knew except her nephew, a herdsman, who brought her bread every three days.

She suffered in fact no harm and lived until 1865. At ninety years of age she herself used to relate these events.

For two weeks after that the aga would leave his *konak* every morning, go down to the mosque, chant the *Lā Allah* and then go on to the *kiosk*. He would ask each of the notables he spoke with:

"Is it true that I've grown pale and thin?"

"There's nothing wrong with you, Aga," they would tell him. "You're a little thin, but you shouldn't worry about it. Go your merry way. You'll quickly grow strong again. The air hereabouts agrees with you—it's invigorating."

So they would answer him. Nor could they answer him differently, because he was ready to raise his long pipe.

By the third week the aga no longer came out of his *konak*. He was no longer strong enough; his sinews were unstrung. He did not even touch the plates that were set before him at table. In vain did the *hanum* redouble her attentions to him. And Fatimeh the negress no longer dared say that her master was black like her own skin. He was in reality pale as wax and white as a sheet.

For two weeks the sick man had not been able to go to the mosque. One morning, in the fifth week after that woman's prophecy, he made a valiant effort and went out, dragging himself to the mosque. Fatimeh, who followed after him, helped him climb on the table. He thrust his head out of the window and began chanting "*Lā Allah ilā Allah, Allah akbar, Mohammed rasūl Al-lah.*" He chanted with all his strength, and his call to prayer echoed down below among the waves of the sea. Off in the distance the steep, hollow rock of the deserted promontory repeated the call in mournful tones.

After he climbed down from the table he felt a great weariness and sat trembling beside it. Without deliberation he opened the Koran that was lying on the table. By a strange coincidence he turned to a page in the third chapter, the third *sura,* and his eye fell on the following passage:

"Man dies when God so decrees, in accordance with the book wherein is inscribed the length of his life's duration."

The aga grew dizzy. He brought his hand to his forehead and closed his eyes. Then he opened them again and read on:

"God hath set you to flight before the face of your enemies . . ."

"It availeth not you abide at your home, be your death inscribed in the book die then you must. The arrow that you avoid in war, the same shall overtake you hereafter."

He gritted his teeth, clenched his fist, and was overcome with rage because he could not go to battle for Islam, could not slaughter the infidel. He leafed through the book and found this passage in the second *sura:*

"O ye faithful! Do battle against the infidels that dwell on your borders. Strike the infidels wheresoever you shall find them. Do battle against them till the time when all evil be destroyed, when all shall be drawn together in the worship of the only God."

After this, supported by Fatimeh, the aga went back up to his *konak,* entered his chamber, lay down on his soft divan, and did not rise again.

The soothsayer Siraino had foretold that he would not last forty days. Indeed, the aga died on the thirty-ninth day after the prophecy. He died from the prophecy, from the suggestion, and from that woman's spell. He died from his sickness. And that sick man with his chronic disease, now four hundred and forty-four years old—who will bewitch him?

Civilization in the Village:
A Christmas Story

NFORTUNATELY ONE
could not apply to the second wife of Stergios that popular saying,
"The first wife serves, the second commands." Thodoria, poor
woman, submitted to all the burdensome tasks imposed on her by
her husband. He was a plasterer, she a baker woman. Although she
was scarcely more than thirty-five, she already looked old. Uncle
Stergios, fifteen years her elder, had made her his second wife by
forcing the issue—that is, by taking her against her family's will.
Their child, Eleftheris, now four years old, had not yet had his fill
of mother's milk. Poor little Eleftheris was scrawny and pale, and
his mother could neither provide him with nourishment from her
own body nor wean him. Her breasts hung withered under her chemise, as if baked dry by the heat of the oven, and the child could
hardly find a drop of milk there.

Her first two children, a girl and a boy, had died, and now all her hopes rested in little Eleftheris. But she lived in fear because this child, too, was sickly. Ah yes, her heart was deeply scarred—yes, the best thing for us humans is not to enter into this world at all. Thodoria remembered with great anguish the moment when her little girl "saw the angel of death." She found her in her cradle livid, motionless, half-dead. Thodoria let out a shriek. The neighbor women ran in.

"What's wrong? What is it?"

"My child! My child!"

They called the doctor, but by the time he came it was all over with the little girl. In our hour, just one hour! One of the neighbors, Katerina "First-Come," wrapped a shroud around the body, and Thodoria began to search for the little girl's clothes. As she was bending over the chest to bring them out, she softly began to sing a lament, but Katerina upbraided her, saying the lament over the dead should not begin before the shrouding. They decked the child out with care, laid her on the rug and covered her so that her brother would not see her and start crying. Haralambakis was two years older and had some understanding of these things. The women of the neighborhood took him away until the funeral procession was over. Later, in the evening, when Haralambakis asked, "Where is Chryso, Mamma? Where did Chryso go?", they answered that she had gone to sleep among the flowers. And Katerina First-Come told him that his sister had gone "to the priest's threshing-floor and garden." The little boy kept on asking, "When will our Chryso come back, Mamma?" until three days went by and then he forgot about it.

Alas! Who could have known that very soon he would go to meet her? A year later Haralambakis fell ill. "Quick," they said, "fetch the doctor to make sure the same thing won't happen again."

The doctor came and examined the child. "It's nothing serious," he said, and sent them medicines, one kind after another. The more medicine the child took, the hotter the fever burned within him. The doctor returned and examined the child again. "In three days he'll be fine." In three days the boy was dead. What strength could Thodoria summon to look for his little clothes? How could her hands bear to deck him out? Fortunately, Katerina First-Come was there—with her untiring helpfulness, with her white kerchief under her printed scarf, with her slight trace of mustache—and was able to relieve Thodoria of this sad duty. How could she lament her own child? What mournful song could she sing? The priests came, took the boy away as they had the other, chanted over him, and carried him "to the flowers" where they had also taken little Chryso the year before.

Now the only child Thodoria had left was Eleftheris. She lay by his side and with her left arm supported his head as it rested on the pillow. She called to mind all that she had endured, and she could not get to sleep. A few hidden embers dimly glowed in the ashes of the hearth. Overhead a vigil light burned before the icons and out-lined the sad features of the saints with its pale gleam. Her husband, lying on her right, had been snoring for quite a while, since nine o'clock, and had already changed his position twice, rolling from one side to the other. As he slept his loud breathing would be inter-rupted from time to time by his grunts and mutterings.

Uncle Stergios was not really a bad man. He did not mind living off his wife's earnings and liked to eat the bread she brought home as payment for her labor at the bakery oven. He used to say that by tending the neighborhood oven his wife was spared the task of kneading her own bread. Whatever firewood was left over at the lime kiln he would load on his donkey and bring home to her. And, it must be said, Uncle Stergios was a hard worker and moreover did not bully his wife overmuch. But if he happened to make some money by selling a load of lime, he would return home with his pockets empty and his insides full of spirits. He would then "paint the town red," and if it was a Saturday evening he would "keep a three-day observance," as Thodoria used to say, and was "in his glory" until Monday morning. But she knew his ways and when she saw him "flying high" would say nothing to him, for if she did, she would risk getting a "whacking." On Monday mornings, however, before he left for the kiln, she would ask him to give her some money—if he had any left—and he would begin to realize to some degree what he had been doing.

During the days before Christmas he was again "making a joyful noise unto the Lord" because he had sold many hundredweights of lime and had a few five-drachma pieces in his hands. And now Christmas was over, the feast of St. Basil was approaching, and he still had not sobered up. This being a Sunday night, he had earlier in the evening been "high on the town" but fortunately had come home early. Thodoria surmised that the drachmas from the last sale were gone. She did not know, however, that during the day Uncle

Stergios had sold some more lime and that he had returned home early because he was a bit tired of being drunk and had a strong headache. Still Thodoria was pleased because with the child ill she would at least have her sleeping husband to keep her company and his snores to comfort her in her anxiety.

The child grew worse, though. Thodoria, sleepless and vigilant by the sick boy's side, suddenly noticed that he was coughing spasmodically and gasping for breath. His forehead was pale, his lips dry, his eyes glazed, and a flush was spreading from his cheeks to his temples. The symptoms were all too familiar from the illnesses of the other two children. Thodoria was overcome by anguish.

She hastily shook her husband awake.

"Get up, Stergios! Are you still sleeping, husband?"

Uncle Stergios, only half-awake, stretched his limbs and yawned. "What is it? What d'you want? . . . Why aren't you sleeping, Thodoria?" And he rolled over on his other side.

Thodoria shook him vigorously. "Didn't you hear me, husband? Are you going back to sleep? What's the matter with you?"

"What d'you say, woman?"

"Get up! Our child's in a bad way!"

"Well, what can I do? If he's in a bad way . . . let 'im get better."

It seemed to him that he was floating over a gaping abyss, his wife's mouth, that was ready to engulf him. He nuzzled his head against the pillow, as if against the edge of a soft, delightful hammock, and like a diver ready to plunge was on the verge of sinking once more into sleep.

"Will you get up, father?" Thodoria uttered the word "father" as the sick child might have. Then unable to hold back her tears she went on:

"Will you get up, father, or will you let me die, me too, like our Chryso and like our Haralambakis? Those two are among the flowers, father, in the next world, where all little children have one Father. But in this world, here, I don't have any other father except you, and you don't have any other child except me."

When Uncle Stergios heard these plaintive words, his heart was moved and, throwing aside the coverlet, he sat up on his bedding and turned his bleary eyes to where his son lay. Thodoria brought him a basin of water and he washed his eyes.

"Won't you go, Stergios dear, and call the doctor?"

"What good will a doctor do? Can you trust doctors? Do they

care? Do you really think, woman, that they feel sorry for us? Supposing I go, I call him, I throw stones against his window . . . he'll play deaf, or he'll get up and give me a scolding and chase me away. 'Couldn't you have come earlier? You come only now? At midnight? To wake the doctor up?' Oh, if you only knew how stony-hearted they are, woman!"

"It doesn't matter. You go, and put all the blame on me. Tell him your wife didn't tell you earlier in the evening that the child was sick."

Uncle Stergios got up, put on his breeches and jacket, wound his broad, yellow, tasseled sash around his waist, pulled on his sandals, clutched his dust-covered fez with its short, frayed tassel, tossed his cape on his back, took the lantern his wife had lit, and went out the door. It was very dark outside. Only a few stars shone here and there, and the sky looked overcast. The north wind that had been blowing mightily the past three days had abated an hour earlier, and the air was unusually calm. Uncle Stergios immediately realized this was the harbinger of a considerable snowfall, which was already making its appearance with an occasional drifting snowflake. "Well! And Thodoria wants me to bring the doctor," the plasterer muttered between yawns. "Will the doctor want to come out at midnight when it's snowing?"

Meanwhile he had turned right and walked about two hundred yards from one group of houses to another. Finally, arriving at the doctor's house, he did just what he said he would. He knocked in vain at the door. Then he threw some pebbles against the window of the doctor's bedroom. He got no answer. After a while a window on the ground floor was half opened, and the housemaid appeared. A lock of her unbraided hair tumbled out the window. She said:

"The doctor isn't here."

"Where is he?" asked Uncle Stergios.

"He's out."

"Out where?"

"He hasn't come back yet. He must've gone to see a patient."

"At this hour?"

"You're looking for him at this hour—maybe somebody else did too."

Uncle Stergios stood there undecided. Suddenly, as if she were talking more confidentially than usual, the maid added:

"Look around and see if there's a shop open in the square,

see if they're playing cards somewhere. But don't say I told you."

She thereupon pulled the shutter to and disappeared from sight.

Uncle Stergios suspected that the cunning maid had thrown him off the scent. "Well, of course, those slaveys make fools of us old men, seeing that we're not worth very much. Still, I'm not very old. I haven't been married more than twice, and if Thodoria were to die on me . . ." He did not pursue this train of thought, which was, in a way, the final symptom of his many days of drunkenness. The picture of the pale child with his gasping breath and the tearful mother appeared before him and froze his sudden youthful ardor. He remembered the maid's words: "See if they're playing cards somewhere." He was now fully awake and was ashamed to return home without accomplishing anything, so he decided to go back through the market place in the hope of running into the doctor somewhere.

ALONG with other evils a plague of cardplaying had descended upon the younger men of the seaside village. Of all the state-appointed functionaries the only ones that did not take part in the frequent evening gatherings at the home of one or another of their number were the assistant customs officer, who was then standing surety for someone; the justice of the peace, who was concerned for his reputation; and the teacher of the junior high school. All the rest, the assistant harbormaster, the health officer, the two assistant accountants at the port authority, the secretary from the justice's office, the telegraph officer, all of them were caught up in the cardplaying fever.

This disease, though of external origin, also infected part of the native population, as was evidenced by the presence at the gatherings—especially during that holiday period when they were held at the snug, well-appointed tavern of Thanasis Moreyios—of a number who were indigenous to the island: the mayor's secretary; two young butchers, who were army veterans; the tailor, who made European-style clothing and acted as the villagers' legal advisor; a barber; and two seamen. The grammar-school teacher came regularly every evening and placed a bet of a few small coins on a game of sixes. If he lost he would leave silently, without drinking even a single glass of rum. But if he won he would sit puffing constantly on his short pipe with one leg stretched out on the bench, the other down on the floor, and would drink two or three glasses of rum, spending exactly the amount he had won that night. When the clock struck midnight, he would get up and go home to bed.

The others would stay up much of the night, usually till three or four in the morning. The proprietor of the tavern, Thanasis Moreyios, was highly pleased with this kind of business, for he received the establishment's rightful percentage of the winnings and also profited from the sale of muscat wine and other drinks. The company would drink as they played, and the winner would graciously treat the others to a round of drinks. Few, however, were willing to admit they had won, and perhaps they acted in sincerity, for according to the wisdom of cardplayers there are only two winners: the one who does not play at all and the one who collects a percentage of the winnings. To the first of these categories belonged Captain Yiorgos Asproudakis, who came every evening. He never played for money, yet he was never absent from the gatherings. Two or three others, standing like ossified phantoms behind the players, represented in their persons Good and Bad Fortune. The group was often joined by Uncle Andonis Priftis, an old boatman, who would stay until someone decided to order drinks for everyone. Then, after he had drunk his rum, Uncle Andonis would leave, taking with him the others, the standees who had been glued to the backs of the players. On those nights, however, when he saw that a free drink was not forthcoming, he would usually slip out unnoticed and go to lie down in his boat. Upon occasion though, Uncle Andonis and Captain Aproudakis would join forces as partners and withdraw into a corner and play a simple game of *skambili* with some others. No money was bet, but there was the usual round of drinks. Captain Asproudakis was always the dealer. If he and his "unlucky" partner lost, the two of them would stay on until two in the morning, playing against each other. Uncle Andonis usually lost in the end and always protested that Captain Yiorgos was cheating him.

On the evening of Uncle Stergios's expedition, as the company was gathered in the snug tavern, the snow began to fall, but so quietly and gently that it seemed to be a white sheet spread by God over the poor and homeless in the streets. The wind had died down and the cold was no longer penetrating. Broad areas of soft whiteness suddenly made their appearance on the ground. One of the cardplayers got up from the table to stretch his legs—it was half past midnight—and went over to the window to peer through the fogged-over pane. But he could scarcely make out anything except a whitish-gray formlessness. At that moment a knock was heard on the bolted door.

"Open up, Mr. Thanasis!"

"Who is it?" called out the tavern-keeper in a voice hoarse from a cold. He was sitting near the table and keeping a vigilant eye on the cardplayers.

"Open up! It's snowing out here!"

The door was opened, not so much in response to the knocker's entreaties as to satisfy the curiosity of the one standing by the window, who was unable to see out clearly and wanted to open the door and find out for himself if it really was snowing. Uncle Stergios stepped into the tavern, shaking his cape, covered as usual with a dusting of white, though on this occasion it was snow rather than lime from the kiln. The ground was now covered with a few inches of snow. It had begun falling thickly during the minutes that elapsed while Uncle Stergios went from his house to the doctor's and thence to the marketplace, where he saw the lights in Thanasis Moreyios's tavern.

"It's snowing! It's snowing!" they all called out as they saw Uncle Stergios daubed in white. Those that were on their feet walked toward the door; those that were seated over a game of *paseta* cried out:

"Shut the door!"

"Where are you coming from, Uncle Stergios?"

"What in the world are you doing here at this time of night?"

"Are you just coming from the kiln—at midnight?"

Uncle Stergios did not answer these shouts. Immediately spotting the doctor, who was sitting between the assistant harbormaster and the secretary from the justice's office, he went over to him, and, bending over, whispered in his ear:

"Would you do me the favor, Excellency, of coming to my house? Someone's sick."

"Who's not feeling well? Your wife?"

"No. My child."

"And you've come at this hour?"

"The woman didn't tell me. The child was fine earlier in the day but got sick during the night."

"Can't you see it's snowing? How can we go out?"

"Come here, Uncle Stergios, come here! Come on over here, why don't you?" said another voice. "Thanasis, bring a glass of muscat wine for Uncle Stergios. Have a drink and warm your bones. Come on! Sit over here by me!"

The speaker was the secretary from the justice's office, a tall, blond young man with a flaxen mustache and prominent, round eyes. He was holding the bank at that moment, and when he saw Uncle Stergios his mustache twitched like a cat's whiskers when it smells a mouse. His strong hand grasped Uncle Stergios's elbow and sat him down next to him with that show of good-natured force that some people like to display toward those of weaker character. The young man's name was Aristides Manganopoulos. During the period of change of government (the year was 188–) he had been hurtled from one end of the Kingdom of Greece to the other. He was a pleasure-seeker, loved to drink, and was a jolly companion. But how can anyone live on only sixty drachmas a month?

Uncle Stergios drank his glass of wine and, leaning over behind the secretary, whispered once more in the doctor's ear:

"Do me this favor, doctor, and may the Lord grant you whatever you wish. My wife's sent me and she's waiting for me. The child is very sick."

"Well, wait till it blows over a bit, wait till it stops snowing," answered the doctor.

The doctor was a fine man, forty years old, youthful, tall, thin, willing to be of help, not excessively stony-hearted or greedy. He was a graduate of the University of Athens and, though he had the means, he had not felt a compelling need to go to Europe to purchase his share of wisdom. Nevertheless, despite these qualities, he sometimes gave in to lassitude. On this particular evening he was annoyed at himself for being caught up in the company of the card-players. If he had gone to bed early, he thought, Uncle Stergios's child would not have gotten sick, nor would this man have come to bother him.

"How did you find out I was here?" he asked Stergios suddenly.

Uncle Stergios at that moment remembered the maid's admonition and answered:

"I was going to your house, and I came by way of the shore where it's sheltered from the wind . . . When I saw the lights in the tavern, I said to myself, 'Let's go in. Maybe the doctor's in there.' "

"And what reason did you have to draw that conclusion?"

"I don't know exactly . . . Something told me you were here . . . I wanted to have a glass of rum to get warm . . ."

"And instead you had a glass of muscat wine."

"Thanks to the kindness of Mr. Secretary. He treated me."

Aristides Manganopoulos had not forgotten about Uncle Stergios. He kept his hand lightly on the plasterer's knee. When he heard these last words, he hastened to join in the conversation.

"Well now! Wouldn't you like to bet a coin or two, Uncle Stergios, to while the time away?"

Uncle Stergios was not entirely inexperienced at cards. When he was young he had been a corporal in the army and had lived for years in various cities of Greece. To please the secretary he began by betting a small coin, which he lost. In a few minutes he had taken out all the change he had, totaling more than a drachma, and lost that too.

To make him feel better Aristides Manganopoulos treated him to a small carafe of muscat wine. Uncle Stergios drank it down and then, leaning over again, said in the doctor's ear:

"Shall we go now, doctor? It must've stopped snowing."

"It's stopped, but it hasn't melted," murmured the secretary very softly.

"Well, we'll see if we can, Uncle Stergios," said the doctor. "Why the devil did your child have to get sick now!"

"Please, doctor . . . may your loved ones prosper."

The secretary, turning to Uncle Stergios, said: "Come on now, Uncle Stergios. Why give it a thought? Play a bit to while the time away . . . to get your money back."

"I don't have any more money, Mr. Secretary."

"Don't tell little fibs, Uncle Stergios. D'you think I don't know that you sold some lime today?"

The simple-hearted man bent toward the secretary's ear and said confidentially:

"You tell the doctor too, so we'll convince him to go."

"To go? Where?"

"To my house. My child is sick."

"There's nothing wrong with him," said the secretary. "Don't worry about it. He'll get well."

"My wife is alone, and she's waiting for me. Think what that means, Mr. Secretary."

"Oh, don't worry about it! Take heart, Uncle Stergios! Don't be afraid. Nothing will happen to the child."

Uncle Stergios lowered his head. At that moment there arose before his eyes the terrible picture of the suffering child, coughing, unable to breathe, with the pallor of death on his forehead, and his grieving mother, clasping her hands and asking for mercy.

"Bring two glasses of wine for Uncle Stergios and me, Thanasis," the secretary called out.

The tavern-keeper brought the two glasses. Manganopoulos poured most of his into his companion's glass.

"I'm not drinking," said the old plasterer. "It'd be too much. I was drinking earlier this evening too."

"Drink up. Don't worry. Don't give it a thought. There's nothing wrong with the child."

Uncle Stergios drank the sweet-smelling wine and slowly the fumes rose to his head. "You're a good friend," he said to the secretary. "You've given me courage. I was really afraid for my child."

"Put up a two-drachma piece and I'll change it for you, Uncle Stergios," said the secretary, spreading out the small coins on the table. "All of this I had lost earlier on . . . I still haven't gotten back all that I lost."

Uncle Stergios brought out his greasy, gray purse tied with a string, undid it, and took out a five-drachma piece. The secretary gave him small coins.

One of the group had stepped out of the tavern and was just then coming back in. "The snow's more than a foot deep. Hey boys, how're we going to get home?"

"Has it stopped snowing at least?" asked the doctor.

"It's still coming down."

"Oh, devil take it!"

"D'you hear, Uncle Stergios?" said the secretary. "Wait till it stops and then you can leave with the doctor."

"Well, what's to be done, Mr. Secretary?"

"Why don't you bet a coin or two on a game?"

Uncle Stergios began by betting one coin, then another, then another. Then they got to the third hand. Then they were even. Then Uncle Stergios won some and bet that as well. Every time they were even the secretary treated him to a glass of muscat wine, and every time Stergios bet his winnings, the secretary treated him to a small carafe. In half an hour Stergios lost his five drachmas down to the last penny. He took out a second five-drachma piece, and in a quarter of an hour he lost that one too. He took out a third piece, his last, and in ten minutes the secretary, who dealt the cards, scooped it up too.

By then it was three o'clock in the morning.

Suddenly there was a knock at the tavern door.

"Open the door! Open the door!"

"What fool is this, at this hour, in all this snow?" exclaimed the tavern-keeper.

"Open up! Please, Mr. Thanasis!"

"Who's there?"

"It's me, Yiorgis Sefertzis."

"What do you want?"

"Is Uncle Stergios the plasterer there?"

"What do you want him for?"

Everyone turned towards Uncle Stergios, who, dizzy from the wine, was smiling like a simpleton at the secretary's mustache and saying:

"I'm not worried! Take it all! Poverty's nothing! Money's not my god! Friendship, that's what counts for me. You're a good friend, really!"

The door was opened and in walked Yiorgis Sefertzis.

Lying against her pillow, Thodoria felt the hot breath of her child. She counted the hours and minutes that had passed since her husband had left. "He'll come soon . . . he's coming . . . he'll be here any minute . . . the doctor'll come with him and he'll make my child well," she said to herself. "Why blame the doctor? Parents are to blame; they're the ones that are hard-hearted. If I had called the doctor in time, my Haralambakis wouldn't have died." She cocked her ears to catch any sound announcing the arrival of her husband and the doctor, but nothing could be heard. The good Lord was quietly sending down snow, scattering flakes to fill the earth with drink, feed the living with her fruit, and cast a white shroud over the dead so that they might lie buried deeper in the ground.

Meanwhile, time was passing and Uncle Stergios gave no sign of returning. Thodoria got up, threw some kindling into the hearth, stoked up the fire, and lay down once more by the side of little Eleftheris. The boy was gasping and moaning piteously. His sleep had been agonized, and when he woke up he was sobbing and coughing convulsively. "There, there, my little one, my sweet, you'll be fine by tomorrow. Your daddy's gone to get you some toys, and you'll have them day after tomorrow on St. Basil's Day to play with, and you'll be happy. And I'll make you a cookie doll dipped in egg, and your godmother will bring you another one, big and lovely with trimmings and little birds and nightingales and no other child will have such a nice one." The child did not seem to comprehend. He had not uttered a word since the previous evening. Thodoria kept on asking him, "Where does it hurt, my little Leftheris? Where does it hurt?" but the boy answered only with moans and gasps.

The log in the hearth began to crackle and toss off sparks. Thodoria recalled a folk rhyme and began to intone:

If it's a friend, let him rejoice;
If it's a foe, let him choke;
If he's from home, let him quickly come.

But the sparks kept on sizzling for a long time. The incantation did not seem to have the power to stop them, perhaps because in this instance the person in question was both a friend and a foe, both from the home and not from the home. Eventually, the sparks died down, but Uncle Stergios still did not return.

Thodoria had not slept at all during those long hours since the early evening. The poor woman had at one point shut her eyes in spite of herself and for a few seconds dropped into that unconscious state when the soul steps into the vestibule of the palace of dreams while the body has not yet surrendered to sleep. But after a moment a crackling sound similar to the one from the sparks in the hearth woke her up. The sound came from the vigil lamp, whose wick was floating in the last drop of oil, struggling to avoid the water below, like a drowning man clinging to a raft, like a soul in its death agony flailing about before it is parted from the body. How uncanny, how lugubrious that sound! What a shudder of fear it aroused! The vigil lamp seemed alive, capable of divining and prophesying. What did it hold in its memory, what could it see or foretell? Perhaps it was weary of being both sacred and profane, of shining on the calm, passionless saints of Byzantium and on the restless, ardent passions of sinful mankind. Perhaps the lamp wished to be extinguished. The lamp wished to be extinguished, but the wick resisted and sputtered.

Thodoria got up, lifted her head, and gazed motionless for a little while at the crackling wick. Her face, chin, and neck took on the expressive pose that one admires in the paintings of the great Western masters. She was tall, dark, comely, almost beautiful. At thirty-five the hair about her temples was already turning gray, as if singed by the oven or dusted with lime. Wretched plasterer's wife! Miserable baker woman!

She then took a jar of oil and lowered the vigil lamp. The grating noise of the rope against the pulley made her shudder. She poured some oil into the lamp and raised it again. She made the sign of the cross three times in front of the saints' icons and prayed for help from the Mother of God. Then she thought, "My husband's very late. I wonder what happened to him. Lord protect us!" It seemed to her that if she were to open the window and look out she would see him coming with the doctor. She went to the window, opened it, and was startled to see the road and all the rooftops standing white in the darkness.

"It's been snowing! Dear Lord! How long has it been coming down?"

She clasped her hands together and felt the burden of her misfortune grow twice as heavy. Until now she was afraid only for her sick child; now she began to fear for her husband as well. What could have happened to him? Had he fallen anywhere? Was he buried under the snow? Was he frozen? Had his heart given in? Oh, God! She blamed herself for sending him out at such an hour to fetch the doctor. It would have been better if she had simply entrusted her child to God's mercy. Lord Jesus and Mother of God! What's happened to Uncle Stergios? Something bad! And what if they brought him to her in the morning, heart no longer beating, frozen stiff, dead? Ah!

She shut the window and pondered a moment what she should do. She felt like setting out herself, just as she was, to find out what happened to her husband. But the child, where would she leave the child? And then, could she, a woman, run about at night in the snow? The streets couldn't be passable. She tried to find explanations to allay her fears: perhaps Uncle Stergios hadn't been able to persuade the doctor; perhaps the doctor had been hard-hearted and Uncle Stergios was ashamed to return in a state of anger without having accomplished anything; perhaps he had found a shop still open at this late hour, had come upon some friends, and started drinking with them. What time was it, anyway? It was a long time since he'd left. Would any shop be open at this hour? There must be something really wrong. She hesitated a bit longer, and then, going to the opposite side of the house, she opened the window that faced west. On that side, almost abutting against their wall, stood the house of Yiorgis Sefertzis, a neighbor with whom, as it happened, they had not quarreled for a long time now.

"Neighbor! Neighbor! Yiorgena!" she called loudly to the wife. She waited a moment, but received no answer.

"Neighbor!" she called again. "Yiorgis!"

A few minutes passed, and then a woman's voice replied:

"What're you shouting about, Stergena?"

"Is Yiorgis asleep?" asked Thodoria, recognizing her neighbor's voice.

"Yes."

"Please—wake him up for me."

"What's wrong?"

Yiorgena opened the window. Thodoria gave a brief account of what had happened.

"And why do you need Yiorgis?"

"Tell him to have pity on me and go find out what happened to my husband."

"How can he go out? The snow's over your head."

"Over your head! Oh, dear woman, what will become of me?"

Meanwhile Yiorgis had woken up. After some protestation on his part, he yielded to the unfortunate woman's entreaties and agreed to go out and search for her husband. The snow stood more than knee-high in some places, but elsewhere, in more sheltered spots, it was only about a foot deep. Luckily, Yiorgis Sefertzis, formerly a seaman, now a land-owning farmer, was the possessor of an old pair of boots that reached over the knees.

RUNNING parallel to the flagstone street was the steep shore road leading to the village's upper quarter, where the marketplace came to an end. There at the top of the hill stood the shop of Mr. Argyros Syrmatenios. If by chance the tax collector or the president of the village council had wished to assess the amount of taxes due from each tradesman, he would have been hard put to decide just what Mr. Argyros's trade was, because as far as one could see, he sold nothing. His store was always open, from early morning until eight o'clock at night, but inside nothing was to be seen except empty display cases, one or two empty barrels, a pair of scales that were used for some unknown purpose, and a small jar that sat next to the scales. Oftentimes, thinking the jar contained tobacco, someone would lift the lid but would find he was mistaken, the jar was empty. It is true, though, that Mr. Argyros Syrmatenios would then graciously offer him tobacco from his pouch. All day long he sat on his stool, taking snuff and chatting with his friends about the politics of the day or matters of local interest.

Mr. Argyros was sixty years old, tall, fair-skinned, with grayish-blond hair, fine features, and small eyes that were all but invisible behind his spectacles. Late in life he had yielded to the demands of the times and had donned European dress, though over his European suit he still wore the island outer coat that reached to his ankles and an embroidered cap on his head. The thumb and forefinger of his left hand were perpetually glued together, grasping a pinch of snuff. He took snuff like every old miser who feels the need to exchange other passions—smoking, drinking, cards, sports, excursions, revelry, even love itself—for this one alone, the cheapest of all. And even though his little jar was empty, Mr. Argyros would graciously offer snuff from his tobacco pouch, reckoning perhaps that with a few dozen pennies he would oblige a large number of people and make them his friends.

While the placid Mr. Argyros passed his time monotonously downstairs in the shop, freely dispensing advice to all present, his wife, a woman of the same age as he, carried on their main business upstairs, selling silk fabrics and gold threads of various qualities to all the women in the village that had marriageable daughters and were obliged to embroider their trousseaux. From this trade Mr. Argyros, with a perfectly clear conscience, reaped a profit of 75 percent.

They said, however, that for close friends he would also lend out money on collateral three times the value of the loan, and at interest that was not higher than 80 percent per annum.

"Times are hard, my good people, and money doesn't come easily these days. And if—understand—you can't manage and you lose your money, then you yourself are lost. And if you go and drink it up—understand—is it right to blame somebody else? I ask you. Why's the other fellow obliged, so to speak, to give you money? It's your fault if you're lazy, Heaven preserve us, and if you can't make a living. Is there enough money around, bless my soul, to help other people? I for my part can't give out money—Lord help us—I can't give out money that'll be thrown away."

That morning, after the snow stopped falling when the clouds dispersed and the sun rose to flood the earth with gentle light and melt here and there the thinner layers of snow, in many neighborhoods of the village men wearing tall boots with shovels in hand were struggling to clear the snow and open up a pathway in the streets. Uncle Stergios, drawn and dejected, with his thick cape wrapped around him, appeared around nine o'clock at Mr. Argyros's shop.

"What's wrong, Stergios?" said he. "You look worried."

"Everything's wrong, Mr. Argyros," answered Uncle Stergios. "Don't ask. Things are very bad."

"What is it?"

"My child died this morning, my one and only child," he said with tears in his eyes.

"How's that? Was he sick long?"

"Only a few days, but yesterday evening he got worse. I went about midnight to call the doctor, and suddenly it started snowing. I couldn't wake the doctor up. I came back with tears in my eyes . . . and by morning the child had passed on."

"Well, why didn't you wake the doctor up if you were in such need?"

"He wasn't at home."

"How could that be? At that hour?"

"Maybe he wasn't at home, or maybe they just told me he wasn't," said Uncle Stergios, avoiding an exposition of the whole truth.

After a moment of silence Stergios continued:

"I've dared to come and show my face, Mr. Argyros, because I'm desperate. I've brought you these trinkets . . . if you could lend me twenty drachmas or so to pay the child's funeral expenses . . . because I have no cash on hand." He showed him two silver earrings and a ring that belonged to his wife.

"How is it that you have no money?" asked Mr. Argyros with a stern expression. "This year, I've heard, you've been very busy at the kiln."

"Yes, I got some money even yesterday," said Uncle Stergios, "but I had some debts and I paid them back. How was I to know?"

"Well, why don't you go to the men you owed and paid off and ask them to make you another loan?" commented Mr. Argyros, without touching the silver jewelry.

Even in his dire circumstances Uncle Stergios was not at a loss for words.

"The people I owed are grocers. They don't lend money," he answered, "I bought from them on credit."

"And what makes you think I lend money?" asked Mr. Argyros.

Uncle Stergios answered sorrowfully:

"If you please, Mr. Argyros. After all, if you gave me credit I could bury my child."

Mr. Argyros picked up the three silver pieces of jewelry and examined them for a long time.

"Who knows if these are really silver," he said. "One has to be a jeweler to tell. But anyway, I don't believe everything you said, Stergios. You owed some money and paid up . . . maybe. But in these times we're living in, my good man, business is bad, many people are hard-pressed. I don't know why there's no money around, why it's just not there at all. And if you go and get drunk, bless my soul . . . when you have money you don't know how to value it. I don't have any to speak of, Heaven preserve us. Let's see if I have twenty drachmas to give you, Lord help us."

He was still examining the three pieces of jewelry and weighing them in his hand. Then he said:

"These aren't even worth ten drachmas. Go and see what else you can bring me."

"I don't have anything else of silver at home."

"Doesn't your wife have any silver clasps?"

"She doesn't."

"A red silk dress, a paisley shawl? A satin jacket, a velvet vest?"

"I'll go and see."

Uncle Stergios went home, gathered whatever silk garments Thodoria had, and returned to Mr. Argyros's shop. The old usurer then counted out twenty drachmas and handed them over to Stergios.

A few hours earlier, at dawn, Uncle Stergios had returned home under the forceful urging of Yiorgis Sefertzis, who had found him in the tavern. The doctor was now ready to go home to bed and was persuaded to pass by the house of the old plasterer. They arrived with Yiorgis Sefertzis in the lead, holding a lantern and stepping in the depressions he had left in the snow on his way to the market-place. The doctor came second, and Uncle Stergios brought up the rear, stumbling and sliding in the snow, constantly falling down and getting up. When they entered the house, the child was breathing his last. They all stood over him during his last moments. The doctor had pencil and paper with him. He wrote the medical examiner's report, handed it to Uncle Stergios, and went home to bed. Thodoria wept and beat her breast.

In the evening a small procession left the church: a little cradle-like coffin carried by two men, the two priests of the parish, Uncle Stergios, Thodoria, and four or five other women who were relatives or neighbors. Opposite the church near the entrance of a general store stood a group of men who doffed their hats when they saw the procession. They were the assistant harbormaster, the telegraph officer, the secretary from the justice's office, and two others. Aristides Manganopoulos, recognizing the old plasterer, asked:

"Hm! What's Uncle Stergios doing there?"

"It's his child that died," said one of the local inhabitants.

"Really? Just think what a good time he and I had together last night! What weather to choose to die in . . . with all this snow!"

A Dream among the Waters

I WAS A POOR HERDS-
man living in the mountains. I was eighteen years old and knew
nothing of the world. Without realizing it, I was happy. It was in
that summer of 187– that I last felt this happiness. In those days I
was a handsome lad. I would see my sunburnt face, prematurely
stern, reflected in the streams and pools. The crags and mountain
sides were exercise grounds for my tall, supple body.

The following winter, Old Father Sisois, or Sisonis, as our coun-
tryfolk used to call him, took me in with him and taught me my letters. He had been a teacher, and to the end of his life everyone would
address him as "Schoolmaster." At the time of the Revolution he
had been a monk and a deacon, but he fell in love with a Turkish
girl and, as the report went, abducted her from a harem in Smyrna,
had her baptized, and married her. After the political situation had
become more stable, when Capodistrias was ruler of Greece, Sisois

taught in various schools throughout the country and acquired a reputation under the name of "Sotirakis the teacher." Later he remembered his obligation of old and, after he had provided for his family, donned the cassock once more, this time as a simple monk since he could not be ordained a priest. He lived out the rest of his life in repentance at the cenobite monastery of the Annunciation, where he wept over his sin. This transgression was mitigated by his many good deeds and, they say, he was able to win his salvation.

After I learned my first letters from old Sisois, I was sent by the monks to a provincial seminary with a scholarship, where I was immediately placed in the upper class. Then I went to the Rizarios Seminary in Athens. I was close to twenty when I began my schooling and was almost thirty when I finally finished my studies at the university. I came away with a certificate in law, second class.

I have not, you must understand, been a great success. Today, I still work as an assistant in the law office of a distinguished Athenian lawyer and politician whom I despise. I don't know why I despise him—but perhaps it is because he is my patron and benefactor. I feel constricted and awkward and cannot make much use of the position I hold with this lawyer, a position resembling that of an attendant at court. As a barking dog tied in his master's yard by a very short rope cannot bite outside the arc circumscribed by the radius of that rope, so I, too, cannot say or do anything more than I'm allowed by the narrow legal concerns of my patron's office.

The last year when I was still a natural man was that summer of 187-. I was then a handsome, brown-haired lad, and I pastured the goats of the monastery of the Annunciation on the mountains that rise straight up from the craggy shoreline and look out northward over the watery expanse. This whole area was known as Xanemo, "Furl-Sails," from the ships that put in when buffeted by storms. All that region was my personal possession. The places along that sheer, rocky shoreline of mine—Platana, the Great Strand, the Vineyard—were spread out in the direction of the north and northwest winds. I, too, seemed intimately bound to those two winds that blew in my hair and made it curl like the bushes and the wild olive branches that were twisted by their ceaseless blasts, the unending whipping of their harsh breath.

Everything there was mine: the ravines, the gorges, the valleys, the mountains, the whole shoreline. The fields belonged to the tiller only during the days when he came to plow or sow, when he would make the sign of the cross three times and say, "In the name of the Father and of the Son and of the Holy Spirit, I sow this field to provide food for strangers and passersby and for the birds of the air, and so that I, too, may reap the rewards of my labor." But I reaped part of the crop without ever plowing or sowing. I followed the example of the hungry disciples of our Saviour and applied the injunctions of Deuteronomy without even knowing them. The vineyard belonged to the poor widow only during the hours when she herself came to fertilize it and prune it and harvest her crop and fill her basket with grapes—if, that is, there were any grapes left to harvest. The rest of the time the vineyard was my property.

The only rivals I had in the usufruct and enjoyment of these fruits were the field constables hired by the mayor's office. Under the pretense of guarding other people's gardens, they claimed the best produce for themselves. They certainly did not wish me well and proved to be formidable rivals.

Even though I often crossed the property lines, my usual haunts were higher up, beyond the boundaries of the olive groves and the vineyards. There, on three mountain peaks separated by two ravines and grown over with scrub brush and wild grass, I pastured the goats of the monastery. I was the monks' ward and worked for five drachmas a month, which they subsequently raised to six. In addition to this pay they gave me leather for my rustic shoes and plenty of dark bread, or *pitas,* "flat cakes," as the monks called them.

My only permanent neighbor on the lower portion of my domain was Mr. Moschos, one of the minor gentry and a very eccentric fellow. Mr. Moschos chose to live in the country in a small, graceful tower with his niece, Moschoula, whom he had adopted because he was a childless widower. She was an orphan with no brothers or sisters, and he had taken her in and loved her as if she were his own daughter. Mr. Moschos had acquired his money in various business ventures abroad. After he already held a fair amount of land in that area, he persuaded some of his poorer neighbors to sell him theirs and had purchased eight or ten contiguous fields. He walled them in and thus created what for our parts was a large estate, consisting of over one hundred acres. The cost of the enclosing walls was considerable, perhaps more than the value of the land, but this did not disturb Mr. Moschos, who wanted to create a sort of kingdom for himself and his niece. At the edge of his property he built a tall towerlike house two stories high. There were springs scattered about his land, but he drained it by digging a well. He installed a winch and used the water for irrigation. He divided his land into four sections: a vineyard, an olive grove, a large grove of fruit trees, and a vegetable garden, this latter surrounded by a stone wall. He settled there and from then on lived continually in the country, rarely going to town. His estate was near the sea, and even though its upper boundary reached the top of a small mountain, the waves almost touched its lower wall when the north wind blew.

For companions Mr. Moschos had his pipe, his hoe, his *komboloi,* and his niece Moschoula. The girl was about two years younger than I. As a child she would leap from rock to rock, run from one inlet to the next down by the shore, gather seashells, and chase after crabs. She was vibrant and restless as a shorebird. Beautiful and dark, she reminded one of the sunburnt maiden in the Song of Solomon, forced by her mother's sons to guard the vineyards: "Behold, thou art fair, my love; behold, thou art fair; thou hast dove's eyes." Her pale, yet dusky, complexion had the golden glow of dawn; her neck, bright and gleaming under the embroidery of her chemise, was much whiter than the skin of her face. To me she seemed like the small kidless she-goat, delicate of limb and feature, with glistening pelt, that I had named Moschoula.

The western window of the tower opened onto a thicket that became denser beyond the top of the mountain. There bushes and sweet-smelling brush grew and the ground was rugged and loamy. This was the beginning of my territory. I frequently descended to that spot and set to pasture the goats of the monks, my spiritual fathers.

One day, I took my usual count of the goats — fifty-six there were that year, in other years between forty-five and sixty. That day I counted only fifty-five and saw that Moschoula, my favorite, was not among them. Somehow she must have gotten left behind. If it had been any of the others, I wouldn't have known right off which one it was — only that one of them was missing — but Moschoula's absence was obvious. I was really frightened. Had an eagle carried her off? But in those low-lying regions eagles didn't deign to visit often. Their principal lookout was high up toward the west on the white craggy mountain that appropriately bore the name Eagle's Nest. Still, it did not seem entirely unheard of or impossible that an eagle might have dropped down unexpectedly, smitten by the charms of my little goat, Moschoula.

I cried out in great agitation:

"Moschoula! . . . where is Moschoula?"

I hadn't even noticed the presence nearby of Moschoula, the niece of Mr. Moschos. The enclosing wall of the property and the house built against it were about five hundred feet away from where my goats and I were. The girl happened to be near her open window. When she heard my voice, she got up, leaned out of the window and called out:

"What's the matter? Why are you shouting?"

I didn't know what to say. Still, I answered:

"I'm calling my goat, Moschoula. It's got nothing to do with you."

When she heard me say that, she shut the window and disappeared.

Another day she again saw me from her window as I lay stretched out in the shade in that same spot. My goats were grazing and I was whistling a tune, a mountain air familiar to goatherds.

For some unknown reason she called out to me:

"That's the way you always sing! I've never heard you play the pipe. A herdsman without a pipe . . . I think that's very strange!"

I did have a reed pipe, but I was not bold enough to play it when I knew she would hear me. On this occasion, however, I felt honor bound to play for her sake, though I was not sure what she thought of my playing. I only know that as a recompense she sent me some figs and a cupful of *petimezi,* candied grape paste.

One evening I brought my goats down to the shore along the rocks where the sea formed thousands of limpid coves and nooks, and where the rugged shoreline shaped itself into jutting crags and hollowed-out caves. The sea, weaving and winding, murmured as it washed in; it danced in unruly splashes and sprays like a babbling child that jumps up and down in its crib, longing to be picked up and dandled in its mother's gentle arms. That evening, as I was saying, I brought my goats down to "get a taste of salt water," as I often did. The sea looked joyful and enticing before my eyes and I felt a longing for it, a strong urge to dive in for a swim. It was the month of August.

I led my herd back up the rugged slope onto a path that was marked out along a ridge between two cliffs. I'd come down by that path and intended to return by it to my mountain fold later that night. I left my goats there to feed on samphire and seepweed, though they were no longer hungry. I softly whistled to them as a signal to lie quiet and wait for me. They heard and obeyed. Seven or eight of them were billy goats with bells I could hear from a distance if the animals grew restless.

I turned and went back down the sharp decline to the edge of the sea. The sun had just set and the moon, almost full, began to shine low on the horizon. It looked as if it were only a few yards above the mountains of the island opposite. The rock at whose base I stood faced northward, and to my left, beyond the promontory to the west, I could see a fold of the sun's royal purple as he made his kingly departure. It was the train of his robe as it follows behind him, or perhaps the carpet that, as they say, his mother spreads for him when he sits down for his evening repast. To the right of the rock there was a small sea-cave strewn with crystalline shells and shiny, many-colored pebbles, as if the cave had been put in order and decorated by sea nymphs. Nearby began a footpath by which one could climb the side of the sheer cliff and reach the lower gate of Mr. Moschos's enclosure, one side of which paralleled the shoreline for a hundred yards.

I quickly threw off my shirt and trousers and plunged into the sea. I washed body and hair and swam about for a few minutes. I felt a tenderness, an inexplicable magic; I thought that I was one with the waves, sharing their essence—liquid, cool, salty. I would have liked to stay in the water forever and would never have had enough of swimming if my flock hadn't been on my mind. No matter how obedient the goats were, no matter how well they would heed my voice when I called to them to stay quiet, they were, after all, only goats, as untrustworthy and unruly as small children. I was afraid that some of them would gambol off. Then I would have to run about and search for them in the dark, in the gullies and mountains with my only help the sounds of the billy goats' bells. As for Moschoula, I'd made sure she would not run off as she had previously. On that occasion some stupid thief—if I could only lay my hands on him!—had stolen her gilt bell with its red ribbon. This time I'd taken some pains to tie her by a short rope to a bush on the rock sloping up from where I'd left my clothes before my plunge.

I ran out of the water, put on my shirt and trousers, and took a step to begin my ascent. I intended to climb up the sea-washed rock, untie my little Moschoula, and rejoin the rest of my flock a hundred yards farther up. The short dash up the slippery incline was only a game to me, like the contests children have jumping from the lower to the higher steps of a marble staircase in their neighborhood.

At that moment, just as I was beginning my climb, I heard a loud splash, as if a body had fallen into the water. The sound came from the right, over near the shell-strewn cave decorated by the nymphs. I knew that Moschoula, Mr. Moschos's niece, sometimes came to bathe in the sea there. Had I known that she, too, was in the habit of bathing by moonlight, I would not have risked approaching her territory for my swim. Without making the slightest noise I took two or three steps up the slope. Hidden by the tip of the rock and some rushes, I peered very cautiously in the direction of the cave and saw that it was indeed Moschoula who had just plunged into the water and was bathing naked in the waves.

I recognized her immediately in the pale moonlight that spread its silvery hue over the calm sea, which was like a stage on which the waves danced with a phosphorescent glow. Moschoula dove beneath the surface and came up again with her hair wet, trailing from her locks a stream of pearls. She swam quite well. She was facing in my direction, playing and floating in the water.

If I wanted to leave, I would have to stand upright for one moment on the top of the rock, then bend over behind the bushes and untie my goat. Only then could I disappear from sight, holding my breath and trying not to make any noise. But for that one moment my tall silhouette would be outlined clearly in the moonlight, and that would be enough: Moschoula would surely catch sight of me, since she was facing in my direction. How startled she would be! She would naturally be frightened, she would cry out, she would accuse me of evil intentions. Then woe to the young goatherd! My first thought was to cough loudly, signaling my presence, and then call out, "I just happened to be here, I didn't know . . . Don't be afraid! I'll leave right away, young lady!"

Yet, for some reason, I was awkwardly irresolute. In my mountain haunts no one had given me lessons in social etiquette. I drew back, descended again to the base of the rock, and waited. "She won't be long," said I to myself. "She'll have her swim, then get dressed and leave. She'll leave by her footpath and I'll leave by the other, beyond the cliff." I remembered Sisois and Father Grigoris, the monks' confessor, who had often exhorted me to avoid the temptation of woman.

So I decided to wait. Now if I wanted to get away without being seen, there was no other means of escape than to dive into the sea as I was, clothes and all, and head westward, away from where the girl was bathing. This would entail swimming the whole half mile to the main beach and harbor of the town, since the shoreline in between was completely inaccessible, all rock and sheer cliff. Only where I was standing was there an inlet, with the sea cradled between caverns and rocks. Furthermore, I would have to abandon my goat Moschoula to her fate, tethered up there on the rock. And then, when I reached the town beach in my dripping clothes, soaked with salt water and sea scum, I would have to walk the half mile back by another path to where I'd left the flock. Then I would have to descend part way down the slope to untie my goat Moschoula. By then Mr. Moschos's niece would have gone away, without, of course, leaving any trace of her presence.

If, then, I carried out this plan, it would require great effort. It would be a real feat, taking more than an hour. And I couldn't be sure that my flock would be safe in the meanwhile. So I had no choice but to wait, holding my breath. The girl did not suspect my presence. Besides, my conscience was clear: I was innocent. Yet, innocent though I was, I did not lack curiosity. I climbed very slowly back up the rock, hid behind the bushes and bent over to look at the swimmer.

She was a delight, a dream, a marvel! She had moved five or six yards away from the cave and was floating on the surface. She was now facing east with her back to me. I could see her hair, dark but dimly shimmering, her slender neck, her milk-white shoulders, her rounded arms, all blurred together, honey-colored and dreamlike in the light of the moon. Between the light and the shadows I caught glimpses of her nimble ankles, her thighs, her calves, her feet, as they dipped into the waters. I could imagine her bosom, her smooth breasts, curved out, receiving the breeze and the divine scent of the sea. She was a breath of beauty, an indescribable ravishment, a dream floating in the waters. She was a Nereid, a nymph, a siren, drifting as a magic ship drifts, a ship in a dream world . . .

It did not occur to me at that particular moment that if I were to step over the rock to go away, if I bent low or even if I stood up straight, it was virtually certain that the girl would not see me. She was facing east, and I was to the west, behind her, and could easily get away. With the moon in the eastern sky, even my shadow would fall westward, behind my perch and beyond the sea-cave. But I stood there entranced, mouth agape, and thought no longer of earthly matters.

I hesitate to admit that wicked, yet childishly foolish, notions came to me, evil wishes disguised as good ones: "If only she would cry out! If only she would see an eddy in the water and think it's a monster, a shark! If only she would call for help!" The truth is that I could not get my fill of the dream floating in the water. But then, strange to say, my first thought recurred . . . that I should plunge into the sea in the oppposite direction, swim all the distance to the beach and flee, flee from temptation! And yet again, I could not get my fill of the dream. Suddenly the voice of my goat brought me back to the demands of the real world. Little Moschoula began to bleat!

Well! This I had not foreseen. I could be quiet myself, but unfortunately I could not easily impose silence on my goat. I knew nothing then of makeshift muzzles—a bunch of twigs in the mouth, grass wound around the snout—since I hadn't learned to steal living creatures, unlike the unknown enemy who had stolen my goat's bell but not cut out her tongue to prevent her from bleating. Affection and anxiety for my poor animal rushed over me. The rope I'd tied her to the bush with was short. Maybe she'd gotten tangled in it, maybe her neck was twisted, maybe the unfortunate animal would be strangled. It didn't enter my mind that the swimmer might see me. Half bending over, I got up and climbed the rock to reach my goat. In a frenzy I grasped her snout. At that moment, precisely because I was trying so hard to avoid her notice, I forgot the swimming girl was there.

I don't know if the girl heard my goat's voice as she was swimming. Even if she had, what was odd about that? What was there to be afraid of? There's nothing unusual in hearing an animal's call as one is bathing a few yards from shore. Whether the girl heard or not—though she apparently did, because she turned her head shoreward—she saw my dark silhouette, the outline of my figure on the rock between the bushes. That one moment I stepped on top of the rock had been enough. In her fright she let out a half-stifled cry.

I was overcome with trepidation, an indescribable anguish. My knees buckled under me. Beside myself with agitation, I managed to utter a few words: "Don't be afraid," I cried out. "It's nothing! I won't harm you!" In my alarm I wondered whether I should dive to her rescue or run away. Maybe just my voice alone would reassure her more than dashing into the water to rescue her.

At that very moment a boat appeared in the distance, coming from the southeast promontory that formed the right bend of the cove. There was nothing unusual in this, since all those coastal waters were frequented by fishermen. The boat seemed to be moving slowly under oars in our direction. Its presence did not hearten the girl; on the contrary, it increased her trepidation. She uttered another cry of even greater dismay. I saw her whole body sink and become invisible under the water.

There was no time to hesitate. The boat was about forty yards away from the struggling girl, but I was only twelve. From the top of the rock I plunged in headlong, clothes and all. The water was deeper than the height of two men and I dove almost to the bottom, which was sandy, with no rocks or stones, thus safe for a diver. Immediately I rose to the foamy surface, less than ten yards from the point where she had gone under. The water there formed eddies and swirls that could mark the instant, watery grave of the luckless girl, those eddies and swirls that are the only traces a human being ever leaves on the sea in his final agony.

With a few strong strokes and powerful thrusts I came in very little time to where she was. I saw her beautiful body struggling below, closer to the bottom than to the surface, nearer to death than life. I dropped down, grasped the girl in my arms, and rose up again.

As I embraced her with my left arm it seemed to me that I felt her cool breath blow faintly on my cheek. I had arrived in time, heaven be praised! Nevertheless she showed no clear signs of life. I shook her with a sudden, rough motion to help her breathe. I drew her across my back and started swimming resolutely toward shore, using only one arm and my legs. My strength increased marvelously. I could feel her clinging to me. She wanted to live. Then let her live and be happy! There was not one selfish thought at that moment in my heart. I was full of generosity and self-sacrifice. I would never ask for recompense!

How long, I wonder, will I remember the soft, tender body of that chaste girl that I once felt against me for a few minutes of my otherwise useless life? It was a dream, an enchantment, a magic charm. And how different from all the selfish embraces, the mean friendships, the base worldly loves, how different was that precious ethereal touch! The burden in my arms had no weight; it was a comfort and relief. Never had I felt myself lighter than while I was supporting it. I was a man who for one minute managed to grasp a dream, his very own dream.

Moschoula lived. She did not die. I scarcely saw her afterwards, and I don't know what she's doing now. Maybe she's a simple daughter of Eve, like all the others.

But I paid a price for her life. My poor little goat, whom I'd forgotten for the girl's sake, did indeed get strangled. She became hopelessly twisted in the rope I'd tied her with and choked to death. I was saddened, but considered that this was my sacrifice for the girl.

As for me, thanks to the support and charity of the monks, I became an educated man with a certificate in law—not surprising, since I had been to two seminaries! I wonder whether that one incident, that dreamlike remembrance of the bathing girl, prevented me from taking religious vows. Alas! It was precisely that remembrance that should have induced me to become a monk. The venerable Sisois was right when he said that if they had wanted to make me a monk, they should never have sent me away from the monastery. The few letters that he taught me were enough, and more than enough, for the salvation of my soul.

And now, when I remember the short rope that strangled my goat Moschoula, I think of that other rope, the one in my simile, the rope that ties up the dog in his master's yard. And I ask myself, aren't those two ropes closely related, are they not for me "the measure of the inheritance," as Scripture says.

Oh! If only I were still a mountain herdsman!

A Shrew of a Mother

HOW IT ALL CAME
about, how he ended up almost mad, nobody knew. Some said that
it was caused by unhappiness in love. Others said that while he was
serving as a recruit in the navy, the captain of the ship punished a
small infraction of his with undue cruelty and severity. Others said
that his own mother had driven him crazy with her curses and
shrewishness.

He used to go along with the men on the boats that went out for
fish and octopus. If they gave him a share of the catch, he took it;
if they did not, he did not ask for it. His mother would then run
around to the houses of the fishermen, screaming and trying to force
his share out of them. She would shout that they were unjust to her
boy—God punish them! The boat-owner's wife would protest with
many an oath that her husband had not caught any fish—not even
a single shrimp. Zakhos's mother would not believe this

at all because she had been burnt many times before.

It was she who forced him to go out on the fishing boats; it was she who made him go till their vineyard because she could not pay for hired hands; and it was she who saw to it that he did all the chores. He gave in to her superior will as if he were still a child, even though he was twenty-five years old.

When he had no work, or when his mother had not found any for him, he would spend most of his time sitting on a ledge across the way from the kitchen window of the mayor's house. This new mayor was unmarried and had taken under his wing the young schoolteacher of the little town, since she was not from these parts and had no one else to look out for her. She lived across the street, behind the mayor's house, which faced the market and the sea. Beneath the windows of the young teacher's residence Zakhos would sit for hours on end, idly strumming his bouzouki, producing monotonous sounds with scant rhythm or melody. There of a summer evening he would sing this song:

My cloak hangs on the willow tree,
Misery, woe, and poverty!

He scarcely was aware of what he was doing, though his real purpose may have been to attract the attention of the neighborhood girls by his singing. Acting as David to his own Saul, he would try to provide entertainment for his addled mind.

On one occasion, however, after he began to intone his graceless song, a shrill terrifying voice was heard coming from a balcony five or six houses away, near the western end of the street.

"He-e-y! Shut up! Get over here—quick! The boat's waiting."

At first Zakhos paid no attention or, more accurately, he scarcely perceived the shout. He went on playing his bouzouki. It was late in the afternoon, and a cool breeze was blowing through the narrow street. With his song he was lulling the afternoon slumbers of the teacher, now finished with the school year and enjoying the easy days of her vacation. With his song he was also accompanying, as though by request, the dishwashing, mopping, and other tasks of Amersa, the mayor's servant. Shoeless, stockingless, bareheaded, she went about her chores, seemingly unaware of the singer and his song. She had never addressed a word to Zakhos. All she would do was laugh condescendingly from time to time when some of the neighborhood women teased him. Akrivo the Weaver would say:

"Ah, poor Zakhos, a lover is always idle. But how can you be idle when that fine mother of yours never leaves you alone?"

Again a shout came from the balcony down the street. Zogara, Zakhos's mother, continued to scream.

"Hey, you! Who do you think I'm talking to? Get moving right away or I'll come down and make your mug as black and blue as your bouzouki."

Zakhos's only answer was his silly, sad laugh. His mother's voice never produced any effect from a distance, though her presence nearby was usually persuasive.

It was August, the time of year when men who wish to get through the winter begin taking steps so they can—men, that is, who imitate the ant and not the grasshopper. Zogara had already made her son available and had hired him out as a carrier. Large boats would soon be sailing to transport firewood from the deserted shoreline, far from the harbor, below the pine groves and forests of the island. Zogara had signed Zakhos on aboard one of these boats. She needed firewood for the winter.

When she saw that her son had turned a deaf ear to her two summonses, she took in hand a long stick that she carried as a cane on her expeditions to the fields. (This cane she also found useful when reaching for figs on the high branches of her trees—and of her neighbors' if they hung over the vineyard.) She now came down along the narrow street and in just a few steps stood before Zakhos.

"Get yourself moving! Enough of that bouzouki! Three men just sitting around, waiting for the likes of you! I told you, you're going to go for firewood now. That's the business we're thinking about now!"

When Zakhos saw his mother with the big stick and heard her voice so close, he jumped up, took his bouzouki, and left on the run. He went home, put on his work clothes, took his knapsack, supplies, axe, and pruning hook—his mother had laid all these out for him—and went off to bring her the firewood so that she could keep warm all winter.

THEY said that his mother had driven him crazy. This was the only child left to her. Two other sons had emigrated from their homeland and gone first to America, then across the Pacific to Polynesia. She sent letters to consulates and officials, to the police of Chicago and Philadelphia. Two or three other women had found their good-for-nothing sons in this manner, but hers did not turn up anywhere. No letter, no explanation, not one peep.

Everyone said that it was her lack of affection that had driven them away, that she was the one who made them good-for-nothings. She was a widow with two daughters, and her sons had deserted her. She wept and she wailed and she was driven to distraction. How could she marry her daughters off? How could she get them settled in life? She cursed those daughters. She wished they had never been born. She wished they were dead.

Oh, yes! In the end Zogara made a good match for those daughters! She decked them out in their finery and put wreaths on their heads, one girl right after the other. She bundled them off, oh yes, and covered them over in the cold earth.

For dower gift they had a tomb,
For mother-in-law a frigid slab;
Instead of handsome wedding groom
The cold black earth they had.

The two girls, it seems, had been consumptive, and they died in the order they had been born, the one eighteen months after the other. And so their mother had no more worries about how she would get them married.

People said that she had done them in with her complaints, with her shrewishness, with her curses and imprecations. And so both girls wasted away and now slept deep in their graves. There was no longer any fear that they would ask their mother for a dowry. Now she called them blessed because they had departed for heaven in all their innocence and purity.

Zakhos was the only remaining child. She said he was daffy and worthless, and she gave him all the hard chores, like bringing her firewood. Well, at least he would never ask for a dowry! His only dowry was the bouzouki with which he entertained his addled wits, a melancholy Saul, a graceless David.

That old bouzouki was a thorn in his mother's side and she would have liked to throw it at him, to fling it away. Let him run after it and find it, if that's what he wanted! She believed that the bouzouki was what kept Zakhos from working and made him unable to do all the chores she wanted to give him. She had hidden it once or twice, but she hesitated to break it or destroy it or get rid of it altogether. Maybe it was all right for Sundays and holidays, but not for weekdays. It was not all right for him to sit around on week-day evenings—at the very hour when Eve hid in the Garden of Eden as she heard the Voice—and sing "the cloak on the willow tree" across from the mayor's house and become the laughingstock of the teacher, Amersa, Akrivo the Weaver, and the mayor himself! So on one occasion, not wishing to do anything drastic, she hid the bou-zouki on the ground floor of the house in an empty storage jar and covered its broken mouth with a sieve. On another occasion she put it in the damp darkness under the divan with the firewood. Both times Zakhos searched for it and found it. He then laughed with un-controllable joy, took it, ran away from her, and began to "live it up," singing "the cloak on the willow tree."

On this particular day Zogara was able to put the fear of God into him and make him go off to gather firewood and bring it back to her so that she could keep warm all winter.

Along with everything else, people thought she was a jinx. She brought them bad luck. When a boat or a caïque was ready to sail and the captain or crew happened to meet her in the street, they turned back and postponed their departure. If a crowd of people was getting ready to go on an outing into the countryside and they ran into her on the way, they stayed where they were and did not go. If someone was setting out on some commercial venture, woe to him if she crossed his path! When there was a betrothal or a wed-ding and Zogara encountered the mother-in-law or the sister-in-law and extended her good wishes, those good wishes were considered bad luck and signified that it was not kismet for the intended mar-riage to take place.

Two days later Zakhos returned from his wood-gathering expedi-tion. When they unloaded the wood, he carried off his share. His mother saw to it that she was present for the roll call, as their neigh-bor the teacher would have said, during the unloading and the dis-tribution, so that Zakhos would not be cheated of half his share. After Zakhos had filled the ground-floor storage room of his mother's house with the wood, he felt the need for some relaxation and decided to "live it up" with his bouzouki even more than before.

He not only disobeyed his mother's orders, but for three days did not even appear before her eyes. He had run away and was hanging around another neighborhood, where her "gracious presence" could not reach him. She chased after him, but could not round him up. She could not find out where he was. He did not come home at night, and where he slept she never knew, whether in small taverns, in another quarter of the town, or in the open air. A group of merrymakers had taken him into their midst. They went about noisily from neighborhood to neighborhood, dragging him along so that he could play "the cloak on the willow tree" and other songs for them. For three days and two nights he ate with them and never left their company. They must have given him the fruit of the lotus to eat and water from the River Lethe to drink, for the poor soul completely forgot about his mother.

Thereupon Zogara became as ferocious as a tigress or a Turk. She bitterly regretted not having smashed her son's bouzouki or thrown it into the fireplace of a winter's day, since it was the bouzouki, so she thought, that made him lose his wits. When angry, however, she was not the sort to fume and fret within herself for long, as other women do. She immediately came to a bold decision. The station of the newly established constabulary was nearby. When she saw two young officers near the barracks, she went up to them and said:

"My boys, do a kind deed for me—may your mothers be blessed by the sight of you once more—go and find that son of mine, the loony one, and take his bouzouki away from him."

"His bouzouki, you say, lady?" asked one of them.

"Yes, his bouzouki—may your mothers find joy in you—because he's become good-for-nothing, he's gone crazy, right out of his mind, and I can't round him up. It's all the fault of that bouzouki."

"All right, lady."

The two young constables did not need much persuasion. It was an easy matter, and amusing too, for two perfectly sane, armed men to snatch a musical instrument away from a crazy man, and a harmless one to boot. And so that evening Zakhos found himself without his bouzouki. The poor fool had lost his instrument, a despondent Saul, a joyless David, and now he wept without rhythm or tune. He mourned for his misfortune, which he bitterly only half comprehended.

He did not set out for the Pacific to find his two brothers. He did not descend beneath the cold slab into the black earth to meet his two sisters. No, he stayed behind, a brute lacking harmony and grace, at his mother's beck and call, carrying firewood as long as his back would bear it. How much more could he bear? How many more winters would she keep warm?

One day he said to her with a very humble look, "Mother, can't you tell Amersa to tell the teacher to tell the mayor, and the mayor to tell the chief constable to tell the officers to give me back my bouzouki?" Did he see, mad as he was, the hierarchical chain by which the whole sane world seemed to be tied together? Did he feel that he, too, was not free of the bonds of this chain?

Has anyone found out if they ever gave him back his graceless bouzouki, the instrument that was his comfort?

After a while it became known that one of the two young constables had been given orders for his transfer. As he was about to embark on a ship for the mainland, a loud dispute over the possession of the bouzouki arose between him and his fellow officer. Both the man leaving and the man staying wanted to keep it. One held on to the body of the instrument; the other pulled it by the neck. The latter was hot-tempered and stubborn, and shouted in a rage:

"I'd rather smash it up! I'll throw it out the window! No! . . . You're not going to keep it!"

No sooner said than done. He was like a disputatious heretic who even under pain of death sticks to a wrong belief so that he will not lose his reputation for infallibility. For in the beginning the constable had voiced his threat somewhat jokingly and not entirely in anger, but then, not wishing to give the appearance of a man that threatens idly, he decided to act on his words. With a violent tug he yanked the instrument out of the hands of the other man, who in his surprise had momentarily loosened his grasp, and hurled it out of the open window.

Just below the upper story was the barred window of a room on the ground floor that was used as a jail. Tied to the bars of the window was a thick-fleeced ewe with her two lambs, perhaps brought in by one of the rural constables. As the bouzouki was flung out it whirled around momentarily in the air, then fell right onto the woolly back of the ewe, which let out a mournful bleat. Losing the momentum of its fall, the instrument tottered a moment there, then slipped to the ground so gently that it suffered no damage.

At the same moment, Alexis, the ten-year-old son of Vaso, a

neighbor, was running by in front of the barracks. He knew the story of the bouzouki and was very fond of Zakhos, who was himself a big child. When Alexis saw the instrument fall, he drew near, bent down, quickly snatched it up and ran straight to Zogara's house, where he called to Zakhos:

"Here you are! Come and get your bouzouki!"

Love the Harvester:
A May Day Idyll

A<small>T DAWN OLD</small> F<small>OTINI</small>
awakened the children, carefully washed their faces, combed their
hair, and gave them some biscuits to munch on "so the donkey
wouldn't take away their appetites." She then took her trim, neatly
woven basket and placed in it her distaff, her kerchief, and some
food for breakfast, and went out with her troop. This was not the
first time that old Fotini had awoken so early, but on this day because of the beautiful weather she was taking along the little children and one other person besides.

This kind old woman spent all her days in the fields. Though she
usually slept in town, she never let a day pass without going into
the countryside. She had a ewe that she cared for tenderly, and the
good women of the neighborhood used to say she slept embracing
the ewe for warmth. Even if she did not actually sleep with her arms
around the ewe, she did at least sleep in a shed with the animal,

a shed that sat at the far end of the courtyard and resembled a hen coop. In the daytime the ewe had her lambs to care for, while Fotini had her children, those of her mistress and those of her mistress's sister, half a dozen little devils that tugged at her skirts, clung to her cavernous chest, and jumped onto her bent shoulders. During the night the ewe's bleats would from time to time awaken her fellow lodger, while the old woman's dreams—bleats from her imagination, one could call them—would cause her to sigh and from time to time awaken the ewe, who then with a little cry would answer in empathy.

Today, however, being a holiday, the May Day Festival of Flowers, the procession was accompanied by the eldest daughter of Fotini's mistress, the lovely Mati. On this account the old woman had assumed that attitude of half-genuine sternness that all old servant women adopt in the presence of their mistresses' daughters. She did not allow the children to hold on to her skirts or pull at them. She scolded them constantly as some ran ahead of her, others off to her side, without paying any heed to her shouts.

Mati walked on the old woman's right. She was tall, graceful, and slim of waist. She wore her hair in the European manner, and she did not cover it in her home. But that morning, because she was going to the country, she wore a thin white veil around her temples, placed so skillfully that it was almost invisible. One could see almost all of her abundant blond hair descending to her waist in two thick braids, like stalactites of gold. Her entire neck was visible down to its base and even a little beyond. She was dressed in a cinnamon-colored bodice and a white skirt that was too short for her. Her mother, it seemed, did not take sufficient account of her growth and continued to make short skirts, while Mati continued to grow. She was now seventeen years old and in the full bloom of her beauty and vitality looked like twenty. Like this May Day itself, she was ready to hand over the scepter to that implacable scythe-bearer, Love the Harvester.

As soon as they left the little town, the girl said she was hot and removed her bodice. Then, with only a long-sleeved chemise over her white cotton camisole, her slender waist, graceful stance, and smooth breasts showed to greater advantage. The swelling flesh beneath the thin camisole hinted that here was a store of pale lillies, dewy and freshly cut, with veins the color of a white rose. Her forehead was framed by her hair, which resembled a reddish-gold cloud powerless to hide the brilliant sunlight; her eyebrows shaded her deep blue eyes like a pale mist that hovers in the morning over the sparkling shoreline, and her lips seemed to murmur "Kiss me!" in whispering tones.

When they had proceeded half a mile from the town, and the countryside began to intoxicate their senses with its numberless perfumes, they came to a narrow way between two fences. They walked along the grass, stepped through a patch of camomile, and every once in a while got caught in a bush. The children ran before them, sometimes invading a vineyard to cut off some shoots, sometimes climbing up uncultivated trees that reached over the fences in search of pigeon nests. All the while old Fotini would shout at them. "Manolis! You children! I'm talking to you. Don't run like a wild goat, Manolis! What are you doing up there, Yiannis? Stathakis, you'll tear your clothes—get down, you little rascal!"

Mati, rousing herself from her reverie, threatened the children with the palm of her hand. "Be still, children! You're going to get a spanking!"

All of this delayed their journey somewhat. Some of the women out for a walk, carrying their little baskets, came up from behind, said good morning, and quickly passed by.

At this point they encountered a young man who, although everyone else was going into the country, seemed to be returning already and making his way to town. He was tall and manly, with dark kindly eyes, a slender, black, twirled mustache, and expressive features. His gait was proud and with its measured pace gave a somewhat studied effect. He was about twenty-four years old. When he saw the two women in front of him, he seemed to slow his pace as if he wished to enjoy the sight a few minutes longer.

As soon as old Fotini noticed this, she gave him a suspicious look, as if she knew something about him, and imperceptibly she shook her head. When Mati saw him, she drew in closer to the side of her aged escort, as though to give him room to pass in the narrow way between the two fences.

The youth drew near with slow steps and cast a long glance at Mati, who lowered her eyes. He doffed his hat, greeted the two women, and moved on as if it cost him considerable effort. He wore a rose in his buttonhole and carried a small bouquet in his left hand. He gave a sign of greeting with his right hand and, in so doing, without thinking, brought the bouquet in front of his breast, as if he wished to offer it to Mati though he dared not.

The old woman responded to hs greeting coldly, and the young woman nodded slightly. A few minutes later the youth disappeared beyond a small bend in the path. Old Fotini turned and glanced inquiringly at Mati. "I wonder where that young swain was. Why's he returning from the country so early?"

Mati looked at the old servant with surprise. "Why do you ask me? What do I know about it?"

"Everybody's going out," insisted the old woman without paying attention to Mati's words. "Everybody's going out, and he's coming back, and the sun hasn't quite risen yet." Indeed, the sun at that very moment peeped out as it rose over the mountain opposite.

Again Mati did not answer. But she appeared deep in thought.

"I know, Mati dear," continued the old woman, "I know why he's coming back so soon."

"Since you know, why do you ask?" said Mati.

"He probably didn't go far out like other people. He must have gone out by The Wells and then turned to the right where the harbormaster and the customs officials and the justice of the peace take their walks. That's why he's returning so soon."

"Maybe he has a garden near here and went to cut some flowers and then came back," remarked Mati.

"He doesn't have a garden near here, Mati dear," contradicted the old woman, "and he didn't go out to cut flowers and then come back. No, he wanted to meet us on the road. That's why he's returned so quickly."

"Meet us? On the road?" repeated Mati, as if she did not understand.

"It's as I say," insisted the old woman.

"Oh, don't bother me, Fotini," cried the girl. "What do I care?"

The old woman did not venture another word.

They left the narrow path and came out onto a grassy meadow filled with myriad flowers from which arose an intoxicating fragrance. The fences around the vineyards were covered with wild vines, honeysuckle, and prickly bushes. Under the first rays of the sun the meadow appeared blood-red from the thousands and thousands of poppies. Camomile, chervil, and mallow vied with one another in presenting their blossoms. Little yellow star-shaped flowers shyly lifted their delicate heads amidst the arrogant abundance of red mushrooms that proclaimed the rich blood of spring.

Included in the boundless wealth of the goddess Flora were wild grain, thorny asparagus, flowerets without names, and a diversity of shoots. It was a heavenly May Day, Spring in the fullness of her life, ready to hand over her scepter to Summer, the scythe-bearing Harvester.

Here and there old women, poor folk, were bent over the ground gathering short-stemmed flowers to be used as medicinal herbs in wintertime. Near the foot of Dragasia Hill, over by the western edge of the meadow, was a rock on which, despite the shouts of Fotini and the threats of Mati, were clambering Manolis, Stathakis, Thymios, and little Kostakis, who was trying to keep up with the others. Stathakis had cut a stalk of wild grain, the "loosener," and was thrusting it up his nostril, chanting:

Loosener stalk, loosener stalk,
Loosen up my nose for me.

The two women were obliged to stop and wait for the children to come down. Mati, who was still somewhat in a daydream, now grew sterner, and finally after much scolding made the children climb down from the rock. They were in any case only a few hundred feet away from Dragasia, the hill that was their destination. On the lower of the two peaks of the hill stood a small peculiar hut with a red banner waving over it, the device of the field constable. The children ran on with graceful bounds like the young of farmyard goats. Finally the procession arrived at Dragasia. There, near the constable's hut, were the fields belonging to Mati's family, vineyard, olive grove, and garden, extending for dozens of acres. The property was entirely surrounded by a wall. There was a well-maintained cabin, a sort of rustic cottage used for storing olives, figs, and pears, and, during the months of tillage, agricultural tools. It also contained a wooden press for making wine.

Mati's mother had stayed at home. She was always indisposed, without ever being really ill. Mrs. Limberena was one of those women that are slow of foot yet averse to riding animals and who consequently do not like the country. Besides, old Fotini had spoiled her. The old woman had been a servant in the family for fifty years and during that time had overseen all of the work in the fields. Mrs. Limberena had inherited Fotini from her mother as part of her dowry, almost as if she were a household slave. The old woman had never married; her betrothed, a young fisherman, went down with his boat and drowned, or, as some said, the sharks got him — a short life, God rest his soul. Even after forty years Fotini still mourned for him and never ceased to see him in her dreams.

Mati's father, Captain Limberios, like all those of his calling, needed a great deal of persuasion to take to life on dry land. He could scarcely breathe if he could not gaze upon the sea. But he found a good buyer for his last big schooner and deposited in the bank his savings from his life at sea, amounting to several thousand drachmas. Thereafter he spent all his days playing Russian *prefa* in the cafes near the harbor. There he would continually find fault with the mayor, the three deputies, and the twelve councilors, and would mock those other captains who seemed fired with ambition to "fix up the town," and thus he would negatively engage in political life without positively running for office.

Fotini placed the key in the padlock and opened the gate of the enclosure. Leaping headlong, the children rushed into the olive grove. It was a fine piece of property, well cared for. Though Captain Limberios never set foot in it himself, he spared no expense in having it cultivated. And Fotini was never absent. She always declared with pride that it was there at Dragasia that they had "cut her cord" as a newborn babe.

Stathakis, Manolis, and the other children immediately ran to the part of the property that was laid out as a garden and began to gather roses and lilies. Along the way they cut wild grape vines and began to weave garlands for their heads with as much enthusiasm as they had earlier searched for the May Day flower and the "loosener." Unknowing little pagans, they were preserving unconsciously after so many centuries the worship of Mother Nature. Mati cut a white rose and with it adorned her virginal breast. The nightingale, sweet songstress, would have been doubly enamored to see that beautiful flower set in such a vase. Stathakis was searching between two plants for an artichoke, which he intended to eat after peeling it and washing it in a stream that flowed from a small spring. He planned to eat it secretly, because Fotini would scold, fearing that it was bitter and poisonous. The other children went ahead a few steps to the small spring, which was in a cleft overhung by rocks in the middle of the property. The property ran along the juncture of the two slopes descending from the two peaks of the hill. One of the slopes was covered with vines, the other with a thick planting of olive trees. Immediately over the spring a huge grapevine spread its branches, tendrils and bunches of grapes already growing profusely on it. A few days before old Fotini, in spite of her great age, had climbed the imposing plane tree that supported the vine and had hung up a large garlic "to keep off the evil eye of strangers."

As Stathakis was bending over near the foot of the enclosing wall, instead of an artichoke he found a piece of paper lying there. He picked it up and ran toward his sister shouting, "Mati! Mati! Look what I found over there, near the artichokes!"

Fortunately, old Fotini was not nearby. She had gone into the whitewashed cabin to rest a bit and to set her basket down for a while. She also wanted to leave her good outer dress there, which she had taken off when she came onto the property so that she could move about more easily in her long vest. She then intended to change the position of her beloved ewe, which contrary to habit she had left tied up overnight in the fields with her two white-fleeced lambs "so that the May Day would come upon them."

Mati blushed. The paper found on the ground was a letter, folded and sealed. "Hush, don't tell Fotini," she indicated by gesture rather than words.

"I won't tell," said six-year-old Stathakis, as though he understood her apprehension.

The girl took the letter and, stepping aside, opened it. It was written on good paper of a reddish hue and went as follows:

Oh Mati, my dearest Mati, you who have stolen my heart from me, the sorceress told me that you are in danger and I have decided to protect you from nearby, just as I have been sighing from afar for so many years now.

"Danger!" whispered the girl with a start. "What does he mean?" Then looking around anxiously she continued to read:

If you find this letter, dearest Mati, that's fine. Don't be too angry. It's bad enough that I can never, alas, find delight with you.

Mati smiled vaguely, a smile that indicated pity, sympathy, unconscious liking, and a touch of irony.

If Fotini finds this, dearest Mati, if you don't wish to lie by saying that it is not from me, tell her the truth, that you don't love me and that I am brazen, brash, and wretched.

At this point the prose section of the letter came to an end and there followed some verses. Perhaps they were the handiwork of the letter writer himself, or perhaps they were patched together and adapted from elsewhere. The verses went:

O portrait painted in my heart
And not by artist's hand:
As talisman nothing do I have . . .

Just at that moment old Fotini emerged from the cabin and walked in Mati's direction. The girl quickly hid the letter in her bosom.

Fotini approached, taking from her basket a pan and a loaf of bread wrapped in a blue-and-white checked napkin. She called Mati and the children to the spring for breakfast. The sun was already "two staff lengths" up in the sky. They sat by the cool spring under the twofold shade from the grape arbor and the plane tree and began to eat their breakfast of cheese, eggs, and fried fish. All the while Fotini had a mysterious look about her. As she was chewing with her ineffectual gums and her two remaining teeth, she said in a low voice to Mati, "I saw that swain once more."

"What swain?" asked Mati with some discomfiture as the blood rushed to her cheeks.

"The one we met on the road."

"Where did you see him?"

"From inside the cabin—from the little window. He was sitting against an olive tree on the property of our neighbor here, Mr. Vasilis, and he pretended he wasn't paying us any heed."

"And why should he pay us any heed?" said Mati. "What have we got to do with him?"

"Why doesn't he go about his business? Why has he appeared in front of us twice this morning? Tell me, Mati, why?"

"People are free to do as they please. Don't bother about him," finished off the girl, indicating by her tone of voice that enough had been said on the matter.

At that moment Manolis, who had gone off unnoticed after eating an egg and a few bites of bread, returned on tiptoe holding a wreath and approached Fotini and Mati from behind. Stathakis and Thymios were watching him, smiling slightly, their mouths agape. Manolis made a sign to them that they were not to speak too soon. Then with a child's triumphant cry he placed the wreath of vine shoots on the head of old Fotini.

Everyone laughed, and the old woman joined in. She got up wearing the wreath, which sat—a study in opposites—on her black kerchief and bedecked the long white wisps of hair that hung from her temples down to her ears. Taking on the expression of a bride pleased with herself, she said, "This is the only wreath I'll ever wear. I'm not even sure any more that they'll put one on me when I'm laid out dead in my coffin."

"And what kind of maiden are you, for them to put a wreath on your head?" asked Stathakis. He had heard from his mother that all who die as maidens are crowned with wreaths.

"As long as you're asking," answered the old woman, "I'm much more of a maiden than some others." The children laughed loudly, though naturally they did not understand what old Fotini meant.

The old woman hurried back to the cabin, picked up her basket, then came out, untied her ewe once more and led her off by the rope. She was going to gather herbs in a far-off section of the olive grove running along the length of the wall that closed in the property on the northwest. The children dashed after her. They began playing hide-and-seek and other games behind a giant olive tree, whose trunk was three yards in circumference, rough and bulging as if compacted of many smaller trunks. They ran about and took turns hiding behind the trunk. Covering their eyes with their palms, they called out to one another:

"I saw you!"

"I'll catch you!"

"I gotcha."

"I see you, you can't see me."

"Catch 'im!"

"I'm Mr. John, Mr. Johnny-Good."

"Gran'dad, where ya 'goin'?"

"To my monastery."

"Up apple, down orange."

"I lost, I lost, I lost the needle."

And many other children's cries. Running and chasing about, they urged one another on: "Walk on cotton, cat won't hear you."

Mati, holding her knitting, to which she had not added one

stitch all morning, heard the children's cries from a distance as she began to make her way to the garden. Then she adroitly turned back, hiding behind some bushes so that she could not be seen from the olive grove where Fotini had gone. With beating heart she entered the cabin. It lay in the northwest corner of the property, almost against the wall of the enclosure, and was shaded by two tall poplars and some dew-covered bushes in front of the entrance. The cabin might have served as an agreeable refuge for someone given to study and solitude, or as a charming nest for a love-smitten soul. Mati went in and peered anxiously out of the small window; a beautiful view extended northward to the higher of the two peaks. From the window one could see Xanemon, a great bay, the domain of the north wind, a perfect place for brigands with its two sea-washed shores. On one side of the bay lay Kefala, rearing itself up into the clouds like the head of a Titan. On the other side lay Platana, a long, unending plateau, grayish-green in the rays of the sun, where the olive tree jostled the fig tree, and the fig tree entwined itself around the apple tree.

Mati looked around to see if the young man Fotini had mentioned was nearby. Nothing. She did not see a soul. Was the old woman mistaken then? Or had he grown invisible? Perhaps he was hidden somewhere? Did he intend to reappear?

The girl took the note her brother had discovered on the ground and read the rest of its contents. The verses read as follows:

O portrait painted in my heart
And not by artist's hand:
As talisman nothing do I have
Except one lovely strand.

Dark sable feathered wings
Those nightly dreams of you,
Like pigeons in a cave
Awaken me anew.

The sorceress informed
Of cloudy danger drear.
The nightingale that sings
Doth shed a mournful tear.

May spring in flowery bloom
Rejoice to look on you.

Its blossoms numberless
Are songs of colors true.

In school you never learned
To write a billet-doux,
Then whence that poison dank
On lips of rosy hue?

In splendrous eyes the god
Of love in ambush waits.
It's heaven knows what drink
My soul intoxicates.

Oh turn those splendrous eyes
To look on me, my dove,
My haughty one, my little bird,
My love, my chosen love.

That dainty precious hand
That works with wondrous ease,
It's heaven knows if it
Received or gave a squeeze.

Deprive me not, my lamb,
Your gracious favors give.
My love, my only love,
So long as I may live.

Two or three times Mati read the letter, which was signed "Kostis." She grew pensive, lost in doubts and suspicions. Though she was inexperienced in life, some of the verses of the fledgling poet seemed vaguely offensive. Unconsciously, she put herself in the position of a third party, someone disinterested, or rather someone concerned about her honor, and she said to herself: If such a person found this letter and read it, how would he interpret it? Wouldn't he suspect that the young woman Kostis wrote to had an understanding with this admirer? It seemed to her that the writer wanted to make her, if by chance the letter went astray, appear as a fellow conspirator. If so, was the writer sincerely in love or was he just a dowry chaser?

The girl remained deep in these reflections, in a rather pensive, melancholy frame of mind. She remembered what the ever-vigilant Fotini had told her a month ago, when the old servant began to comment after she first noticed the youth circling their house.

"Now there's a proper young swain! Ah, there's one who's really sweet on you."

To tease the girl, whom she had caught on two occasions glancing at the youth through the half-closed window, she added:

"Can this be love? Why's he eating his heart out?"

As Mati was turning over in her mind the old woman's words, she was suddenly frightened by a dull thud. She raised her eyes. A form leaped into the cabin through the window (only a man's height above the ground) and hurtled toward her. Mati's heart throbbed; she thought it was Kostis. But suddenly she let out a cry of fright. It was not Kostis. The invader was a wild, disheveled man, about thirty years old, broad-chested and powerfully built. His face was not altogether ugly, but his eyes were dull and expressionless and were overhung by reddened eyelids. He wore coarse, ragged garments. He lunged toward the girl, who retreated, pressing her back to the wall. He tried to muzzle her with the palm of his hand. It appeared as if he intended to choke her. She managed to utter a second cry.

AROUND eleven o'clock the night before a young man had knocked at the low window of a humble cottage in the town, not far from Mati's house. The whole neighborhood was asleep at that hour. The man that knocked did not look like one who roams at night, nor did he look like a chicken thief. Perhaps he was one of those bothersome cavaliers, those guitarists and serenaders of provincial towns that periodically annoy families whose portion it is to have marriageable daughters. The nightwalker saw a small dim light through the cracks of the shutter. It was not light from a vigil lamp burning in front of the icons of the saints. It came from a smoking oil lamp whose thin wick was burning low. The light appeared to be moving and one could hear a soft footstep. The door opened with a doleful sound.

The visitor hurriedly went in. He nodded a greeting to the woman who opened the door and walked toward the sofa, which was the only large article of furniture in that poor dwelling. The mistress of the house lived alone. She was a fifty-year-old widow, tall and bony, with a dark complexion. She wore shabby clothing and gray strands of hair peeped out from under her kerchief. Her gaze expressed something irregular and unearthly. The visitor sat on a low stool, the woman opposite him. He was tall, dark, and well dressed, with a thin black mustache and attractive dark eyes.

"Sorceress, O sorceress: I've come for you to tell me the fate that awaits me—awaits her and me."

The woman looked at him with curiosity. He seemed agitated and impassioned. Her face registered surprise, an ingenuous confession that she had expected nothing so extreme. The thought came to her that seldom in her long career had she met such a manifestation.

"I laid out the cards three times," answered the sorceress slowly. "I found only black signs."

"Black?"

"Only black. The Jack of Clubs is threatening her."

"What Jack of Clubs?"

"The Jack of Clubs is her enemy. The Queen of Hearts is not looking out for her interests."

"Who is the Queen of Hearts?"

"The Queen of Hearts is from her family, because she herself is the Queen of Diamonds. That's how I have designated her. I have studied the cards many times. The Jack of Clubs and the Queen of Hearts are always against her."

"So the Queen of Hearts is . . ."

"Her mother, of course," said the sorceress. "I was wrong when I said she's not looking out for her interests. I should have said that the Queen of Hearts is not looking out for your interests . . . because a mother naturally can't be against the interests of her own child."

The lover cried out. "And yet, how many mothers . . . ," he began, but cut himself short. After a moment he asked again, "The Jack of Clubs? Who can that be, Mrs. Asimenia?"

"The Jack of Clubs," repeated Mrs. Asimenia, "is danger, a storm arising for the first time. It's a hostile stranger who will come on the scene in order to threaten her; he is now nearby. Fortunately, alongside the Jack of Clubs I find the Jack of Spades."

"The Jack of Spades?"

"The Jack of Spades," affirmed the sorceress, emphasizing her words, "is her friend and will be near her at the right moment to rescue her from this danger."

The youth breathed a sigh of relief. "And who might the Jack of Spades be?" he whispered, with the hope of the superstitious.

"The Jack of Spades," answered Mrs. Asimenia quickly, "I don't know who he might be, unless he's you . . ." The sorceress said this with a trace of irony, but the youth did not even notice it. He was ready to cry out in triumph.

"That's what the cards told me," concluded the sorceress. "Opposition from the mother, danger from an outside source, friendly intervention: that much and nothing more. The same things appeared in the egg but . . ."

The young man reached into his purse and placed a silver piece in the hand of the sorceress. He was getting ready to leave when he heard those last words of Asimenia.

"The egg? Ah! Did you consult the egg too?"

"Yes, the egg," said the sorceress. "Do you want me to show it to you?" She got up and went to the hearth. A small shelf held a cup containing an egg with a round opening in one of its sides.

Kostis—for indeed the young suitor was he—gave the sorceress the look of a gullible child. He was easily convinced, like all who are in love—and he was in love, or at least two-thirds of the way.

He was a student, though actually more of a seaman than a student. He was romantic, like all of his generation, the one that came to maturity between 1862 and 1880. When he finished three years of high school, he interrupted his studies and went to sea for four years. Then, having seen the world and having forgotten what he had learned in his classes, he returned to school on the strength of his earlier grades and, a bearded man, received his diploma. For two years now he had been enrolled in the law school in Athens, but having no taste for dusty writing tables, he spent most of the year on his cool island. His reputation in town was not a good one: people criticized him for neglecting his studies, for being lazy, for wasting his father's modest means, for nocturnal serenading, for drinking too much.

Some months earlier he had fallen in love with Mati. Her father was a friend of his family, and when Kostis was younger he was a welcome visitor in her home. But when Mati grew up, he no longer dared enter the house. So awkward was he that once when Mati, in all innocence of course, pressed his hand during a visit for a family celebration, he lost his bearings and in turn rather too warmly squeezed the hand of her aunt Chrysi as he greeted her. The aunt, a woman over thirty and the mother of four children, looked at him in bewilderment and disapproval. Many months later he called to mind the pressure of that dainty lily-white hand with its azure veins and hinted at that squeeze in his verses.

The incomprehensible character of his letter should be attributed to the youth's excitability and hotheadedness, as well as to his nervous instability arising from an irregular life. He was, of course, not acting from ulterior motives; he was merely heedless.

The sorceress took the egg from the shelf over the fireplace and brought it to the youth. Through the hole in its side could be seen the yolk and the white, part of which had evidently spilled out. The sorceress showed the superstitious youth certain indications in the yolk.

"Here's a large black mark and here's another smaller black mark. The one is danger from the outside, which now threatens Mati; the other is help, which will come to her, and that red mark you see is resistance, which she'll meet from her own people, her own blood."

The youth sighed.

"But there is also something else," continued the sorceress slowly.

"What else?" asked Kostis.

"The black mark, the smaller one, seems to be overcoming the red one."

"Ah," exclaimed the youth.

"In summation," continued Asimenia, who had taken to official parlance because her husband had been an officer in the constabulary, "in summation, it appears that her friend, who wishes her well, even though her mother does not want him, will in the end be successful."

The youth's face was aglow with happiness. He took a second silver piece and cheerfully gave it to the sorceress, who laughed discreetly.

"They named me Asimenia, the silver one," she thought to herself, "because they knew that it was right for me to get silver. A person's name," she concluded to herself, "is connected with his fate."

"So, Asimenia, Asimenia," said the youth, "what was that you said?"

"I said that there's hope you will succeed."

"Tell me again, Asimenia, tell me so I can hear it. What was it you said?"

"As the egg says," reiterated the sorceress, "before much time has passed, you will find joy in her."

"Really? Really? I thank you, my dear Asimenia. Let me kiss your sweet hand." Seizing the large hand of the sorceress, he kissed it noisily.

"Calm down, calm down," said the widow with annoyance. "If somebody was passing by and heard, he would say that . . ." She guffawed loudly.

The youth was so absorbed in his single purpose that he did not even notice the new turn in the sorceress's behavior. He rose, said goodnight, and went out with a hurried step. He felt the need to pour out his great joy and abundant hope into the open air. The sorceress closed the door, blew out the lamp, prepared her bed and got into it. When she fell asleep her expression was the same as it had been while she was awake. It was the virtual imprint of the words that formed her recollection of the day just past: "Two silver coins in my pocket and a kiss on my hand."

THE strange man took his hand off Mati's mouth and began to entreat her by gestures and movements of his head not to cry out and to listen to him.

"What do you want?" Mati asked, regaining some of her composure.

The wolf-man looked to the right and to the left, as if he were afraid that there was somebody hidden, listening.

"Why did you come here? Go away!" said the frightened girl.

The weird creature held his mouth agape; his front teeth looked grayish and far apart, and the four canines were very sharp. He said nothing. He moved his lips two or three times, as if he wished to articulate a word but found it difficult. Finally, after strenuous effort, he uttered a few sounds that were not genuine words but tattered shreds of words.

"Lez go my 'ut," he brought out, stuttering and stammering.

The girl did not understand what he was saying. Bewildered, she looked at him fearfully. For the first time her eyes took him in. Then she remembered what she had often heard Fotini mention, that there was a young man, a real wolf-man, known commonly as Wildman, who lived in a goatherd's hut not far from their property. He never came to town but lived alone with the goats he pastured for his master, who had made him a herder as an act of charity. He was hardly ever seen by anyone. He spoke few words and was almost a mute. Only in unusual circumstances and with much effort was he able to utter articulate sounds. His master communicated with him through gestures. Women were afraid of him and said that he sometimes bothered them. Mati surmised that this must be the strange man before her. Now at the height of springtime he must have grown weary of his isolation and felt that he too was a male. Within him, too, nature was stirring, poor man!

"Lez go 'way," repeated the wolf-man. "You go wi' me, wi' me?"

The girl continued to look at him, torn between curiosity and pity. From his gestures she began to understand better that he wished her to follow him. Poor wolf-man!

"Dere, 'ut . . . gib you yo'urt, kweem, puddin'."

Mati did not answer. Her fear had almost left her, for his dull gaze aroused pity instead. She looked at him intently, as if he were an unusual phenomenon beyond anything she could imagine. The wolf-man was encouraged by the girl's attitude and took it to be a favorable response.

"Lez go," Wildman said again. "Wound 'ut, have twees, ga'den, fiel's, spwing, well, runnin' wa'er. Shady twees, you lie, beddy-bye, in gwass. Me too, beddy-bye, next you."

The girl made a gesture of revulsion when she heard the wolf-man's proposal and his pastoral description. Wildman moved a step closer, stretched out his hand and tried to caress her arms. Terrified, Mati tried to push him away. A shudder of repugnance ran through her body.

"Go away from here!" She turned toward the door. Wildman lunged after her.

"Go away, foolish man. The constable will come and kill you. I feel sorry for you. I'll call the children and they'll throw stones at you."

The wolf-man continued to come at her.

"The children are coming now and so is Fotini," she said, threatening him with her hand. "Go away or they'll bash your head in. Didn't you hear me? They're coming. I'll start screaming."

Wildman flew at her and encircled her with his arms. The girl screamed loudly for help. She struggled desperately to extricate herself from the strange man's embrace, but the wolf-man was strong and threw her down onto the straw mat near the fireplace. He thrust his rough left hand below her soft arm and pressed hard on her virginal breast. With his right hand he grasped her throat and threatened to choke her if she let out the least sound. Pale and weak, her hair in wild disorder, with her delicate hands she tried to detach Wildman's paws from her body, but he curled his fingers with their long black nails into an eerie claw. Mati gasped under the painful pressure. He panted in expectant agitation and uncontrollable desire. For one instant the girl managed to free her neck and let out a choked cry, but the wolf-man immediately grasped her throat again and at the same time immobilized her resisting arms. With his legs, tough-skinned as a turtle's shell, he tried to enclose her tender limbs in a viselike grip. The girl choked, gasping and moaning. Twice she spat in his face and twice tried to bite him on the shoulder, but so bestial were Wildman's impulses that biting him would have aroused him more. He bellowed, growled, and laughed uncontrollably. With a sudden movement he began to tear at her clothes. A little more and the violence of the wolf-man would have triumphed over her virginal resistance. At that moment a dull thud was heard, as if a body had fallen from the top of the outside wall.

The girl directed her glance as best she could toward the small window. She hoped that help was coming. She could not understand why Fotini and the children had not come after she cried out three times. She regretted that she had not listened to the old woman, who tactfully suggested, just before she left to gather herbs, that it would be a good thing for Mati to accompany her. But Mati had smiled condescendingly, saying that there was no danger, and if the Kostis Fotini mentioned should appear, she was able to take care of herself.

Poor old woman! She did not realize that by speaking about the young man to Mati she aroused the girl's curiosity and fed her imagination. What harm could Kostis do if Mati was not willing? But where was Kostis now? Where was Fotini? If only Kostis would appear, since Fotini and the children were not coming!

Fotini's absence, however, could probably be explained by the distance that separated them. She most likely did not hear Mati's cry. The old woman was on the higher ground at the edge of the olive grove, and Captain Limberios's holdings stretched out for great distances. The cabin was situated in a lower section of the property, where a human voice could not carry beyond the four walls of the enclosure, its echo lost in the thickets. Perhaps the wind, which was blowing from the northeast and growing stronger as the day went on, also contributed to the muffling of the girl's cries. Its unceasing, whistling breath took up Mati's voice on its wings and dissipated its resonance toward the southwest, over against the nearby hills and valleys.

Meanwhile, Fotini continued to gather herbs and the children went on playing behind the trunk of the giant olive tree. Mati's first and second cries had indeed gone unheard. The old woman gathered herbs and did not cease to ponder on the affairs of men and women. She reflected that of all those she had loved up till now with hardly a thought of recompense, the ewe alone had not fallen short of her expectations. The ewe not only fed her with her milk and clothed her with her wool, but was also faithful to her, as faithful as any of God's living creatures could be.

Her mistress, Limberena, a virtual hypochondriac, sickly and self-indulgent as are all women that are chronically indisposed, placed as much value on the old servant as she did on Fotini's ewe. And this was actually a great sign of goodness on Limberena's part, reflected Fotini, because the ewe was really much more valuable than people thought. As for Mati, little Mati, whom Fotini had brought up with love and devotion, whom the ewe had nursed after Mati was six months old because Mrs. Limberena never had enough milk, the proud and beautiful Mati had also acquired some secrets recently. Previously she had trusted Fotini unquestioningly, had confided everything to her, but for some time now she had been concealing something.

And so it is that all affection and trust grow weak and decay. As Fotini bent over to pluck her medicinal herbs, she would from time to time turn her eyes to the carefree children playing farther off. Would they love her till the end? she asked herself. Would they always continue to trust the old, devoted servant who had tasted few of the world's joys and pleasures except those that come from self-sacrifice and devotion?

Thymios and Kostakis were just then absorbed in a game. Thymios was bending over the ground. He had placed the smaller child against his shoulders, back to back, and was clutching the little boy's hands tightly against his chest. These were the words they exchanged:

"What d'ya see?"

"Sky."

"What'ya walkin' on?"

"Land."

"What'ya eatin'?"

"Cucumber."

"Fall down like a donkey," said the older child, and let go of the little one, who merrily rolled around on the soft grass.

At the same moment a shrill voice was heard coming from the direction of the cabin. It was Mati's third cry, the one that reached the ears of Fotini:

"Fotini! Stathakis! Help!"

Fotini cocked her ear. "Quiet, children, so we can hear. Did you hear a cry?"

"We did!"

"Quick, let's go, children, Mati is calling us," said the old woman on the run. "What could it be, dear Lord?"

"I'm comin'," said each of the children. Among them was Yiannis, recently arrived from a village on Mt. Pelion, the adopted son of a childless woman named Argyri. He, too, said "I'm comin'."

In her struggle Mati heard the dull thud that sounded like a body dropping from the top of the enclosing wall into the garden. Immediately afterward she heard the running footsteps of a man. The half-closed door of the cabin was thrust open and Kostis appeared on the threshold.

Apparently the youth had decided, subsequent to his last meeting with the sorceress, which we described above, to keep close watch over his beloved. And, behold, the sorceress had spoken the truth this time, perhaps even without intending to.

After he left the sorceress's house that May Day eve, Kostis roamed about until midnight, went home, and wrote the letter to Mati, adding the verses about the sorceress's predictions to the lines he had composed a few days before. Then without undressing he lay down on a sofa and slept uneasily for an hour or two. At three o'clock in the morning he got up, bathed in cold water, and went out immediately. He walked into the countryside in the direction of Captain Limberios's lands, where he knew Mati always went on May Day. Trusting to luck, he threw his love letter over the wall and withdrew. He planned to spend the day in hiding nearby, prompted as a superstitious man by the fear the sorceress foretold and as a lover by a desire to feed his gaze on his beloved Mati. But he could not resist the temptation to make his way back into town in order to experience the boundless pleasure of encountering Mati and wishing her good day.

After the two women had gone past him, Kostis turned back again by a side road and followed them at a distance. He looked ahead and saw Mati's slender figure and white dress outlined in the sunlight against the horizon and felt an inexpressible joy, as if she were right there beside him. Is it not said that love shortens distance and flies over space? And so he returned once more to the area near Mati's property and cautiously made the rounds of Dragasia's higher peak. That was where Fotini caught sight of him sitting behind a tree trunk.

After a while, Kostis went further off and sat in the shade of a rock on the hill's western slope. There, though about a thousand paces away, he had a clear view over the wall and into a part of Captain Limberios's garden and olive grove. At a certain moment he caught sight of Mati ascending from the spring in the ravine and walking toward the cabin, whose roof alone was visible to him. Then he saw Fotini and the children, small as puppets in the distance, going up to the olive grove. But the next moment he also saw a man, a peasant as it seemed from his dress, circling the property and examining the wall of the enclosure in a suspicious manner. Kostis saw him approach, retreat, stop, look, and approach again. Finally, he saw the man bend down toward the wall and busy himself with something as if he were searching for a chink or removing a stone. Then the strange man lifted one leg, placed his foot in an opening he must have made, lifted the other leg, climbed up, jumped over the top, and disappeared behind the wall.

It was Wildman, who had seen Mati from the high peak of Dragasia where he was pasturing his goats. He had also seen the old woman and the children walking away. He had evidently observed the girl on many another occasion both from a distance and nearby, in hiding as befits a wolf-man, and the girl had aroused his desire. He now hastened to act upon the age-old herder's impulse, "when a goatherd looks upon his bleating she-goats covered by the male . . . " He left his herd and ran down to the place where he had seen the beautiful, dreamlike being. Poor wolf-man!

Meanwhile, Kostis lost no time. He got up and ran as quickly as a deer. He ran and ran and then heard Mati's cry. He came to the enclosure and found the place where Wildman had removed a stone with his eerie nails. Kostis climbed up the same way, jumped over the three-foot wall, and landed inside the property.

"In the nick of time," as the European story writers say. Wildman had not choked Mati yet but he would have done so in a very short while. When Kostis entered the cabin he saw a strange tangle of limbs in front of him. The next thing that caught his eye, even before he climbed up the five steps inside the cabin, was a short-handled axe with a glistening edge, a handy weapon. Actually, Kostis was carrying a loaded double-barreled pistol in his pocket but was afraid to use it lest he hit Mati. He seized the axe and ran up and began hitting Wildman's arms. Wildman released his victim and lunged at Kostis, who found it necessary to give him a blow on the head. Wildman lost his bearings and rolled to the ground.

At the same moment Fotini and the children arrived. When the old woman saw Kostis she assumed he was the evildoer. She turned a fierce gaze on him, glaring wildly, and, ignoring the weapon he held, raised her arms ready to tear at his face. But the youth nodded in the direction of Wildman, who was stretched out half-dead on the floor with his head all bloodied. The old woman began to understand.

"Bring some water," said Kostis. "Help Mati."

The girl was lying still, almost unconscious, so weakened by her fearful struggle that she could not move. The old woman threw herself grief-stricken on her beloved girl and felt for her pulse and her heart. The frightened children ran to fetch water. Kostis produced two shining white fragrant handkerchiefs, which were wrapped around some flowers pressed against his breast, and began to bind Mati's wounds. Fotini raised no objection. The girl had two deep gashes on her neck and another on her arm. The left side of her long-sleeved chemise was stained with blood, and the old woman, groping, discovered a third gash on her left breast. The youth doffed his thin jacket, tore off two wide strips from the front of his clean white shirt and gave them to the old woman to bind the wound.

The children brought water. Mati recovered little by little, but she was still very weak. She gave Kostis a grateful look. Fotini, as an act of charity, also washed Wildman's wound and bound his head with an old rag.

Kostis was considering what he ought to do with Wildman. The field constable was probably not far off and had to be informed. The constable would see to it that Wildman was taken to a police station, where he would be duly hospitalized or jailed. And Kostis would have to go himself, find the field constable, and report the event. But how could he leave the two women and the children alone with Wildman, who would still be dangerous when he recovered consciousness. Kostis was therefore about to suggest to Fotini that they all leave the cabin and lock Wildman inside so that he could then go in search of the constable.

But no sooner had Kostis reached this decision than he saw Wildman moving very slowly. He sat up on the straw mat, arose, limped to the door and went out, headed for the gate of the enclosure. Kostis followed him out of curiosity and saw him push the bolt and open the gate. At the last moment he turned around, threatened Kostis with his fist and cried out:

"You wait—you come sometime to 'ut! I show ya'!" He then disappeared.

Captain Limberios found out what happened, and because Mati conceded that without Kostis's help she would have become the victim of her boorish attacker, her father asked her if she wanted to marry her rescuer. The girl replied innocently that since she was in any case going to get married, "better to him than someone else."

And so the wedding of the passionate lover, Kostis, and the beautiful, tender Mati took place three months later. Thus virginal beauty, wondrous and heavenly, the culmination of springtime, was destined to hand over the scepter to that inexorable harvester, love.

The Voice of the Dragon

O NE EVENING KRA-
tira Diomena, a spinster in her forties, settled down to spend the night in the lowly hut that stood in her olive grove, where she had worked all day gathering olives. At close of day she would temporarily put sacks full of olives in the hut. The following morning the load would be carried by mules to the olive presses of Dimos Maniatis down in the country district of Kehrea. On the nights when the harvested olives were in the hut she would sleep there to guard against a possible theft, although such incidents were actually rare in that area.

She found repose in her small shelter and slept soundly during the night, tired as she was from her continuous excursions around the countryside and the chores she ceaselessly performed up and down her various fields. The spinster held a considerable amount of property, though it was encumbered with debt. She had hopes and expectations that after so many years she would finally manage to pay off the debt, which stuck like mange and multiplied like caterpillars on a plant. Her comfort and joy was to run from vineyard to field and from field to olive grove. At the appropriate times and seasons she never ceased performing alone the tasks that women perform: sulfurizing the fields, picking the fruit, harvesting the grapes, and, above all, gathering the olive crop during the fall and winter months.

On the evening in question she was not alone; she had as her companion her thirteen-year-old nephew, Kotsos, her sister's son. The boy was not only the son of her sister's travail but a child of sorrow for both women.

Kratira and her younger sister Sofoula had been orphaned as girls. The years went by; at first Kratira probably did not wish to marry and later, perhaps, she was not able to. Like a good mother, however, she arranged her sister's marriage and provided her with a dowry. She gave the bride half of the family property and because the groom demanded cash, she in addition mortgaged the other half for three thousand drachmas and handed that over to him. After the wedding the husband, a seaman, spent some months that winter at home and in February embarked on the ship he owned and sailed away.

Sofoula had become pregnant. The husband returned. After a short stay that summer he went to sea again. Shortly afterward Sofoula completed the term of her pregnancy and bore this child, Kotsos, not exactly nine months, but nine months and three days after her husband's first departure. Then the old gossips of the neighborhood and of the whole village carefully counted out the months, the weeks, the days, even the hours. "So many in February, and March has thirty-one, and that makes . . . and thirty in April . . ." and so on. When they had added up all the months to October, the nine months would be completed. But Sofoula sat on the birthing stool not on the seventeenth but on the twentieth of that month, not therefore, on the 270th but on the 273rd day after her husband's departure.

Hence arose scandal and ill-repute. Then came the return of the husband and the divorce. They said that Sofoula had brought this child into the world by one of her cousins, who as a relative was looked upon as a protector of the two orphaned girls. Sofoula had engaged, therefore, not only in adultery but also in incest.

"Look what we've come to! Somara-Gomara!" said a simple-minded old man, shaking his head.

"People of Sodom and Gomorrah," corrected Mr. Anagnostis, son of Evgenitsa, who was the cantor of the Church of the Holy Virgin.

"God will destroy us, my child!" concluded an old woman.

Kratira never believed that her sister was guilty, nor did she ever choose to question her. She preferred to be uninformed and to have faith in innocence. She merely asked the priest to "instruct" her sister and told Father Ioakim, an eccentric wandering monk, to "give her good advice." Kratira was inclined to believe that the three additional days of the pregnancy were an exception of nature, a mistake in the numbering of days, since the laws given by God in his goodness did not seem to her as rigid and niggardly as the accounts of usurers and the reckoning of the old women of the neighborhood. A gynecologist from Athens, it was said, upon hearing a report of the affair, revealed that it does happen, though very rarely, that the fetus through some sluggishness or injury stays in the mother's womb a few additional days.

At the trial, Sofoula's attorney, a clever man with words, made the following remarks:

"Must we, then, consider as touchstone of a woman's fidelity the particular circumstances and disadvantages accruing from the occupation of her husband, rather than her character, her inner convictions, her understanding of what is good for her? If that is the case, are we then to say that the wives of country folk, farmers and shepherds, should be considered faithful only because their husbands do not leave home and because it is not possible to make a public accounting of months and days? And yet such an accounting is made improperly and haphazardly for the wives of seamen."

This learned man, moreover, added the following argument:

"Sacred Scripture itself tells us, 'In those days Elizabeth conceived,' meaning 'on one of those days' or 'about that time,' and does not specify that the mother of the Baptist conceived on exactly such and such a day."

In reply to the testimony from Scripture brought forward by the aforesaid lawyer, the opposing lawyer retorted that the actual passage from the Gospel does not say "In those days," but, to be exact, "After those days Elizabeth conceived." And as for the first argument, the syllogism framed by the counsel for the defense, continued the plaintiff's attorney, it is a fact we all know that the judgment meted out by man is of necessity imperfect. There is no reason, he said, though we know that human justice is imperfect, to allow it to surrender its claims and to disappear altogether. For justice would indeed be dethroned and sent into banishment if one were to apply the syllogism of the opposing attorney. When a proven thief or murderer or adulterer is sentenced, everybody knows that there were, and are, and probably will be, other thieves and murderers and adulterers, be they many or few, who are not caught and who escape the axe of human justice. But that is no reason for the guilty persons that are caught red-handed at these crimes to go scot-free. "I shall judge thee by thine acts." Justice, fighting in defense of mankind, will punish today all the perpetrators she is able to catch, and waits in readiness for those who have perhaps escaped her grasp for the moment until she can apprehend them on the morrow.

In his reply the attorney for the defense remarked with fine sarcasm that according to the thread of his opponent's argument, one might surmise that the Goddess of Justice was giving advice and instruction to those women who wished to sin, that she was telling them: "If you wish to take a lover, see to it that you do so while your husband is at home and not when he is away." But the plaintiff's attorney answered that these instructions would be unnecessary, for the advice contained therein was self-evident and the daughters of Eve do not need such instruction. (Laughter in the courtroom.)

Finally, after many difficulties, the divorce was granted. Sofoula had for a long time been in a state of agony, exposed to the cruel vilification of society. Afterwards she returned with her child to her sister's house, as in earlier days without a man, but now a mother without a husband and a widow without the intervention of death. While still a young and comely mother, Sofoula was fortunate enough to fall prey to a disease and slowly waste away until, fifteen years after giving birth, she died. But she did not leave her Kotsos behind her to wander through life exposed to the slings and arrows of mankind.

As he grew older, that child of sorrow had become strong and tall, bold and fearless. He climbed trees, rocks, cliffs, peaks, wherever it was difficult for rumor, shame, and the malice of other children to reach him. For at the slightest vexation, or on the least pretext, or even without a pretext, the children would hurl at him the disreputable name of bastard. Rarely, however, did they do this to his face, for Kotsos had powerful arms, and they knew that if in his rage he caught any of them, his fists would break their bones. He would run here and there like a wild goat scampering up tree and rock, wherever he thought the echo of that dreadful word could not reach him. Yet the echo resounded more loudly on those heights and pursued him wherever he went.

"Go off somewhere, my child, and hide so they won't see you or hear you," an old woman told him one day. She lived in the neighborhood and was a hard, perverse soul. And thus the fate that had rocked his cradle from infancy with the song of calamity was bound to take him and hide him deep in the bowels of earth so that there people would not see him, nor he them. Nor would they hear him, nor he them. For, one day, when he was fourteen, he climbed up a very tall cypresslike poplar, the kind used for ships' masts. He had almost reached the top when a boy who often annoyed him ran by and took the opportunity to shout up at the climber the usual opprobrious name. Kotsos, evidently enraged at the boy's insult, let go with one hand and glanced furiously down. Within a few seconds he was hurtling down to the ground from a height of sixty feet. The unfortunate Kotsos lay unconscious for only a few hours and then breathed his last.

Kotsos had been about ten years old when he first heard, or rather, first noticed, the name that one of the boys hurled at him in a quarrel over a game of pebbles. The boy ran away, and Kotsos, sensing that the name was an insult, chased after him but was not able to catch him. The boy went up the hill to the "Upper Quarter," got two of his playmates as allies, and taking advantage of the height began to throw stones at Kotsos. Kotsos was forced to retreat.

Immediately he ran home to his mother.

"Tell me, Mother, what does *moulo* mean?"

Sofoula grew pale and said haltingly:

"Where did you hear . . . that word?"

"Yiannis, Famelou's son, called me that just now when we were playing, and we started fighting, and he ran away and kept on calling me *moulo! moulo!* I couldn't catch him to get even with him . . . Tell me, Mother, what does it mean?"

"May their mouths plug up! May they break out in sores!" Kratira began this cursing in a low voice, as she came to the aid of her sister.

"Aren't you going to tell me, Mother, and you, Auntie, what does it mean?" insisted the boy, crying and noisily beating his feet on the floor.

Then his aunt took it upon herself to explain, forgetting that her answer was inconsistent with the curses she had just uttered.

"Well, look, they see you're blond . . . and your hair supposedly makes you look like a little mule, that's why they call you *moulo.*"

Kotsos was not convinced.

Kratira added: "Just like Boulina's son, who's a redhead, they call him 'Red,' and Yioryis, Melahro's son, who's dark, they call him 'Blackie.' Now, d'you see?"

The boy began to calm down. He was soothed more by his aunt's gentle voice than by the meaning of her words.

"Like Nikos, Kontoula's son, who's called 'Little Bee' because he's big as an ox?" he said.

"Yes, that's it," Kratira assured him.

"And Mihalis, Koronios's son, is called 'Grizzly,' the way goats are?"

"Exactly so."

Kotsos was appeased for the moment. But he noticed that they flung that name at him with much more malice than was shown to those called "Grizzly" and "Little Bee." A short while afterward he began to question his aunt privately:

"Now come on, Auntie, won't you tell me why my father left my mother and married another woman?"

"It's none of your business, asking about things like that!" answered Kratira, trying to conceal her discomfiture under a tone of severity.

"It's none of my business?" repeated Kotsos on the verge of tears. "Why do they call me *moulo?* It's not because of the color of my hair, is it? Is it because I supposedly haven't got a father?"

Then Kratira thought for a moment. Being a sagacious spinster, she decided that it would do no good to hide the truth from her nephew, since nowadays, when there is no authority anywhere, children learn everything before their time. If she were silent, the boy was sure to learn much more than was right for him to know from the children in the village and from the language of the street and the rumors of the marketplace. Therefore she said to him:

"Listen, Kotsos dear. When your mother had you in her belly she got sick and was very weak and could not give birth at the right time. During her sickness, both when she was awake and when she was asleep, she kept on calling out 'My child! My child!'—Do you realize how much she cares for you? Do you understand how much pain and sorrow she felt when she was bringing you up?—when that first illness came on, before she gave birth, she kept you in her belly two or three days longer. Then the nasty gossips—busybodies that they are—counted the months and the days and said that—so they claimed—your mother did not have you by her husband because he was away at sea for nine months and you stayed in her belly those extra two or three days. Then your father—I don't want to say anything against him—he who made my life miserable and forced me to mortgage my property to give him three thousand in cash because he insisted and kept on demanding 'Hard cash! Hard cash!' and up to the last minute didn't want to go through with the wedding if I didn't count out the money, so that after I gave your mother half of the property, all her share, I was forced to mortgage my share also to get cash to give him—in short, your father believed what people said and refused to recognize you as his child. But you, like all other orphans, have God as your father, and you should love your mother, who never did anything to harm you, who suffers pain and sorrow to bring you up. You should be a good boy, and those who've done wrong will be judged by God. Even if your mother did have you by someone else, still it wouldn't be your fault, and they shouldn't taunt you for that. But they're only children and you shouldn't mind them, because they don't know what they're doing. Just be good and you'll see that these things can't hurt you. May God help you to prosper and become a useful man, and those same people who insult you now will some day come and bow down before you in repentance, and you'll act stern with them. Only, Kotsos dear, be careful not to hurt your mother, who loves you so very much. And may Christ's blessing be upon you. But if you behave stubbornly, like a child . . . well, her heart is bleeding anyway for all those other reasons."

AND so on that autumn evening in question Kratira and her nephew stayed in the olive grove and shut themselves in the small hut to sleep. Near her property was a large wooded area, a deep forest of splendid, towering oaks. By the edge of the forest on the northwest boundary of the olive grove there were a number of ruins and a cavern of a peculiar form and structure, called the Dragon's Cave.

Its entrance was an opening in a rock, whose base had served as a cornerstone for one of the ruined buildings. The cave led upward inside a high cone-shaped mass of rock that was the peak of the formation. They said this passageway was many yards long, with a way out at the top. They said that within the cave one could always hear a strange, loud rumbling sound, and that in days gone by a dragon dwelt there, whose hidden treasures were guarded at night by numerous black slaves.

Scattered around outside the cave were the ruins of three or four buildings, and at night from out of these ruins came a crowd of specters, ghosts, and spooks. A narrow, shaded ravine dropped down from the ruins and plunged into a deep hollow. Within the ravine, a little below the ruined buildings, there was an ancient spring at the foot of an old tree. A cup was attached by a chain and hook to its aged trunk. The spring was called "Cold Well," and indeed it was cold, not only because of its water but also because of the damp air in the dark, shaded hollow of the small glen. Many people refused to drink from the spring, for they claimed it was haunted. Old women who had been born around the turn of the century would greet the ancient spring whenever they were obliged to pass through the narrow hollow and would utter this formulaic phrase:

"Greetings to you, Cold Well, and to your creature!"

Some would say, "Greetings to you, dear Cold Well," and others, more euphemistically, "Greetings to you, good Cold Well, and to your creature." Everything in this place, the ruins and the stream, was thronged with fairies by day and hummed with spooks and phantoms by night. Many people reported that they had seen a Black Man seated near the Cold Well holding a long pipe. A number of tender beings, village boys, young shepherds and shepherdesses, had been "stricken" because they happened to be near the Cold Well at an ill-omened hour. One night Kambanahmakis's wife, a shepherdess and mother of ten children, had been stricken with paralysis and muteness.

Kotsos, the child of misfortune, had learned from his aunt to love the countryside, and he frequently accompanied her on her expeditions. His mother stayed at home. Since her son's birth she had been weak in body, and her spirit was pierced by the barbs of defamation. But her sister was virtually a denizen of the open fields.

Kotsos not only loved the countryside, the mountains, fields, springs, and ruins; he even loved the phantoms themselves. He had become a misanthrope from the shame that his playmates heaped on him. He stopped attending school because of his mates' behavior, which with some effort he might have controlled if he had been the sort to "tell the teacher on them." But among children this is an act of foulest treachery. And so Kotsos had no other recourse than to be frequently embroiled in quarrels and to beat up his schoolmates — sometimes, too, he would get the worst of the blows.

After one incident in which he beat up two or three boys, they reported him to the teacher. Since Kotsos did not wish, either through shame or reticence, to mention the epithet the others had aimed at him, the weight of the teacher's wrath fell on him. Not only was he whipped with the teacher's thin, stinging rod, but he was also temporarily suspended from school. In vain did his aunt, seeing his unwillingness to tell on the boys, offer to report the children to the teacher and explain that they said such and such and called him so and so. Kotsos of his own volition turned the temporary suspension into permanent desertion and never stepped into the schoolhouse again. This happened in his thirteenth year.

On other occasions as well Kotsos had gotten a whipping from the teacher though he did not deserve it. Conversely, he had sometimes gone unpunished when he actually was at fault. The wandering monk, Father Ioakim, would then counsel him, saying that in this world "in some things we are at fault, in others we are sorely vexed," and he would try to explain the meaning of the maxim "Wrongdoers there are many, wronged there are none."

Kotsos thus learned to love the wilderness, the ruins, and even the spooks and phantoms. Ah, they at least did not wish him ill; they had done him no wrong. They had never thrown at his face or at his back that terrible social stigma. He was seized by a deep desire, an uncontrollable curiosity about one thing: he longed to enter the opening of the cave that appeared to descend into the earth but then rose to the peak of the rock. This particular place, the Dragon's Cave, held a great fascination for him.

Earlier on the day in question, in the afternoon, he had made an attempt to approach it, but his aunt, who watched him vigilantly, ran toward him and called him back.

"Don't do it, my child! Did you want to go into the Dragon's Cave? God forbid! Don't be reckless!"

"Is there really a dragon in there, Auntie?"

"Even if there's no dragon, who knows? You may hurt yourself. It's dark, and who knows what sharp rocks there are in there? You may have a bad time or get the shivers or the frights. They say the cave has a terrible rumble when a man creeps into it."

Kotsos seemingly listened to his aunt's advice and returned with her to the olive grove. But his longing and curiosity were even stronger than before. He had heard from other children and from old women that the dragon who had lived there in olden times could make a man rich at his whim, just as he pleased, unless he pre-ferred — and this happened more often — to harm the rash intruder and maim him for life. The dragon had stored up a vast number of coins, countless florins that a Black Man took out at night and tossed up and down near the mouth of the cave, where they glittered brightly in the moonlight. Kotsos dreamed that he could escape the Black Man's notice and seize as many of the florins as possible while they were dancing in the air. And with those florins he would, first of all, pay off the mortgage on his aunt's property because it made her unhappy. Then he would give the two women enough money for them to live well, and then he would build himself a beautiful three-masted vessel. He would go on voyages and return with "bushels of five-drachma pieces," as he had heard tell of ships that sailed up to the Black Sea during the Crimean War: they had returned, holds laden with drachmas, which were distributed by the bushel to the crew — the boatswain, the seamen, even the cabin boy. With the dragon's money he would be the center of those hateful boys' atten-tion, those boys that were now his enemies, and they would come and bow down before him, as his aunt said.

That night he lay down in the hut, and when he was sure that his aunt was sleeping soundly (as was natural for someone as tired as she), Kotsos got up silently, took a box of matches and a thick section from a wax candle, opened the door very carefully and stepped out. He closed the door without making a sound and ran towards the Dragon's Cave. The sickle-shaped moon had just risen. It was almost midnight. He quickly reached the ruined buildings, passed through them and stopped at the cave's mouth. He lit the candle with a match and, making the sign of the cross, entered the opening. The gap easily held a man standing upright, and Kotsos, though a boy, filled it with his tall, husky body. He felt a cold, damp wind against his face. He was stepping on something like dust or sand. He bent over and took a few steps forward. He could see only a black wall, as smooth as if it were chiseled. He heard an undefinable hum coming from within, like the buzzing of flies or the delicate beating of small birds' wings. He caught sight of dark shapes; some looked like melted drippings from a tangle of wax candles, others like crystalline icicles that hang from roofs in time of frost.

Suddenly his path was blocked. The wall that up to that point had formed a vault over his head seemed to have descended to the ground and halted his progress. Kotsos held the candle up and traced a circle with it to see if there was a passageway, but a blast of air suddenly fell on the candle and snuffed it out. At the same time Kotsos heard, he thought, a subterranean rumble, a muffled voice that came violently out of the depths of the cavern and seemed to say:

"*Mou—lo! Mou—lo!*"

So! Even the phantoms knew of his misery! So then! Even the spooks, all of them, knew his vulnerable point! Even the dragon gave an approving word to the cries of the hateful children!

Kotsos wanted to escape. Turning round in the dark toward the cave's mouth, hoping to find a friendly ray of moonlight to brighten his way, he struck his head violently against the rock vault and momentarily grew dizzy. Ah! He should have beaten his head against the wall before, when he first considered entering the Dragon's Cave. Or rather, even earlier than that . . . before he ever was born. At that moment there appeared in his mind's eye the figure of the wandering monk, Ioakim, smiling and twitching, who had once told him about the innocent curiosity of the disciples of Christ: they had asked whether the man who was blind from birth was himself a sinner or whether his parents were sinners and caused him to be born blind. Kotsos himself was something worse than a man blind from birth—he was a man condemned from birth.

When he recovered from his dizziness he returned trembling and shaking to his aunt. He found her awake. She had started up in her sleep, and once her eyes were open she saw to her surprise and dismay that her nephew was missing. She got up and opened the door. She suspected that Kotsos, that reckless boy, had gone toward the ruins and the Dragon's Cave. She began calling him.

"Kotsos! Where are you?"

Hesitating only a moment, she was getting ready to run out there half-dressed and barefooted, when she saw Kotsos coming back.

He was pale with agitation and looked paler still in the light of the moon.

"What's wrong? Where were you?"

The boy recovered quickly.

"Nothing . . . nothing, Auntie. Don't worry."

"Didn't I tell you not to go into the Dragon's Cave? Tell me what happened."

"I heard a voice."

"A voice? You must have heard the sound they say comes up at night. Were you very frightened? Make the sign of the cross, my child. Come, go to sleep, and be careful. Next time don't be so reckless."

"The voice I heard . . . "

"The voice? Well, what about it?"

"It kept saying . . . a word."

"What?"

"It kept saying . . . 'Mou—lo!'"

Kratira was pained but at the same time could not help laughing. She explained to her nephew:

"When somebody is reckless enough to go into the Dragon's Cave at night, at midnight, that's what he'll hear. They say that the sound in that cave has this peculiarity: to everyone it repeats what his heartache is. Whatever sorrows he has in life, it's as if it tells him in a human voice. That's what people said in days gone by, but nowadays there probably hasn't been anybody who's tried to enter the cave. You thought you heard 'Moulo.' If I went into the Dragon's Cave, I'd think I heard 'The debt! The debt!'—that's my heartache. If your mother went in, her ears would hear 'The child! The child!' And if that fine fellow your father went in, he would hear the voice saying 'The cash! The cash!' That's what the voice of the dragon is."

A short time after the hapless death of the boy, the two bereaved sisters, dressed in black, went out early one morning and headed for the countryside. The mother was pale and weak and walked with difficulty—indeed, she was destined to die a few weeks later—the aunt, thin, sunburned, enduring, and long-suffering.

Outside the village they met the wandering monk, Ioakim. He greeted them with sympathy, shaking his head, and addressed the childless mother:

"Eh, well! Courage, Sofoula! What can we do, my dear? There, in the other world, you'll find many, many others and your

Kostandakis too. What can you say, poor woman? Of course, you must have said it was an evil moment! Ah! much more evil, Sofoula, is the moment of sin! Ah! the wages of sin . . . that's why the blessed Theodore the Studite said 'May your right hand, Lord Jesus, guard me from all evil plots.'"

Then, when Sofoula turned her head away, weeping, the wandering monk said to the older sister:

"Ah, Kratira, if only she were innocent! She would join the holy martyrs. Whatever it was, I believe the Lord will have mercy on her."

Because Kratira looked at him in perplexity, the monk continued in a low voice so that Sofoula would not hear him:

"Of the two evil moments, the one when a creature fell into temptation and brought another creature into the world, and the one when that second creature fell from a tree and was killed, the second moment would not have happened without the first—the more evil of the two moments, Kratira, was the first."

The Marriage of Karahmet

WHEN THE PASHA-ADMI-
ral brought his fleet in and came to anchor between the Great Strand
and the Little Strand, the watery domain was filled with ships and
the whole sea grew black. Some cast anchor along the coast line by
Kouroupi and Lehonia as far as the rocky islands off Kastri, while
others, the smaller craft, were moored by the shore of Ai-Sostis,
where it was calmer and more sheltered from the wind. On that
occasion, at the end of June, the etesian winds were not blowing
and the sea was still, but even if a wind had arisen, it would not have
blown severely along that sheltered northwest coast.

There was no harbor along the coast. It was a place of dreamlike
beauty, a glorious expanse of waters, the kingdom of the north
wind. All the day long, from early dawn till evening, the waves
rolled their lengthy course over the whole of the northern Aegean,
between the Straits and Mount Olympus, between Mount Athos

and Euboea, and only toward dusk did they reach their destination and come to rest by Kastri, the citadel of the north. A great crowd of people, the thousand or so inhabitants of Kastri, gathered toward evening by the canon of Anangia on the highest, northernmost part of the citadel and gazed out to sea. They gazed with insatiable eyes on the monster newly come: so many huge, three-masted vessels with two or three decks. The monster lay anchored at the pleasure of the sultan, the infidel dog, their lord and master. It lay anchored there among the rocky islets of Kouroupi.

In those parts dwelt a multitude of evil spirits and phantoms. Between the crags farther inland and the rocks along the shore was a strip of wave-washed sand, where goblins descended and appeared in the shapes of women, widows lamenting amidst the jagged outcrops. There pebbles, red, purple, rosy, blue, rolled trilling to shore as priceless gifts of sea nymphs to delighted children. Two or three humble ships stood on the sand, and on the evening in question two or three little boats timidly floated out from that spot towards the side of the sea monster. They circled it at a distance with oars poised over the charmed waters. The sailors from the decks called down to the little boats in Greek, "Come on! Come on!" But the boys at the oars did not dare to approach because the admiral's ship was anchored nearby, among the small islands opposite the citadel.

In addition to the Turks, Egyptians, Arabs, Berbers, Tunisians, and Algerians on board the ships, one-fifth of the crew members were Christians, the usual Greek complement. Hydra, Spetses, Psara, Kasos, the Sporades, each had furnished about one hundred and fifty men, and there were a few from other islands. Also on board was Pasha Ahmet's secretary, a Phanariot Greek of the family of M——. He had recently fallen into disfavor with the authorities and the pasha had secretly engaged him as his secretary after making him change his name. This clever Greek was naturally devoted to his master, as any man in his circumstances ought to be.

The first to pay an official visit to the commanding pasha was his old acquaintance Koumbis Nikolaou, the leading notable of the little town. Koumbis, dark, strong, and imposing, with his long pipe and his long, swaying sleeves and his baggy felt trousers, usually presided over the *kiosk,* the pavillion near the Big Cistern and the mosque. The *kiosk* was the meeting place of the notables and stood right next to the residence of the Turkish sergeant (whose presence there was a mere formality). Here the notables discoursed and took counsel with one another. At these meetings it was the opinion of the most animated speaker that prevailed, that of the speaker who on each occasion was forceful enough to bend the will of the others. Koumbis was amply endowed with this capacity. With his dark looks, robust frame, and abrupt manner, he insisted on having things as he wanted them. And as he wanted them was the way things usually went, for—though his character did not allow him to engage in flattery and though he was a straightforward and plain-speaking man—his relations with the local agas were excellent.

At home, however, Koumbis was being sorely tried. That particular year he had taken it into his head that he must separate from his wife, because after fifteen years of marriage she had not borne him a child. Koumbis would not think of taking a concubine—"whoremongers and adulterers God will judge." This was about the only verse he knew from the whole of Scripture. On the other hand, how could he adopt another man's child? "Don't feed a stranger's flesh," went a common saying. Would not his nephews and nieces curse him after death if they were disinherited? Yet how could he leave his property to all of them? After he died they would quarrel over who should get the most, and maybe they would not even bother to hold memorial services for him. That, too, would be a dire weight on his soul. The Lord was right: "Sell that thou hast, and distribute unto the poor." And the monks, for whose benefit the Lord evidently said this, they, too, are waiting for someone to sell his possessions, or else give those possessions to them as a gift, so that they will have enough to gobble up. In fact the monks also lay a voracious claim to what they declare "monastery property," so that the bishop and the churchwarden and the deputy governor and the secretary and so many others can eat their elegant fish and their suckling pig.

At this point Koumbis felt it was absolutely necessary to make some changes in his life, to draw in the rope, adjust the yoke, and shift the burden. Although he was generally a stern man, Koumbis, too, had a weak spot: he wanted to have a dear, sweet little baby, an angelic being to dandle on his lap. Seraino was forty years old, and after many years, about fifteen, she had not borne a child. "Neither pup nor chick nor child." Koumbis was around fifty. His comely neighbor, Lelouda, was only about thirty, fresh as a rose, a modest, humble, poor woman, with a spotless reputation, all alone in the world with no one to protect her. She did have one uncle, but he was altogether incapable of serving as her protector.

Koumbis considered abducting her, bribing a priest or even threatening him with force—everyone knew he was on good terms with the Turks—to perform the marriage rite over him and Lelouda. And what would happen with the first marriage? Neither he nor his wife had ever dishonored their vows. "Whoremongers and adulterers . . ." He would do this deed only so that he could obtain, God willing, an heir.

And so, when the pasha sailed in with his fleet on that occasion, Koumbis decided to act. During his visit to the flagship, he had an hour's talk with Ahmet Pasha. What passed between them? Evidently Koumbis asked a favor and the Turkish admiral made him a promise.

The next evening, when it grew dark, Koumbis fitted out a launch with six oars. He persuaded two fishermen of the shallow waters, who were his men and devoted to him, to climb up the steep, precipitous mass of rock that led from the shore to the citadel. A rough-hewn bridge went across to the citadel, and all who traversed the deep chasm that gaped beneath were seized with vertigo and dizziness.

That morning, after Koumbis stepped down into the lower section of the main room from the raised platform where he slept, he summoned his wife. He was wearing his native baggy trousers, embroidered sashes, and wide sleeves, and was sipping his morning sherbet. (Coffee had just then been introduced to the island by Mr. Alexandros Logothetis, another notable, who traded in the provinces of the Danube, but Koumbis was not yet accustomed to that beverage. He was not one for innovations—except in the case of matrimony, and there what he sought with his dubious project was not innovation but revolution.) He summoned his wife and said:

"D'you hear, Koumbina? This evening at dusk, you go light the vigil lamps in the Church of St. Procopios down in the ravine. I made a vow to do it some time ago. Tomorrow is the saint's feast day and then it'll be hard for you to wait your turn, so many others will be bringing jars of oil. Take our neighbor Lelouda along. She's a poor woman and doesn't get out, and she has no other comfort except you. You go light the vigil lamps when there's nobody around, and you'll have a nice walk too."

"Listen to me, Koumbis, if I may say something too," answered Seraino. "Lelouda doesn't go out, as you say, and now that the fleet is in, who knows if the Turks won't come ashore and start walking around the gardens and fields? Lelouda will be afraid to come with me."

"Listen to me, Koumbina. You just persuade her to go with you. Who would harm you, whether Christian or Turk or anything else, even if he's the devil with horns? Don't you know that I'm on good terms with the agas? Do they have any other representatives in the town to look after their interests and their comfort? I'm right here. Who would dare to harm you?"

Even though Koumbina could not entirely dismiss a peculiar suspicion that had entered her mind, she complied with her husband's instructions. She was a simple, guileless woman. "And the wife, see that she reverence her husband." The she-goat's horns, it would seem, are bent as a sign of her subjection to the straight-horned billy-goat. The chicken's comb is dark and low, whereas the rooster's comb is red, tall, and erect, and his whole body stands upright on his long legs. Everywhere, the submission of the female to the male.

When the humble Lelouda was asked by the preeminent lady of the town to go with her on a small excursion outside the citadel, she was persuaded because she, too, felt an unexpressed need for a change of air after so many months of seclusion in her modest cottage. Koumbina told her that they need not fear the Turks since there were many Christians from Hydra and elsewhere among the ships' crews. And even if the Turks did come ashore—but it was not likely they would because when the wind shifted the fleet would set sail—yet even if the wind were still and the Turks did come ashore, Koumbis "wielded a sharp sword" and was on good terms with the agas for the benefit of the Christian community, and they did not dare harm anyone.

Lelouda wore a red chemise embroidered with silk and a handsome overdress of striated moiré silk. That it would be appropriate to go dressed as a bride never crossed her mind, though in her hope chest she had a dress with an elaborate gold-embroidered hem and silver belt-clasps inlaid with gold. She took up her basket, placed in it a jar of oil, some incense wrapped in paper, and also something to nibble on—bread and olives because it was Friday—and went out to join Koumbina.

Koumbis, meanwhile, had gone to see Father Stamelos, his parish priest, pastor of the Church of Christ, and he said to him:

"As soon as it's dark, get your stole and your prayer book. We're going to the frigate, where you're going to perform the rite of blessing."

The priest looked at him with surprise.

"You shouldn't be surprised. There are a lot of Christians on board those ships. The pasha's secretary is a Christian, a fellow Greek; the boatswain is a Christian, and there's practically a whole army of Greeks on the other ships. They're a third of the crew on the frigate. The pasha himself is a god-fearing man and calls upon Saint George and Saint Demetrios and Meriem-Ana (the Virgin). Take along the Gospels too, because I think you'll have to read a few chapters over the boatswain. He's sick with a fit of melancholy and doesn't know what ails him."

The priest listened frowning. Koumbis continued.

"If, that is, you wish, Father. I preferred you because you're my parish priest. If you don't want to, I'll get Father Frangoulis, your brother in Christ, or Father Danielos from St. Nicholas. Don't be afraid one bit, Father. I've got an order from Ahmet Pasha. You'll get a five-drachma piece and more for your trouble. If you don't go, the pasha will be angry at me and at your priests because I didn't do his bidding."

By the time Koumbina and Lelouda left St. Procopios's Church, where they had lit the vigil lamps, it was already twilight and darkness was spreading over that part of the precipice. In the distance, to the west, lights were visible in the little Church of St. Kyriaki, where an all-night devotion had evidently just begun. The two women had visited that little church just before sunset and had then gone on to St. Procopios's. From this church they followed the path that led down to the shore, at which point it began to climb again, making a winding ascent by stages until it reached the entrance to Kastri by the bridge. The women made their way through the speckled shadows in utter solitude. There was no sign of life anywhere.

Indeed, it would have been better for Koumbina and Lelouda if there had continued to be no sign of life in that place, for they were frightened nearly out of their wits when two men, hidden behind a rock by the side of the path, addressed them in Greek:

"Stop! Don't be afraid."

"Oh! What is it? Oh! Lord protect us! Saint Procopios! Oh! Holy Virgin!"

Before they could utter another word, a third man emerged from behind the rock. It was Koumbis.

"Don't be afraid, gentle Lelouda. Koumbina, go back home! Lelouda, you come with us."

Koumbina had the courage to stammer:

"Come with you? Come where? What's wrong with you, Koumbis?"

"Go on home, Koumbina," her husband said again. "Lelouda, come, we're going to the frigate."

"The frigate!" echoed Koumbina.

To avoid frightening the women excessively, Koumbis had decided that it would be more judicious if he himself took part in the drama of the abduction. Seraino, divining immediately what was going to happen, went back home in all humility and resignation, fell to her knees, and prayed before the icons. A woman of the neighborhood came in and was indiscreet enough to ask what had happened to Lelouda, why she had not returned with her from the country church. Seraina gave this explanation:

"She stayed at St. Kyriaki's. Father Frangoulis is conducting an all-night devotion, and there are people there. If I could have, I would've stayed too. But Koumbis hadn't given me permission."

The six-oared launch was waiting at the foot of the sea-girt citadel near a low, well-worn rock that formed a natural dock. Father Stamelos, frightened and confused, was waiting, seated in the stern, tightly wrapped in his cassock, with his conical headdress pushed low over his eyebrows and the tips of his ears. The six oarsmen, all Greeks from among the crew, took up the oars. Lelouda, as if in a dream, pale and trembling, faint and looking almost dead, was helped on board by Koumbis. The two individuals who were the accomplices in the abduction followed along. One sat in the prow and the other headed for the rudder in the stern.

"No!" said Koumbis. "I'll do the steering."

The man returned to the prow. The island notable took hold of the tiller, the oars struck the water, and after twenty minutes the boat came alongside the admiral's ship.

There was no sign of Commander Ahmet Pasha, neither while the guests were on deck nor later when they went below. After they came on board Koumbis disappeared for three minutes. By the light

of two big lanterns hanging from the mizzenmast the priest and
Lelouda looked at each other, at the sailors with their Turkish fezes,
at the tall masts and the complicated rigging. Koumbis soon reap-
peared. He had gone to do the customary obeisance to the Turkish
admiral and to give him an account of the proceedings so far, proceedings for which Koumbis had asked his goodwill and protection.
To this request the pasha had nodded assent and had given orders
to his Greek secretary to represent him.

The Phanariot made his appearance and led the guests down to
his own cabin. There the first object that Lelouda noticed as she
gradually recovered her presence of mind was an icon of the Virgin
with the Christ Child. Below it was Saint Nicholas, a prelate with
a round gray beard, holding the Gospel and giving his blessing.

After the guests were offered *loukoumi* and *mastiha,* which
Lelouda did not touch, the Phanariot coughed and opened the
conversation:

"So, Father, if you please, put on your stole now and open your
book."

The priest obeyed mechanically. At that moment one of the seamen who had acted as oarsmen on the launch came down the stair-
way of the cabin. He placed in Koumbis's hands a small, flat, round
package wrapped in silk cloth.

"I found this in the boat," he said.

"Ah! I forgot them," said Koumbis.

They were wedding wreaths that Koumbis himself had made on
the sly while Koumbina was on her way with Lelouda to St. Procopios's. He had taken two slender tendrils of the flourishing vine in
his courtyard, wound cotton around them, and attached a little gold
foil he found in the drawer where his wife kept the materials for her
handiwork. The foil was left over from wreaths made for other wed-
dings, inasmuch as Koumbina liked to perform certain social func-
tions and often served as *koumbara* for a couple and as godmother
to their children. On these occasions she would hear those common, yet heartfelt, expressions of good wishes: "As you have come
with the oil, *koumbara,* so may you come with the vine," thus
phrasing the hope that she would live to be in turn *koumbara* to
those infants she had just baptized.

Koumbis set the wedding wreaths on the table under the holy
icon, made the sign of the cross, and gave his hand to Lelouda.

"Come, my love."

The young woman rose mechanically. She was not willing, yet she was unable to resist. Koumbis stood on her right in front of the icon.

"Now, reverend Father," said the secretary, "you will perform a marriage rite in the manner of the Patriarchate, the rite we from the Phanar are accustomed to. Ask the bride and bridegroom if they wish to pledge themselves to each other."

The priest, in a state of fright, remained motionless.

"Did you hear me, Father?" the admiral's secretary insisted.

"I came here to read a blessing," stammered the priest. "I didn't know that it was a wedding, to bring my Gospel and censer and my chasuble."

"We have a censer here," said the Phanariot. "And I also have the Gospel."

"Didn't you bring your Gospel, Father, as I told you to?" asked Koumbis.

The priest was silent. The secretary said again:

"It doesn't matter. I have the Gospel."

They lit the candles that were under the icon stand. The Phanariot stood behind the couple as *koumbaros*. The priest mechanically opened the small prayer book he was holding and began to mumble prayers appropriate for times of drought. Before he could finish his first prayer, the Phanariot became aware of what was going on and interrupted:

"We haven't had a drought this year, Father, heaven be praised! It's rained a good deal. You've made a mistake. Find the prayers for the marriage rite."

The priest turned over a few pages in his book, hesitated, coughed, and began to mutter again in an even lower voice. This time he was reading the prayers for the dying.

"I told you, Eminence," said the Phanariot, "you forgot to ask the bride and groom if they wish to marry each other."

The priest turned to the couple and asked mechanically:

"Do you, Koumbis, wish to take Lelouda as your wife?"

"I do."

"Do you, Lelouda, wish to take Koumbis?"

Lelouda stood still and did not move her head one bit, keeping it bowed in all simplicity and modesty. From behind the *koumbaros* gave the bride's head a gentle thrust forward. She had the air brides usually have, but she had even more the muteness of a sacrificial victim being led to slaughter.

"Read, Father, the rite of the betrothal and then the service of the wedding wreaths."

"Well, so be it," said the priest. "I shall read the service for the second marriage."

The Phanariot thought for a bit and then said:

"Why for the second marriage? The bride is a virgin. This is her first marriage. You'll read the rite of the betrothal and of the wedding rings.

"I don't care what goes on at the Phanar. I'm going to read the service for the second marriage," insisted the priest.

The pasha's secretary yielded. (The story goes that he threatened to hang the priest from the sailyard. But that is all conjecture. The fact is that in the end the Phanariot gave in.)

"Well, so be it. Read the service for the second marriage."

The priest intoned the invocation, "Blessed be the name of the Father . . .," and began the rite. Koumbis had four or five gold and silver rings on his fingers. Only two were required; he removed one from his ring finger and one from his little finger. The priest alternately placed the rings on the bride's and groom's fingers and then went on to the service of the wreaths without saying "Blessed be the Kingdom . . ." With great devotion he began to read the first blessing, where there is reference to sins and human weakness. Next he blessed the wreaths and showed the *koumbaros* how to exchange them on the couple's heads. Then he gave the bridal pair to drink from a common chalice, led them in a circle in "the dance of Isaiah," and finally read the dismissal.

At the very moment when the Phanariot was exchanging the wreaths over the heads of the bride and groom, three loud blasts thundered up on deck from cannons at the sides of the ship. The entire sea quivered, and the citadel opposite shook from the noisy reverberation. The night watchman sitting on the cannon of Anangia at the northernmost corner of the citadel saw the flash and smoke under the brilliant starlight—it was midnight and the quarter moon had just set—and he made the sign of the cross:

"Why are the agas firing their cannon at midnight?" he wondered. "Are they celebrating Ramadan?"

Two women of the vicinity who were resting uneasily and only half-asleep jumped to their feet. One, lying in the upper story of a house near Anangia, rose, looked out the window, and asked the night watchman what was going on.

"The agas are celebrating Ramadan," answered the man.

"What does Ramadan mean?"

"Who knows?"*

The other woman, who was in a country house a little farther off, had a baby in her arms. The child woke up and began to cry and would not be quieted in spite of its mother's soothing words and lullabies. The cannon blasts resounded far and wide across the area called Echo, the battlements of Anangia and the two white islets opposite, and amidst the rocks and caverns all around.

Down by the *kiosk,* in the quarter of the notables near the Church of Christ, Seraino was keeping watch in Koumbis's house. She was the only one to give the correct explanation when she heard the cannon shots:

"May they be steadfast and fortunate!" she murmured with scarcely any bitterness. "May you be blessed with sons, Koumbis!"

At that moment Seraino reckoned with certitude that within two hours at the most the couple would be back at the citadel, for it was unthinkable that they should stay on the admiral's ship until morning. It occurred to her that she must ask Lelouda for the key so that she, Seraino, could spend the rest of the night in the little house across the way. Then she remembered that Lelouda had left the key with her, and it was precisely there, in the eastern chamber where she was sitting at that moment, that Lelouda had hung the key under the icons. Seraino looked and saw it in the glow of the vigil lamp. Without reflecting, she made a movement towards it. But she checked herself and said: "It will be better if I ask her for it when she comes."

Finally, around one o'clock, the bride and groom arrived calmly and in the utmost silence. Koumbis, always a man of influence but now more so than ever because of the presence of the Turkish fleet, had informed the notables and the town guards beforehand. He explained to them that he had important business aboard the frigate, and that he would return very late at night: therefore they should lower the bridge and open the gates of the fortress.

Seraino opened the door at the first knock. She stood there with composure and with a slight smile gave them her good wishes:

*Fasting by day, feasting by night [Papadiamantis's note].

"May you be steadfast and fortunate!—with sons, Koumbis!"

"How do you know?"

"A little bird came and told me."

She turned to Lelouda:

"Shall I take the key to your house and sleep there tonight?"

Lelouda nodded tearfully. Then she ventured:

"Forgive me!"

"You are forgiven. May Heaven bless you!" said the former Koumbina with forbearance.

The following morning, as Koumbis was leaving his house and passing by the door of the humble little dwelling, he called his wife and told her:

"Seraino (he no longer called her Koumbina), take your clothes, your belongings, everything that's yours, and some of my things too, as much as you want, and go live in your house over in Pregadi. I'll send you some workmen today to fix it up, to do whatever is necessary. And I ask you, as best you can, to be on good terms with Koumbina."

"I'll be on good terms with the new Koumbina, as I was with Lelouda," answered the simple soul. "And I ask you, Koumbis, to let me stay in your house to bring up the children that you'll have."

"Yes, God must be guiding you to act this way, saintly soul," answered the hard man, unable now to hide his emotion.

From that time on, the people of the little town called Koumbis, son of Nicholas, "Karahmet," from the name of the Turkish admiral, and to this day his descendents are called the Karahmets. For Lelouda bore, and Seraino reared, Konomos (Alexandros), Moskovos, George, Thomas, and an equal number of girls.

A few months after the wedding Lelouda made a terrible mistake, one fraught with danger. It was on a great feast day, on Palm Sunday. Koumbis had woken early to go to the Church of Christ to attend the liturgy. The new Koumbina had laid out on the divan the clothes he was to wear. In her haste and excessive zeal, however, and confused as she often was and frightened by her husband's sternness and shouts, she had not laid out his silk shirt with its wide embroidered sleeves, the kind the notables then wore. In its stead she had placed one of her own gold-embroidered chemises. Koumbis's eyes were still half-shut from drowsiness, and by the faint light of dawn and the fluttering candle he put the chemise on. He then donned his baggy trousers, his fine silk sash, and his velvet jacket and went out the door.

When he entered the church, the notables near the choir stall noticed the mistake. They looked at the woman's chemise Koumbis was wearing and some of them whispered and bit their lips so as not to smile. Koumbis realized something was amiss. He looked down at his chest, torso, and arms and discovered the mistake.

He rushed out quickly. He was in a rage. He ran on with the intention of killing Lelouda.

The two women were dressed. The former Koumbina wore a modest unadorned frock; the new Koumbina was in her wedding dress, the one she had not worn at her wedding. They were both ready to leave for church.

With one glance at Koumbis, Seraino realized what had happened. He had already raised his thick, iron-tipped cane at Lelouda:

"Filthy woman!"

Seraino threw herself at the cane and fell at his feet.

"Mercy, Koumbis, mercy! Poor thing, she didn't mean it. She made a mistake in her haste and confusion. She hasn't learned your ways yet, Koumbis, your wishes. Forgive her this time, dear Koumbis, forgive her. Mercy, Koumbis, mercy!"

Koumbis yielded.

Seraino lived on for ten or twelve more years, as many as sufficed for her to rear the children of Koumbis. She came to her final rest and was buried outside the little Church of St. Demetrios, near the great mulberry tree, a little way down from the huge clump of bulrushes that was bent over in the shape of a hut and dropped tears of incense. Opposite the grave, over the lintel of the church, was the beautiful, resplendent image of the saint. Three years later, when they went to disinter and transpose Seraino's remains, a delicate scent, as if of basil, musk, and rose combined, wafted to the nostrils of the priest, the gravedigger, Lelouda, and two other women who were present. Seraino's bones had become fragrant.

The American:
A Christmas Story

THAT EVENING THE SHOP
of Dimitris Berdes was like a boat that appears to be caught in a gale
with the wind abaft the beam, its one side washed by waves breaking over the gunwale and spattering the unhappy passengers, while
its harried skipper and deckhand give and take orders in an incomprehensible language, the one strenuously guiding the tiller, the
other taking in and letting out sail and plying a helpful oar on the
leeside, both of them running fore and aft, frightening the less
seasoned passengers, bespattered as they are with foamy water and
constantly assailed by the smell and taste of salt. For it was Christmas eve and every customer had in mind that there was shopping
to do. Mr. Dimitris Berdes, with a storm raging on his countenance
and calm stored away in his heart, was running back and forth. To
some of his customers he poured adulterated drinks, and to others
he sold short weight. He was delighted by the noise of the clientele,

overjoyed by the ringing of coins as they fell through a slot into his
securely locked drawer, like so many sparrows into a trap. His
helper, Christos, his sister's fifteen-year-old son, scarcely had time
to fill the bottles from a barrel, mis-weigh butter from a jar, and
pour honey out of a leather bag. With an apron tied high over his
chest, he kept yelling "Right away!" in a number of different tones
and pitches—a phrase that as time went on he managed to truncate
to "Rightay," then to "Right," and finally to a simple "Ri!"

In one corner of the shop sat a group of five men. They were
drinking their *mastiha* before leaving for their evening meal at
home. All shipowners of the island, they were waiting until after the
Feast of the Immersion of the Cross was over so that they could sail
away. One of the group, Captain Yiannis Imbriotis, had that very
evening put in safely with his schooner, and they were welcoming
him back. Each man treated the party to drinks in honor of the captain, and he in turn ordered a round to wish them good health.
Then each friend insisted on treating the party to a second round,
and again Captain Yiannis reciprocated. By this time the men were
in the midst of an animated conversation about the affairs of their
calling, about freight, business good and bad, the loading and unloading of cargo, damages, and shipwrecks. Captain Yiannis was
recounting in great detail the events of his last trip and the perversity
of Turkish officialdom that had forced him to spend a few days in
Volos, where he had put in to unload some cargo. Then he
remarked:

"Ah! I forgot to tell you about the shipmate I took on in Volos."

"You took on a passenger in Volos?" asked one of his friends.

"He doesn't want to disembark. He's still on the schooner. I invited him to come to my house, but he didn't want to."

"Where's he headed for?"

"For here, as of the moment. I asked him, but he didn't want to
tell me."

"What's his business here?"

"What sort of man is he?"

"What did he look like to you?"

The questions of the skippers came in quick succession.

"He's clean-shaven except for a fringe of beard along his jaw and
under his chin. He looked to me like an Englishman or an American, but not really English or American. The few Greek words he
said were spoken with hesitation and a lot of effort—not exactly

like a foreigner, more as if he once knew Greek but had forgotten it. Most of the time we got along with the little bit of Italian that I know."

"Did he tell you his name?"

"I put him down in our book as 'John Stathison, with an American passport.'"

At that moment Captain Yiannis, who was sitting with his back to the wall facing the door, suddenly cried out:

"Ah! There he is now!"

Everyone turned toward the door.

There entered a tall, well-dressed man about forty-five years old. He was handsome, with an open, frank expression, and clean-shaven except for the fringe of hair along his jaw. Across his chest he wore a thick gold chain, from which were dangling a pendant and some small lumps of gold. It would have been difficult to guess what latitude or people claimed him. He seemed to have acquired, like a film over his face, a sort of mask from another part of the world, a mask of cultivation and good living under which his true origins were concealed. He walked in hesitantly, glancing with uncertainty at the faces and objects around him, as if he were trying to get his bearings.

Before sunset the stranger had been unwilling to go ashore on the island, as Captain Imbriotis had said, but when night came on he asked the seaman who was standing guard on the schooner (this crewman was not a native and therefore had no place to go) to take him ashore. He left his baggage, three very large trunks, in the cabin near the prow, and the seaman rowed him to land. He found himself in the seafront marketplace. He looked around as if he did not know where he was. Because of the bitter cold there was no one out of doors. The mountains all around were capped with snow. It was the 24th of December 187–.

The stranger looked inside a couple of taverns and cafes, then inside two shops that sold both dry goods and groceries, the sort usually found in villages. But evidently he did not recognize them and so appeared dissatisfied. He went on and ascended the lane to the small square in front of the Church of the Three Hierarchs. There, apparently, he did recognize the place. Although he did not cross himself when he saw the church, he raised his hat in the darkness and put it back on, as if he had just met an old friend and was greeting him. Then he glanced to the left, saw Berdes's small tavern and general store, and went up to it. He stood still for a few minutes looking inside and finally entered. He had not, in fact, seen Captain Imbriotis. The captain, though facing the door, was hidden from view by his drinking companions, who were looking the other way, and by another group standing and drinking at the counter, before which stood bottles of liquor. Had the stranger seen the captain, perhaps he would not have entered.

"There's the American," repeated Captain Imbriotis, pointing out the stranger to his companions.

The four merchant captains turned their eyes toward the newcomer and gazed at him intently.

"*Bono pratigo, Signore,*" cried out Imbriotis. "You decided, I see, to come ashore."

The stranger raised his hand in greeting.

"Please, Captain," said one of the skippers in English. This was Captain Thymios Kourasanos, the owner of a large brig, who had made two ocean trips to London and had learned a handful of English phrases.

"Thank you, sir," replied the stranger politely in English.

Tossing a ten-lepta piece on the counter, he spoke only one word to the boy: "Rum." He took the glass in his hand and, so as not to give the impression that he was systematically avoiding his fellow man, he approached the group and with some awkwardness and effort spoke in Greek except for one English word:

"Thank you, gentlemen. I am not sitting to make *talk* and hard for me to make *talk* in Greek."

"What's he saying?" asked Captain Thymios Kourasanos, furrowing his brow. "He wants *tocca* with us?"

The stranger heard and hastened to undo the misunderstanding.

"Please excuse me, sir; I meant, make *talk,* make *conversazione,* how do you say it?"

"He means," said Imbrios, comprehending, "that he finds it difficult to carry on a conversation in our language."

"Ah, yes! conversation," said the stranger in Greek. "I forgot the Greek word."

"And where you come?" said Kourasanos in broken English.

"For the hour I come here," replied the American in Greek. "After, I don't know. I'll make other trips."

Captain Kourasanos could not grasp his meaning and simply looked at him.

"Why don't you sit down, *Signore?*" said Imbriotis. "You won't find better company anywhere."

"I won't sit down. I go to make *walk,* to *walk* around, how do you say it?"

"To go for a *spazio?*"

"Ah, yes, *spazio,*" said the stranger. "Yes, I see. You talk Italian word, so I understand Greek word."

He nodded farewell and turned to the door. The five shipowners were all at sea, in a greater ocean of ignorance after this exchange than they had been when they were being informed by their fellow captain, Imbriotis.

Leaving the shop, the stranger headed for the column. It stood opposite the Church of the Three Hierarchs, and around it in days gone by seamen tied the stern cables of ships wintering in the harbor. He kept glancing to the right and left, and finally fixed his gaze on a small house, which he stared at for a long time as if he were trying to remember or recognize something. Finally, he turned into a narrow lane leading through the neighborhood and disappeared from sight.

If someone had followed him, however, he would have seen that the stranger walked on a few paces, then turned up the hill and came to a spot that was four houses beyond the small dwelling he had previously been staring at. There, between two houses, was an empty space covered by the debris of two half-ruined walls, rubble apparently from a building recently torn down. After looking around to see if anyone were observing him, the stranger stepped hesitantly into the ruins. In the corner where the two walls met, a blackened recess indicated that there may once have been a hearth there. The stranger took off his cap and held it in his hand. Then, kneeling down, he touched his forehead to the cold stones forming the corner. He remained kneeling for a few minutes, then rose, wiped his eyes, and slowly walked away.

He retraced his steps downhill and stopped in the middle of the lane not far from the little house he had been staring at before. Again he cast his eye around to see if anyone were observing him and then he stood still, evidently trying to catch some sound. What, one wonders, was he listening to? Perhaps it was the voices of the children of the neighborhood, who were going from house to house singing Christmas carols. Their songs collided with one another and drifted off in various directions like the twittering of winter sparrows. At one point these verses rang out:

Christ's mass, Christ's birth,
First mass of the year.
Come and hear and learn,
Christ is born this day.

At another point, these:

Lady of the house
With your daughter fair,
Lady of the house
With your precious one . . .

and at still another point:

Be bright and white as Olympos,
As bright and white as a dove.

Voices of innocence, joyful, without color, full of a child's mirth and happiness.

Suddenly, the stranger was obliged to step aside because two youngsters, one carrying a lantern, had just climbed down some stairs and were coming toward him. He took a few steps back in the direction he had come from. The children came near, but hardly noticed him. They went up the staircase of the very house he had been gazing at so fixedly. When he saw this, he turned back again with a marked show of interest and stood poised to listen.

The boys knocked on the door.

"Shall we come and sing for you, Auntie?"

After a moment, footsteps were heard from within. The door was opened; an old woman with a black kerchief appeared and said in a mournful tone:

"No, my children. Why should you sing to us? Do we have anyone? Have a good year, but go and sing somewhere else."

She put a five-lepta piece in their hands. The boys left, satisfied that with no other effort than the climb up and down the stairs they had earned five leptas.

The stranger, hidden behind a corner, saw the wrinkled

countenance of the old woman and heard her sorrowful voice. Oddly enough, he let out a sigh of relief and seemed to be pleased. At that moment an idea came to him, and without much reflection he proceeded to act on it.

When the door was shut and the old woman was out of sight, the boys came down the stairs exchanging a few words.

"Hey, Gli'oris, we've got one sixty-five now."

"How much does that make for each of us?" asked the other, who held the cash. "That makes eighty lepta each."

"Aren't we going to share that old woman's five-lepta piece?"

"Yep, we'll share it, Thanasis. Eighty for me and eighty for you."

"Let's buy some walnuts with it, Gli'oris, and we'll share them."

"An' if they give us five walnuts, how'll we share them?"

Suddenly the stranger appeared in front of the boys. He held out his hand and showed them a silver dollar.

The boys, who had never before seen a man without a mustache and full beard, were startled. The one holding the lantern let out a small cry, while the other, whose pockets were well filled, turned and fled. Then Thanasis, suspecting that if Gligoris went off, he might hide out the next day and not give him an accounting of the money, placed his lantern on the ground and was about to start running after the fugitive. Acting quickly, the American managed to show the dollar he was holding in the light of the lantern and said:

"Wait. Take this dollar."

The boy, torn between two fears and two wishes, with trembling knees and frightened look, stood motionless, not knowing what to do.

"Two words I wish you to tell me," said the stranger. "This house you went up, who lives?"

The boy could hardly understand.

"What did you say, Uncle?" he asked, beginning to take courage.

The stranger put the dollar in his hand and tried to explain more clearly.

"You went up now to house. The old woman came to door. Who other lives in house with her?"

The boy did not fully understand, but after receiving the dollar he entirely lost his fear.

"Auntie Kyratso lives up there," he said, "and she gave us a five-lepta piece. There's another woman there too. I don't know how they're related."

"Her daughter is up with her?"

"She must be her daughter. Yes."

"Her daughter is married?"

"I don't know if she's married. It doesn't look like she has a husband."

"And how many years is her daughter?"

"I don't know how many years she's been her daughter. I guess from the time she was born till now."

The boy took up his lantern and left on the run, clutching the dollar in his fist, not wishing to entrust it to his pocket. He ran to find Gli'oris to ask him for his share of the money. The stranger did not try to stop him.

After this the American departed and went down to the marketplace by the shore, where lights could be seen in two or three of the cafes. He looked to see which had the fewest customers and entered the one where he saw only one individual, the proprietor. The old man was freshly shaven, had a twisted mustache, and was wearing short baggy trousers, tall boots, and a clean apron. He was preparing to close his shop. When he saw the American coming in, he looked at him with curiosity. The stranger ordered a glass of rum and tossed a ten-lepta piece on the counter. Seeing the coin old Uncle Anagnostis wanted to give him five leptas in change, but the other said "No! No!" in English. Then the proprietor poured him a second glass of rum for the value of the other five leptas, properly, as he thought. But the stranger threw another ten-lepta piece on the counter.

"He probably doesn't know Greek," thought Uncle Anagnostis. To try him out, he addressed him:

"Have you just arrived?"

"I come today with ship Captain Yiannis."

"Of Captain Yiannis Imbriotis?"

"Yes. Can you make punch?"

"Gladly," said Uncle Anagnostis.

Making an effort to recall to memory some ancient bit of knowledge, the old man tried to prepare some punch, but the rum would not flame up. He offered it as it was to the stranger, who made no complaint, and tossed a silver shilling on the counter.

Uncle Anagnostis took it up.

"What's this worth?"

"I don't know money here," said the stranger.

The old man opened his drawer to see if he had enough for change, but he did not find more than eighty leptas in small coins. Nevertheless, his conscience did not allow him to cheat his customer and he said:

"Haven't you a twenty-kreuzer piece, sir?"

"I have not other money except for England and America."

"I haven't enough change, sir. Take your silver piece. This must be worth about one drachma thirty-five or forty. You can give me the twenty leptas tomorrow."

"Keep the shilling. I don't want change."

Uncle Anagnostis stood with mouth agape, looking intently at the stranger. At that moment, however, a group of three men came in and, standing in front of the counter, ordered three drinks. One of the three men was singing with drunken abandon:

Come, my beautiful Vasilo,
Make your arms my nice soft pillow . . .

The second man, bare-chested and barefooted despite the bitter cold, began to scrutinize the stranger.

"I've seen that man somewhere," he mumbled indistinctly.

These three were the town porters and also its criers, a jolly trio that spent its time drinking away at night the money earned in the day. The singer suddenly changed his rhyme and tune and went on:

Come out, you slut,
Come out and see
This flesh you cause
Such misery.

"Your health, friends!" They noisily clinked their glasses. The bare-chested, barefooted fellow continued to look intently at the stranger, whereas the first went on with his singing:

Vasilo, hey, Vasilo,
You've something that allures,
But loaded, damn it all,
Those heavy kegs of yours!

At that moment heavy footsteps were heard above a wooden staircase leading to the living quarters upstairs. The staircase was closed in by a frame that cut off a corner of the cafe. By the upper part of the frame under the ceiling a little door opened, and a head with a white cap, white mustache, and coarse features peered out of the opening.

"How many times have I told you, Anagnostis," came a voice from the head in the little doorway, a voice coarse enough to match the features. "You just won't listen. You keep disturbing the quiet of good settled folks. Think of what day it is tomorrow, and here you are singing and carrying on again! What time is it anyhow?"

It was half past eight. The singer of the porters' triumvirate took up the conversation and said with mock gravity:

"We're leaving now, Captain Anastasis! We wouldn't think of disturbing your quiet!"

"Quiet, you lout!" shouted Anastasis.

The shopkeeper called out:

"Right away, Captain Anastasis. I'm closing now. Y'see, I can't turn these people out."

"Such honest faces!" guffawed Captain Anastasis from the little door. "But sure to treat 'em with politeness!"

"We didn't insult you, Captain Anastasis. I see your worship, though, is insulting us," said the porter.

And in a low voice he mumbled:

"But you want every last bit of the rent, and you know how to ask for it even ahead of time. If this poor man doesn't make a few pennies, how'll he be able to pay you?"

"You be quiet now. He's right; it's Christmas Eve," said the conscientious proprietor. "It's at other times that he seems harsh, God bless him!"

The head with the white cap had meanwhile disappeared behind the little door, and Uncle Anagnostis was getting ready to close his shop. The three porters left arm-in-arm, singing. The stranger had nodded farewell and gone out ahead of them, but the proprietor called him back and said:

"Where are you going to sleep tonight? Do you have a place? Where are you staying? I'm sleeping here. If you're going back to the schooner, fine, but if you're not, you can stay here if you'd like. It's warm."

"I'm not sleepy," said the stranger. "I'll take a walk and then we'll see."

"Any time you want. Knock on the door, and I'll get up to

let you in. I have some bedding to give you, too."

This time the American headed for the same neighborhood by another, narrower street. Now he could see the little house that was the object of his attention from the other, southwestern side. Opposite the house, at the corner of a neighboring residence, was a pile of rocks and wood that had lain there for an unknown number of years and appeared to be the rubble from a building that had been torn down or fallen to ruins. Light from a small window shone in that direction. One of the two shutters was open, and if someone wanted to step onto higher ground he could see through the glass into the interior of the house. When the stranger was satisfied that the street was deserted, and that not even the shadow of a passerby could be seen, he climbed to the top of the rubble and with beating heart peered into the house.

Against the wall opposite the unshuttered pane was the hearth, where a log was sputtering in a slow-burning fire. Above, higher up, was a vigil lamp lighting the holy icons. A woman, who appeared to be still in her youth, was sitting by the hearth, resting her head against her hand and wearing a sorrowful, troubled expression. Her lips were moving, and she could be heard murmuring something, a faint warble, sung in a voice that was clear and virginal, yet at the same time feeble and wilted. The stranger's ear caught these two verses clearly:

Misery me, and misery more,
The sailor's gone to far-off shore . . .

The stranger's heart was pained, and tears came to his eyes. He suddenly felt the urge to descend from the pile of rubble and run over to the house. To do what? He himself hardly knew. He restrained himself, however. At this moment he heard a faint creaking, as if someone were climbing an interior staircase, as if a trapdoor were being shut. Another woman, old, bent, wearing a black kerchief, came over to the hearth and, kneeling in front of it, threw kindling into the fire. It was the same old woman who had given the five-lepta piece to the two boys and sent them away.

"Well, daughter, when will you come to your senses? I'd like to know, are you going to spend all your time weeping? Well! What a thing! To listen to you! Why, we've become regular hermits! Do you think you're the only one? While you had some marriage proposals, while there was still time, after that fine fellow of yours went to America, why didn't you accept anyone? Didn't I tell you? Why don't you listen to your mother? I told you so, time and time again. Now you're too old, and whose fault is it? But it's not as if you're the only one. There are other girls older than you. Mygdalio, Mahou's daughter, and Krystallio, Yioryena's daughter—your age isn't even close to theirs!"

The stranger was all ears. He appeared, curiously enough, to understand what the old woman was saying more from inspiration and an awareness of the situation than from the seemingly little Greek he knew. At that moment steps and voices were heard coming from the end of the street. Two men were approaching. The eavesdropper hurriedly came down from his vantage point and went on. He reached the end of the narrow street, turned right, and found himself once more in the small square in front of the Church of the Three Hierarchs.

The shop where this narrative began was still open. Dimitris Berdes did not scorn small profits and did not reject even a five- or a two-lepta piece. He called these "small catches." The other profits, those of the early evening, he termed "net-catches." Whatever one pulls in, he would say, either with a dragnet or a small casting net, is satisfactory. Berdes was at the moment attending to the bailiff and the constables, who were night watchmen, and was serving them diluted wine. They permitted him to keep his shop open until eleven at night, since they found it more comfortable to sit there in the warmth than to make the rounds of the town out in the cold.

The shop owner stood at his counter, reckoning up the ten-lepta pieces, the twenty-five lepta pieces minted under Otto, and the twenty-kreuzer pieces. The boy Christos, his apron tied high under his arms, was asleep on his feet. His head bobbed back and forth like a two-oared dinghy rocked by a gentle breeze from the south as it lies alongside an anchored sailing vessel. From time to time the boy was suddenly aroused by the stamping of the shopkeeper's foot and his even louder voice repeating the orders of the customers. Then like a sleepwalker Christos would move about, serve the drinks, take the ten-lepta pieces, throw them mechanically into the counter drawer, return, and fall asleep again.

Just then, with loud cries and shouting, dancing and thumping, the merry confraternity of the three town porters invaded Berdes's shop, the next shop after their expulsion from Uncle Anagnostis's cafe. One of the three, Stoyiannis Dobros, whose origins were in Serbian Macedonia, was playing the role of a bear and was dancing around, while one of his companions, Pavlos the Smith, had smeared his face and was acting as the bear trainer. Carnival time, to be sure, was far off, but the morrow was already Christmas, "Saint Basil comes" after Christmas, and after Saint Basil's feast it would be Epiphany, and after Epiphany it would be only a few weeks until Carnival time. The third man, Vangelis Pahoumis, the leader of the confraternity, hairy-chested, barefooted, with his trouser legs rolled up over his calves—perhaps from his long practice of wading into the water to unload small boats—could not stop thinking about the American. "I can't get him out of my mind," he kept saying.

But lo! A few minutes later in walked the very man who was the object of his meditations. The stranger went to the counter, ordered a glass of rum, and tossed a silver shilling on the counter top. Berdes took it.

"What does this go for?"

The American made a gesture indicating indifference and said: "I don't know money in this place."

"This doesn't tally with our money and isn't good here," said the shopkeeper. But if you want, I'll take it as worth a drachma."

"I don't care," muttered the American in English, and then repeated his words in Greek.

Berdes gave him ninety-five leptas.

All the while Vangelis Pahoumis had not ceased looking at the stranger. Just then he turned to the others in the shop and said loudly:

"Hey, fellows, do any of you remember Yiannis, the son of Uncle Stathis Mothonios, the one who's been in American nigh unto twenty years?"

When the stranger heard this name he started and instinctively turned towards the speaker. Nevertheless, he restrained himself and, feigning indifference, went over and sat in a corner of the shop. He lit a cigar and began to smoke.

No one answered the porter's question. Its hidden allusion escaped everyone present.

Vangelis continued:

"No wonder you don't remember! You're all younger than me, except for Uncle Triantafyllos, who's not from these parts. I'm almost forty now. I was eighteen years old when the son of Mothonios left his country; he must have been about twenty-five then. Why, I think I'd recognize him if I saw him now. Both his parents died in their longing for him, both Uncle Stathis and his wife, may God rest their souls! And their house fell to wrack and ruin. It's a little ways up from here, near the church, with two ruined walls and a black hollow in the corner where there was once a hearth. But the son's left for good. Well, a lot of people get lost in America. Did you know that he was even betrothed?"

"Who was the girl?" asked the mayor's bailiff, chief of the night watchmen, without interest.

The stranger was listening very attentively, but refrained from turning his eyes toward the speaker.

"It was Melahro, daughter of Auntie Kyratso, Mihalis's wife. After he left and a couple of years went by, lots of men wanted to marry her, because she was very pretty and people respected her and she was good at her handiwork, the only embroideress in our village, and she had fine things in her hope chest. But Melahro didn't want anyone, and so the years went by and she's now a spinster. With all her weeping and wailing she's grown thin and pale. Still, when a woman's got a good shape, she doesn't grow old so easily. You oughtta see her, fellows, she's still easy on the eyes. She must be more than thirty-five but she looks like twenty-five. I happened to see her one day when I was bringing them a sack of flour. The more you look at her, the more appealing she gets."

"Come on, cut that out, Vangelis," said the mayor's bailiff sternly. "It's not right to talk in taverns about women and girls."

"You're right, Uncle Triantafyllos," said the porter. "But I meant no harm."

The American's expression showed his joy. A ray of happiness, piercing the masklike layer mentioned earlier, lit up his whole face.

Uncle Triantafyllos, the constable, and the two citizen watchmen got up and picked up their guns. The bailiff turned to the shopkeeper and said:

"Hurry up, Dimitris. All of you fellows, quiet down. That's enough of all this singing and dancing. This isn't Carnival time. Think of what day it is tomorrow. Close up quickly, Dimitris, so people can go to bed. They'll be getting up at two in the morning to go to church. The gentleman, he has a place to sleep, I suppose?" he asked, indicating the American.

"Don't worry, Uncle Triantafyllos," said Vangelis. "Uncle Anagnostis, the cafe owner, told him to spend the night in his shop. Anyway, there's no reason for you to worry about him," he added, winking at the bailiff. "If he wants a place to sleep, he can get one very easily."

"How's that?" asked the bailiff softly, with curiosity.

"He's from these parts, a native," whispered Pahoumis into his ear.

"How do you know?"

"It wasn't easy, but I recognized him."

"Who is he?"

"The man I was telling you about before, Yiannis, the son of Uncle Stathis Mothonios. When you came and settled here, he was already gone. That's why you don't remember him. But I think you must've run across his father, Uncle Stathis."

"I did. Well, hurry up, Dimitris," the bailiff said again in a loud voice and went out of the door.

Vangelis's two fellow porters had stopped singing and dancing and were getting ready to leave. Suddenly Vangelis went up to the American and said in a low voice:

"What'll you give me, Chief, if I go and deliver the good news?"

The stranger did not put his hand into his pocket. Instead he took the British sovereign he was holding with his thumb, index, and middle fingers, and he quickly dropped it into Vangelis's palm. This was done with such eagerness and joy that the stranger appeared to be the receiver, not the giver.

When the neighbors of Auntie Kyratso, Mihalis's wife, woke up after midnight to go to church, as the church bells were ringing out noisily, they were indeed surprised to see the poor widow's house ablaze with light. This was the house where children were not welcome to sing Christmas carols, but were sent away with "We have no one" and "Why should you sing to us?" Now all the shutters were open, open glass panes were sparkling, the door kept opening and closing, two lanterns were hanging over the balcony, shadows flitted back and forth, and voices and sounds rang out joyfully. What was happening? What was going on? It was not long before those neighbors found out. Those who did not find out in the neighborhood found out at church. Those who did not go to church found out from worshippers returning at dawn after the end of the divine liturgy.

The groom who had left for foreign shores, who was absent for twenty years, who had sent no message, left no trace for ten years, who had not associated with a compatriot or spoken Greek for fifteen years, who had wandered over many places in the New World, had worked as a contractor in the mines and as a foreman on the plantations, that very man had now returned with several thousand dollars to his place of birth, where he was reunited with his faithful betrothed, older now, but still in the prime of her life.

The only news he had heard, fifteen years earlier, was of the death of his parents. As for his betrothed, he was almost certain she would have married long ago; yet he still had a faint hope. Out of superstitious fear, as he drew nearer to his native land, he grew more and more hesitant about asking directly about his betrothed and therefore did not identify himself to any of the compatriots he met when he arrived in Greece. He preferred to remain ignorant about his betrothed until the last minute, when he would disembark in his birthplace and pay a reverential visit to the ruins that had once been his father's house.

Three days later, on the Sunday after Christmas, the marriage of John, son of Eustathios Mothonios, and Melahrini, daughter of Michael Koumbourtzis, was celebrated in all solemnity and joy.

Auntie Kyratso, after many long years, wore again for a few minutes her purple flowered kerchief in order to kiss the wedding wreaths. And on the eve of Saint Basil's feast day, she stood on her balcony and was heard calling to the passing groups of children:

"Come, children, come and sing!"

Notes

Fortune from America (Ἡ τύχη ἀπ' τὴν Ἀμέρικα, 1901)

P. 2 ANCIENT COMIC POET . . . : A reference to Aristophanes' *Clouds,* 629–31, where Socrates voices his impatience at old Strepsiades, the latest pupil of the "Thinkery."

P. 2 VLACH: In Papadiamantis's day fixed surnames were not yet in general use in the countryside. The second name used was either a patronymic or a matronymic, or denoted social position, place of origin, a physical or character trait, or other peculiarity. John's ethnic origin was Vlach, a division of the Romance-speaking peoples of the Danube region. Many Vlachs were settled in Greece, particularly in the north.

P. 3 SEND LAZARUS!: Luke 16:24.

P. 5 RACHEL: Genesis 29:6–31.

P. 5 EPARCHINA: I.e., wife of the *eparchos,* or subprefect.

P. 10 SMALL MONASTERY . . . : Monasteries were used occasionally as convalescent homes both because of the more healthful country surroundings and because the prayers and care of the holy men were considered beneficial to the sick.

P. 14 KOUMBAROS . . . : The *koumbaros* is the principal witness at a wedding and has a religious function in the marriage sacrament. He slips the wedding rings on the fingers of the bride and groom and crowns the couple with the traditional wedding wreath.

P. 14 KOURAMBIEDES: Dense butter cookies covered with powdered sugar.

P. 15 LOWERED IT . . . : An ambiguous gesture. The lowering of the head from time immemorial among Greeks has signified assent, but here it could also indicate nothing more than bridal modesty.

The Homesick Wife (῾Η Νοσταλγός, 1894)

P. 22 NATIVE VILLAGE: As is clear from some of the geographic features and place names, Lialio's village was on Skopelos, the larger island to the east of Skiathos.

P. 27 FAREWELL . . . : These lines are from a poem by Ioulios Typaldos (1814–83), a native of Cephalonia in the Ionian Islands, which are also known as the Heptanese. The Heptanesian poets are the most eminent representatives of Greek Romanticism.

P. 29 BOTH TESTAMENTS . . . : Genesis 2:23; Matthew 19:6 (cf. Mark 10:9); 1 Corinthians 11:3.

P. 31 NEREID . . . : In ancient Greek myth the Nereids were sea nymphs, the fifty daughters of the sea god Nereus. They were benign divinities, who danced and played in the waves and helped voyagers on their way.

P. 39 TRITONS . . . : The Tritons of myth were mermen, the male counterparts of the Nereids, and followers of the great sea god Poseidon. They appeared singly to mariners, usually to bring help, as a Triton did to Jason's Argonauts. But they could also be harmful if provoked, as described in Vergil's *Aeneid* 6.171–74.

The Haunted Bridge (῾Η Στοιχειωμένη Καμάρα, 1904)

P. 41 WASTING AWAY . . . : In Skiathos and other parts of Greece a prolonged deathbed agony is considered the sign of a grave sin that has not been expiated.

P. 41 ARETI: In the Greek text the main character is variously called Areto, Areti, Aretoula, and Aretaki. Areti ("Virtue") is the standard form of the name; it appears thus in the folk song below. Areto is a dialect form. Since the affectionate diminutives Aretoula and Aretaki are used in the story with ironic effect, I have retained the variants in my translation. In other stories I have for simplicity's sake generally used only one form of Christian names.

P. 42 A BRIDGE . . . : Variants of this folk song, known in Greece as

"The Bridge of Arta" from its most common version, are widespread throughout the Balkans and the Greek islands. Its theme, found in folk belief in many parts of the world, is the necessity of a human sacrifice to provide a sound foundation for a new edifice, usually a bridge. The sacrificial victim, invariably the master builder's wife in the Greek versions, is said to be the spirit (*stihio*) that dwells in the bridge. Presumably the sacrifice was demanded by a supernatural power—here represented by the bird—as a recompense for the builder's privilege of constricting the river. Until very recently, in many parts of Greece animals, or, in a symbolic gesture, the shadow of a man, were immured in the foundations of edifices.

P. 43 KARAMOUSALIS: A prominent family of Skiathos.

P. 46 RIGHTEOUSNESS . . . : The words quoted are from Psalm 36 (37), verse 6. The psalm treats of the problem of evil, God's vindication of the righteous, and the punishment of the wicked in this life—applicable here to both Areti and her father.

The Matchmaker (Ὁ πανδρολόγος, 1902)

P. 52 AUSTRIAN COINS . . . : It was, and still is, a custom in Greece for revelers and dancers to press coins against the foreheads of musicians as a sign of approval. The money drops to the ground, of course, and is subsequently gathered by the musicians.

The Bewitching of the Aga (Ὁ ἀβασκαμὸς τοῦ Ἀγᾶ, 1896)

P. 57 KASSANDRA: The province of Thessaly was ceded to Greece in 1881, but Turkey did not give up Macedonia, where Kassandra is located, until the end of the Balkan Wars in 1913. The events narrated in this story (as in "The Marriage of Karahmet") take place in the period of the Ottoman occupation of Greece, before the Revolution of 1821 and before the establishment of the independent monarchy.

P. 58 RIPE FRUIT . . . : The fruit of the wild fig tree is host to insects that leave pollen in the cultivated figs where they deposit their eggs.

P. 58 KONAK . . . : Most—though not all—of the following Turkish and Arabic words and phrases that appear in the original Greek text of this story would have been understandable to readers of Papadiamantis's day. Their translation is as follows, in the order of their first appearance:
konak: The residence of the Turkish official.
Lā Allah, ilā Allah: There is no God but Allah.
kiosk: The town pavillion, a sort of gallery.
Lakirdi soilé: To have a conversation (faulty Turkish).
hanum: Woman, wife.
Axám hairolsoún: Good evening.
Astaghfir-u-llah: God help me!
Lā Allah ilā Allah, Allah akbar, Mohammed rasūl Allah: There is no God

but Allah, God is great, Mohammed is the messenger of Allah.

P. 64 KORAN . . . : The passages from the Koran are as follows: Koran 3:145–46, 154, and 2:190–93. I have translated Papadiamantis's version of these passages.

P. 64 SICK MAN . . . : The "sick man" (*homme malade*) was a term coined by Tsar Nicholas I to characterize the Ottoman Empire of the mid nineteenth century. The term was in common usage (especially as "the sick man of Europe") in the period before 1918. The calculation of 444 years is made from the fall of Constantinople to the Ottoman Turks in 1453, signifying the end of the Byzantine empire. It should be noted that in the year Papadiamantis wrote this story Greece was preparing to enter a war against Turkey in support of the still subjugated Cretans.

Civilization in the Village:
A Christmas Story (Ὁ πολιτισμὸς εἰς τὸ χωρίον, 1891)

P. 66 THRESHING-FLOOR . . . : Katerina is here using the language of Greek folklore. "The marble threshing-floor" is in folk songs the site of the wrestling match between the legendary Byzantine hero Digenis Akritas and Charos (Death).

P. 67 FEAST OF ST. BASIL . . . : In the Orthodox Church the feast of St. Basil falls on January 1. It was, and to some extent still is, the custom to exchange gifts on that day.

P. 70 FUNCTIONARIES . . . : The civil servants were appointed by the central government in Athens. Such functionaries, especially in Papadiamantis's time, were hardly ever natives of their place of assignment. Papadiamantis often expresses disdain for these better-educated, Westernizing, supercilious outsiders, whose presence tended to change local ways.

P. 71 SKAMBILI: A card game similar to pinochle. There are two to eight players paired off as partners.

P. 72 PASETA: A game of chance played with all fifty-two cards of the deck. The dealer, who "holds the bank," turns up the cards one by one: if the card turned is even-numbered, the other player(s) win and the dealer loses; if odd-numbered, the dealer wins and the other(s) lose.

P. 77 CRACKLE . . . : It was a widespread folk belief that the sputtering of the fire in the hearth presaged someone's arrival. It is interesting that the English poet Coleridge alludes to virtually the same popular superstition in his poem "Frost at Midnight," where a "film . . . flutter[s] on the grate." In a note Coleridge explains: "In all parts of the kingdom these films are called *strangers* and supposed to portend the arrival of some absent friend."

A *Dream among the Waters* (*Όνειρο στὸ κῦμα*, 1900)

P. 84 REVOLUTION . . . : The beginning of the Greek Revolution against the centuries-old domination of the Ottoman Turks is traditionally dated to March 1821. The success of the Greek cause, marked by extreme factionalism among the Greek leaders as well as stirring examples of valor and self-sacrifice, was uncertain until the favorable intervention of the allied French, British, and Russians. Count John Capodistrias, a Corfiot Greek who had served as a joint foreign minister of Russia, governed Greece with an able, though autocratic, hand from 1828 until his assassination in 1831. Greece was established as an independent kingdom in 1833.

P. 85 . . . A PRIEST: According to the canons of the Orthodox Church, a married man can be ordained both a deacon and a priest. He cannot, however, marry *after* he has been ordained. If he does, as the deacon Sisois did in this instance, he is considered to have broken his vows and is therefore defrocked.

P. 86 HUNGRY DISCIPLES . . . : Matthew 12:1: "At that time Jesus went on the sabbath day through the corn and his disciples were an hungered, and began to pluck the ears of corn, and to eat." Deuteronomy 23:24–25: "When thou comest into thy neighbour's vineyard, then thou mayest eat grapes thy fill at thine own pleasure; but thou shalt not put any in thy vessel. When thou comest into the standing corn of thy neighbour, then thou mayest pluck the ears with thine hand; but thou shalt not move a sickle unto thy neighbour's standing corn."

P. 87 KOMBOLOI: A string of beads ("worry beads"), often made of amber, that men in the Balkans and the Near East still carry with them and run through their fingers to while away time.

P. 87 MOSCHOULA: The girl's name is of course a feminine form of her uncle's. *Moschos* means "calf" and was clearly chosen by Papadiamantis for its associations. It appears in ancient Greek pastoral poetry.

P. 94 SCRIPTURE . . . : The quoted phrase appears in the Old Testament, e.g., Deuteronomy 32:9 and Joshua 17:14. In an ironic play on words Papadiamantis equates *schoinion,* the common Greek word for "rope," with an ancient cognate *schoinisma,* which appears in the Septuagint translation of the Old Testament with the meaning "a measurement or allotment of land or property."

A *Shrew of a Mother* (*Στρίγγλα μάννα*, 1902)

P. 96 BOUZOUKI: From the Turkish *büzük.* A musical instrument similar in appearance to a long-necked mandolin, with three pairs of strings, usually played with a pick. It was indigenous to the easternmost part of the Aegean, though in nineteenth-century Skiathos and other islands it was not one of the primary folk instruments like the violin and lute, or *laouto* (see, for example, the musicians mentioned in "Fortune from America" and

"The Matchmaker"). Since World War I the bouzouki has become a standard instrument of Greek popular music. Now, as then, bouzouki music is associated with feelings of deep sorrow, world-weariness, and social rejection.

P. 96 DAVID: I Samuel 16:23.

Love the Harvester: A May Day Idyll (Θέρος-Ἔρος, 1891)

P. 103 MAY DAY: May Day is celebrated throughout Greece with picnics and excursions into the countryside expressly for the gathering of wild flowers. On Skiathos men, women, and children bind their waists with wild grapevines so that their bodies will be "strong as iron," and, as Papadiamantis describes in this story, make wreaths of vines and wild flowers for their heads. Wreaths and bouquets are also hung outside each door.

P. 103 DONKEY . . . : Local belief requires everyone to eat a little garlic or biscuit or Easter bread early on May Day morning to ensure good health for the coming year. And if someone should hear a donkey's bray before he eats, the bray is believed to "stuff his mouth," i.e., take his appetite away.

P. 107 "LOOSENER" . . . : On Skiathos children do this to draw a little blood from the nose, to "loosen" it, as they say.

P. 108 PREFA: A card game similar to bridge, popular throughout Greece.

P. 111 "I SAW YOU!" As is clear from the fragments of their chants, the children are at first playing tag and hide-and-seek. Then they play a game somewhat similar to our "London Bridge" ("I'm Mr. John"), in which the players pass under the raised arms of two children; a teasing game, in which one child pretends to be an old man who chases the other children; and a game in which one child throws a ball to the accompaniment of a rhyme ("Up apple, down orange").

P. 123 "WHEN A GOATHERD . . . ": The quoted words are from a poem (1.87) of Theocritus, the greatest of the ancient pastoral poets (third century B.C.). The herder Daphnis, dying of unrequited love, is taunted by the fertility god Priapus, who declares Daphnis is no better than a goatherd that is erotically aroused by the sight of his mating animals.

The Voice of the Dragon (Ἡ φωνὴ τοῦ Δράκου, 1904)

P. 128 MONK . . . : Father Ioakim, though called a "monk" and addressed as "Father," is strictly speaking not a monk, since he does not belong to a monastic community, and he is probably not a priest either. This type of wandering holy man is the equivalent of the Russian *starets*.

P. 128 GOSPEL: Luke 1:24.

P. 138 THEODORE: (759–826), abbot of the monastery of Studius. An eminent Byzantine saint, he was known for his opposition to the Iconoclasts and his codification of monastic rule. Perhaps Father Ioakim quotes him because of his strong opposition to the emperor's adultery.

The Marriage of Karahmet (*Ὁ γάμος τοῦ Καραχμέτη*, 1914)

P. 139 "THE MARRIAGE OF KARAHMET": . . . This story was left unrevised by Papadiamantis at his death and was published posthumously. I have chosen the more detailed of two openings and have in some places silently eliminated certain inconsistencies.

P. 140 PHANARIOT: The Phanariots were a group of Greek families who in the seventeenth and eighteenth centuries rose to positions of great prominence and power in the service of their Ottoman rulers. Their name is derived from the Phanar, the district of Constantinople where the Orthodox Patriarchate is located. The most distinguished of the Phanariots, a few members of the Mavrokordatos family for instance, held the titles of Great Interpreter (in effect foreign secretary of the sultan) and of prince of the Danubian provinces of Moldavia and Wallachia. It is a historical fact that the position of interpreter to the admiral (*kapetan pasha*) of the Ottoman fleet was one of distinction and influence.

P. 141 WHOREMONGERS . . . : Hebrews 13:4.

P. 141 SELL . . . : Matthew 19:21; cf. Mark 10:21, Luke 18:22.

P. 142 DISHONORED . . . : In Greek Orthodox canon law the only sure basis for divorce was adultery.

P. 143 "AND THE WIFE . . . ": Ephesians 5:33.

P. 146 ST. NICHOLAS: The patron saint of seamen. Greek sailors often display his icon. Moreover, appropriately enough for this story, there was a legend attached to this extremely popular saint that he furnished the dowries for some penniless girls who could not otherwise have married.

P. 146 LOUKOUMI: a sweet made of gelatin, sugar, and fruit flavoring, still popular in Greece. In English it is sometimes called "Turkish delight."

P. 146 MASTIHA: an alcoholic beverage made of spirits of wine and flavored with the resin of the mastic tree.

P. 146 KOUMBARA: The *koumbaros* (*koumbara* if a woman) is the principal witness to the wedding and has a religious function in the marriage sacrament. After the priest has placed the wedding wreaths on the heads of the bride and groom, the *koumbaros* switches them alternately from head to head three times.

P. 147 GENTLE THRUST: Among Greeks a forward movement of the head has from Homer's day to the present been a sign of assent.

P. 148 SECOND MARRIAGE: The rite for the second marriage is briefer and more austere than the regular rite, used for a first marriage. The term for this shorter rite is in Greek *digamos*—also the word, appropriate here, meaning a bigamist.

P. 148 "DANCE OF ISAIAH": The "dance of Isaiah" is enacted by the priest, groom, bride, and *koumbaros* as they walk in a circle three times before the altar. It is so called from the opening words of the priest's chant, "Isaiah, dance for joy," referring to the prophecy of Isaiah 7:14.

P. 151 FRAGRANT: It was believed that a sign of sanctity was that the body, instead of putrefying, gave off a fragrant odor. It was, and still is, customary in Greece to disinter the bones after three years and place them in an ossuary.

The American: A Christmas Story (Ὁ Ἀμερικάνος, 1891)

P. 153 FEAST . . . : On January 6, the feast of the Epiphany, when the Orthodox Church celebrates the baptism of Christ in the Jordan, it is traditional for a priest to bless the sea and thus make it safe for sailing. During the rite of the blessing the priest throws a cross into the water and a group of boys competes to retrieve it and receive a blessing and reward.

P. 155 "BONO PRATIGO": The *pratigo*—or, in standard Italian, the *pratica*—is the authorization given by a sanitary official allowing sailors to dock and come ashore. Here, obviously, the captain is using the expression as a jovial greeting to one newly debarked.

P. 155 TOCCA: From the Italian *toccare,* to touch, used in Greek to mean a "handshake" or a "clinking of glasses" in a toast.

P. 163 OTTO: The first king of the modern Greek nation, who reigned from 1832 to 1862.

P. 164 SAINT BASIL'S FEAST: celebrated on January 1. On the eve of the feast day it is customary for children to go from door to door singing carols, just as they do at Christmas (see the end of this story). "Saint Basil is coming" is the first verse of one of these carols.